Love Life

Ukrainian Research Institute
Harvard University

Harvard Library of Ukrainian Literature 12

HURI Editorial Board

Michael S. Flier
Oleh Kotsyuba, *Director of Publications*
Serhii Plokhy, *Chairman*

Cambridge, Massachusetts

OKSANA LUTSYSHYNA

LOVE LIFE

A Novel

Translated by
Nina Murray

Introduced by
Marko Pavlyshyn

50 years ■ 1973–2023

Distributed by Harvard University Press
for the Ukrainian Research Institute
Harvard University

The Harvard Ukrainian Research Institute was established in 1973 as an integral part of Harvard University. It supports research associates and visiting scholars who are engaged in projects concerned with all aspects of Ukrainian studies. The Institute also works in close cooperation with the Committee on Ukrainian Studies, which supervises and coordinates the teaching of Ukrainian history, language, and literature at Harvard University.

Copyright © 2024 by the President and Fellows of Harvard College

All rights reserved
Printed in India on acid-free paper

ISBN 9780674297159 (hardcover), 9780674297166 (paperback), 9780674297173 (epub), 9780674297180 (PDF)

Library of Congress Control Number: 2023950140
Library of Congress record is available at https://lccn.loc.gov/2023950140

Cover image by Anya Styopina, https://zemla.studio
Book design by Andrii Kravchuk

Publication of this book has been made possible by the generous support of publications in Ukrainian studies at Harvard University by the following benefactors or funds endowed in their name:

    Ostap and Ursula Balaban
    Jaroslaw and Olha Duzey
    Vladimir Jurkowsky
    Myroslav and Irene Koltunik
    Damian Korduba Family
    Peter and Emily Kulyk
    Irena Lubchak
    Dr. Evhen Omelsky
    Eugene and Nila Steckiw
    Dr. Omeljan and Iryna Wolynec
    Wasyl and Natalia Yerega

 You can support our work of publishing academic books and translations of Ukrainian literature and documents by making a tax-deductible donation in any amount, or by including HURI in your estate planning.

To find out more, please visit
https://huri.harvard.edu/give.

Contents

A Peninsula of Desire: An Introduction to *Love Life*
Marko Pavlyshyn • IX

Love Life • 1

The Key to *Love Life* • 227

A Peninsula of Desire:
An Introduction to *Love Life*

Marko Pavlyshyn

The Ukrainian poet, prose writer and literary scholar Oksana Lutsyshyna was born in 1974 in Uzhhorod, the capital of Ukraine's westernmost region, Transcarpathia. In Uzhhorod, she completed her undergraduate studies in English philology and received encouragement from local literati to begin publishing her works. "I still consider myself to be a Transcarpathian Ukrainian writer," she said in 2008, having lived in the United States since 2001.[1]

Lutsyshyna's early collections of poetry, *Usvidomlena nich* (Night Comprehended, 1997) and *Orfei Velykyi* (Orpheus the Great, 2000) announced themes that would be characteristic of much of her poetry and prose: a dark and threatening world and the anxious and exposed predicament of human beings within it—and, counterbalancing these, the poet's intuitive and privileged grasp of a transcendent, indeed divine, presence. The early poems, generally traditional in form, are rich in allusion to the literary and philosophical heritage of Europe, both ancient and modern.

In the course of her postgraduate studies in the United States, Lutsyshyna engaged with literary and cultural theory and, especially, the work of feminist scholars and thinkers. "Postcolonial Herstory: The Novels of Assia Djebar (Algeria) and Oksana Zabuzhko (Ukraine)" and "The Great Phantasmagorical Season: The Prose of Bruno Schulz in the Framework of Walter Benjamin's *Arcades Project*" were the titles, respectively, of her master's thesis at the University of South Florida (2006) and her doctoral dissertation at the University of Georgia (2014). In the 2000s, prose genres—the novella, the short novel known in Ukrainian as the *povist′*, and the novel *per se*—came to the fore in Lutsyshyna's literary output. *Ne chervoniiuchy* (Without Blushing, 2007), her collection of short prose works, contained darkly satirical representations of gender relations in both Ukraine and the United States, and of the trauma that migration imposes, especially on women.

The predominantly realistic premise of much of Lutsyshyna's prose of this period did not preclude shifts into the realm of fantasy. One such transition occurs in the *povist′* "Tsvirkun" (The Cricket, 2008), where the husband of the female central figure begins to shrink—"grow in reverse"—as his wife discovers new sources of self-fulfilment and pleasure that do not include him. Likewise, Lutsyshyna's first full-scale novel, *Sontse tak ridko zakhodyt′* (The Sun So Seldom Sets, 2007), interweaves a plot set in a realistically portrayed post-Soviet Uzhhorod (whose representation, however, is not free of grotesque, even surreal, elements) with a narrative that unfolds in a mythologized Florida. *The Sun So Seldom Sets* is at once a crime novel with sensational plots involving mafias on both sides of the Atlantic, an explicitly feminist text critical of the patriarchal orders of Ukraine and the United States, and an exercise in fantastic prose in the spirit of E. T. A. Hoffmann.

In the free-verse, almost prose-like poems of the collection *Ia slukhaiu pisniu Ameryky* (I Listen to the Song of America, 2010), Lutsyshyna explored the emotional costs

LOVE LIFE   XI

that accrue when the power disequilibrium between the genders is amplified by the social disadvantages suffered by the immigrant. The lyrical subject, a Ukrainian woman of intellect and cultural sophistication, observes these traumas with an analytic eye even as she struggles to come to terms with being abandoned by her American lover. The theme of asymmetrical love and betrayal across a cultural and power divide is elaborated in Lutsyshyna's next novel, *Liubovne zhyttia* (Love Life), published in Lviv in 2016.[2]

Virshi Felitsyty (The Poems of Felicitas, 2018) returned to the philosophical ground of Lutsyshyna's early poetry. Awed by the grand but imponderable nature of the universe, the lyrical subject of these poems searches, often prayerfully, for connection to the divine—not only as a means of understanding the world but as a guide to action in it. The question of how to be and act in the world, and the attendant question of the human person's responsibilities to society, is also at the heart of Lutsyshyna's novel *Ivan i Feba* (Ivan and Phoebe, 2019), for which she was awarded Ukraine's most prestigious literary award, the National Taras Shevchenko Prize in the literature category.[3] *Ivan and Phoebe* was a novel of education—a *Bildungsroman*—in reverse. The classical *Bildungsroman* as exemplified by its prototype, Goethe's *Wilhelm Meisters Lehrjahre* (Wilhelm Meister's Apprenticeship, 1795–96) traces the evolution of a young man through a sequence of learning experiences toward an adulthood marked by self-knowledge and useful contributions to society. The story of Lutsyshyna's Ivan is the opposite. The historical event that propels the novel's plot is the Revolution on the Granite of 1990–91, the first of the protracted public protests in Kyiv that punctuated Ukrainian society's determination to establish and later protect a just and democratic political order. The protest, mainly by students supported by former political dissidents who had returned to public life after years of imprisonment, presaged the later and better-known Orange Revolution of 2004 and the Revolution of Dignity, or Euromaidan, of 2013–14. Ivan, inspired by the libertarian ideals espoused by some of his peers, joins the heady, if risky, protest on the granite slabs of Kyiv's main square. Thereafter, his story is one of decline and degradation. Smothered by the expectations of his provincial family, dispirited by the political compromises entered into by his former comrades, and blackmailed by agents of the old Soviet regime who have not conceded defeat, he abandons his ideals and vents his frustrations by psychologically abusing his wife, Phoebe.

Ivan and Phoebe documents, and is itself a manifestation of, the enervation and sense of powerlessness that afflicted part of the Ukrainian creative intelligentsia in the years after the Russian Federation occupied Crimea and began its war with Ukraine in 2014—a mood that, it should be said, evaporated with Russia's full-scale invasion of February 24, 2022, yielding to an upsurge in public determination to defend the Ukrainian state and its independence.

Love Life, the second of Lutsyshyna's "American" novels, reflects the worldview of a period of hiatus, of the calm in the eye of the storm, when it appears possible to look beyond the perturbations of the moment—*zloba dnia*, the evils of the day, as the Ukrainian phrase has it—and focus on matters of greater generality. For *Love Life*, on the surface a tale of an unequal love gone badly wrong, is also a moral reflection of consequence and a novel that demands and repays careful reading.

Keys—to What?

We should read *Love Life* attentively. The author makes this suggestion by placing at the end of the novel a "Key: for professional players of the glass bead game." Like other works by the German-Swiss writer Hermann Hesse, *The Glass Bead Game* (1943) achieved a degree of countercultural popularity in the 1970s for its esotericism and its evocation of the idea of arcane and privileged knowledge. In Hesse's novel, the glass bead game is a pursuit engaged in by a special caste of monk-like adepts whose lives are dedicated to training for, and then playing, the game.

Like much else in *Love Life*, the allusion to Hesse compliments erudite readers for their erudition and adds to the riddles with which the novel confronts its audience. The reference to the glass bead game implies that there are encoded, hermetic meanings in the novel that are not easily penetrated but add to its philosophical weight.

What, then, is this Key? It is a set of paragraphs, most of them numbered, each of which discusses parallels between the figures of the tarot card deck and characters (or, in a few instances, situations) encountered in the novel.[4] In public discussions of *Love Life*, Lutsyshyna sometimes conceded that these parallels were not essential for its interpretation; the Key, she confided, was intended chiefly to warn intending critics against excessively naïve readings of the work. By means of the Key, Lutsyshyna, well versed in contemporary literary theory, reminds us of approaches to literary interpretation that examine a text through some conceptual paradigm external to it. Lutsyshyna's own PhD thesis was a work of this genre: it read the works of the Polish-language Jewish writer Bruno Schulz who lived and worked in what today is Ukraine with the help of ideas developed by the German cultural critic Walter Benjamin (1892–1940) in his reflections on urban modernity. Justifying her adoption of such an approach, Lutsyshyna warned against excessive dependence on interpretive structures too obviously suggested by the text itself, observing that "look[ing] at [Schulz's] prose in broader theoretical and historical contexts [...] will, eventually, offer parallels and explanations that were not expected before."[5]

The logical precondition of such freedom in the selection of interpretive tools is the idea that no approach to understanding a text can claim sole validity. It is possible, but not essential, to read *Love Life* with the aid of the tarot deck as a "key." One might, for example, choose instead to read the novel in the light of Lutsyshyna's dissertation, noting that the latter work gives attention to ideas and symbols which also figure prominently in *Love Life*.

Mimesis and Mastery

In his *Poetics*, Aristotle contended that we derive pleasure from a work of art because it recreates reality, and because of the masterliness of that recreation.[6] As to the mimetic veracity of *Love Life*, both critics and general readers have remarked on the persuasive realism of parts of the novel (only parts; in places it is patently unrealistic). One reader praised the novel's representation of the dire plight in which the novel's central character, the emigrant woman Yora, finds herself, as follows: "The book is really very frightening. Because it is frightening to be sick and alone and without money or insurance in the middle of a North American city in a cheap rented apartment. [...] I saw a very accurate, honest, and merciless description of the psychological state of a young emigrant."[7]

Indeed, notwithstanding Lutsyshyna's statements about placing little emphasis on depictions of the mundane

LOVE LIFE   XV

details of life, there is a good deal of social realism in the
novel: critical representation of the vulnerability of unem-
ployment, the harshness of poverty, and the consequences of the new colonialism of the age of globalization, including its exploitation of migrants. Here and there, such
critical remarks take the form of wittily worded satirical
barbs ("What's she doing when she isn't singing—studying management, right? How to sit in an office and go to
shopping malls?"; 141).[8] A significant part of this social mimesis is undertaken from a feminist perspective. The novel
depicts men being violent toward women (if not physically, then mentally), men treating women with disrespect,
men refusing to take responsibility for children, or for the
emotional harm they inflict on women. These abuses are
shown to be as characteristic of the New World as they are
of the Old. The assertion of one reader that "the novel is
a unique encyclopedia of contemporary life" is somewhat
hyperbolic,[9] but there is no doubt that part of the pleasure
engendered by reading it rests precisely upon its lively,
convincing, and critical depiction of aspects United States
society, the setting in which Yora's tribulations play out.
In the late nineteenth century, the Ukrainian novelist Ivan
Nechui-Levyts´kyi demanded that Ukrainian literature
describe all the territories settled by Ukrainians and all
the social and ethnic groups on those territories. That is
the spirit in which *Love Life* may be seen to "colonize" for
Ukrainian literature the state of Florida, hitherto beyond
that literature's horizon.

Florida, *à propos*, is nowhere named in the novel. It is
systematically called "the Peninsula." Such abstinence
from the naming of names is one of the devices by means
of which the novel signals that it is not consistently realistic. Rather, it establishes a tension between the imitation of
a recognizable reality and mysterious generalization. Such

tensions in the novel—there are a number of them—are among its manifestations of the technical "masterliness" that Aristotle regarded as the second of the sources of pleasure afforded by the work of art. In *Love Life*, there exist delicate balances between various narrative tones (mundanely informative vs. elevated and generalized), various levels of consciousness (ordinary daytime awareness vs. dream and hallucination), and various options for understanding events and states of affairs. The subtle management of these tensions allows the novel to formulate a complex worldview and, simultaneously, to grant the reader intellectual pleasure.

Constructing the tension between realism and non-realism in the novel, the text, on the one hand, naturalistically depicts actual places in the USA. One can readily ascertain that locations where the action takes place closely resemble the (unnamed) city of Tampa and its environs: the tollways, universities, hospitals, and shops that are mentioned in the novel have exact counterparts in Floridian reality. On the other hand, the novel, in places, creates the impression that the action is occurring on some transcendent plane that is mysterious, mystical, and symbolic. Neither Tampa, nor Florida, nor the United States are referred to by their proper names. We are not even told the surnames of the main characters (we know them only by their given names). Such accidental connections to the everyday, we must conclude, are too mundane for this novel. And yet, the tension between the triviality of realistic details and the dignity of abstraction and generalization makes it impossible for readers not to notice that the novel is playing games with them: where it presents them with the entourage of weighty significance, it is often unclear whether it does so in all seriousness, or parodically. Consider the beginning of the novel:

LOVE LIFE XVII

> The man Yora could not stop looking at was dressed with no apparent care—he wore a gray T-shirt, with a burn hole on the chest and faded Hindi lettering across the shoulders, a basic pair of shorts, a bracelet made of fruit stones on his thin wrist—but his face glowed like the face of a saint on an icon. His entire head glowed, especially when he leaned over the water, studying a particular bird, or peering into the thickets on the far side of the river, and fell into the sunlight that came down in a neat cone. You could think it was the halo of his hair that burned, in a tremulous contour, a myriad tiny darts of heat. (3)

The excerpt is reminiscent of Hermann Hesse's sweetish, Orientalizing discourse of wisdom with its Buddhist coloration. It is hard to say whether this mode of narration crosses the boundary into kitsch or not. On balance, it seems that Lutsyshyna generates such Hessian echoes with parodic intent. As will become evident, the novel presents many quasi-philosophical statements and structures of meaning in ways that make it difficult to say whether they articulate the "stance" of the novel, or parody the very idea of such a stance. In her dissertation, Lutsyshyna quotes Karen Underhill's observation that Bruno Schulz's texts "preserve the dual poles of *irony* and *messianic poetics*, seeking an aesthetic mode in which the modern—present—world in ruins can still be the messianic world."[10] The same occurs in Lutsyshyna's novel: every argument that it constructs can be taken either seriously or ironically.

In the novel's first sentence, Yora, who is referred to by name, gazes upon an individual who is not named and called simply "the man," a device that endows him with generality and, possibly, symbolic portent. He is carelessly dressed: the "gray T-shirt, with a burn hole on the chest," the Hindi lettering and the bracelet made of fruit stones suggest that this man is indifferent to material things and somehow connected to the wisdom of the Orient; there could scarcely be louder proclamations of his sacral exceptionalism than his face, glowing like that of "a saint on an icon," the cone of sunlight illuminating his head, or the burning "halo" of his hair. He is surrounded by sunlight, water, a bird, the thicket across the river—all phenomena of nature named in the most generalized way, eschewing particularity. They must, surely, be symbolic of something.

Or perhaps the very opposite is the case. Might not the accumulation of these somewhat clichéd images of light be a deliberate strategy to suggest that the "deep meaningfulness" that they seem to proclaim does not in fact exist? Furthermore, the man's sartorial carelessness is only "apparent" (that is to say, inauthentic); perhaps the same is true of the rest of his staged attributes of significance. After all, as readers will soon learn, the man is a former cinema actor, an intellectual of dubious stature, and Yora's future exploiter. His name, revealed to be Sebastian, likewise seems to carry special meaning, evoking associations with the early Christian martyr and the tradition of eroticized representations of the saint in agony, his almost naked body penetrated by arrows. But this, too, proves misleading: the status of the injured victim will descend upon Yora, not her future lover and tormentor.

Tensions between meaning and parody on meaning, between substance and triviality also exist at the level of plot. The story of Yora is extraordinarily simple. She falls in love with Sebastian. Sebastian treats women as instruments of his erotic pleasure and maintains parallel relationships with several, including Bonnie, who is barely of age, and Mumtaz, who belongs to a cultural minority. The discovery that she is but one of Sebastian's lovers causes Yora to lose her capacity and will to act, and even to live. She develops an illness that puzzles physicians: bleeding ulcers appear on her feet. After a failed attempt at suicide, Yora forces herself to take steps to avoid ending up destitute in an economically unforgiving America. Yora's interlocutor in the first half of the novel is Inga, like her an immigrant from "Eastern Europe" (characters' countries of origin belong to the category of facts which the novel keeps concealed). When Inga leaves Florida, the role of Yora's mentor and supporter passes to a young woman of the Goth subculture called Raven. Yora's passion for Sebastian finally subsides, as attested toward the end of the novel by her commitment-free erotic adventure with a certain Jimmy and, possibly, Justin (the situation is described ambiguously), both of whom she scarcely knows.

On the one hand, this narrative has the appearance of an embodiment of the sentimental genre of the "romance," where a woman's achievement of happiness in a heterosexual relationship is at first thwarted by the Villain, but, despite all obstacles, the heroine eventually arrives at her desired happy ending. On the other hand, in the story of Yora, we can also detect the exposition of a worldview, tragic or simply resigned, which concedes that it is difficult to live a good life (that is to say, a life that is both righteous and one in which the human being's spiritual and material needs are met), and yet affirms the existence of virtues that are binding upon a person of good conscience.

The seemingly simple tale poses difficult questions. How do we judge the actions of human beings who, independent of their conscious will, have fallen under the power of another person or their own psycho-sexual drives? Why must human beings suffer as a result of circumstances over which they have no control? How should human beings live in conditions of such undeserved suffering? In these questions, where the words "human beings" appear, they could in each case be followed by the phrase, "and, in the first instance, women." The novel formulates these questions in the course of narrating the experiences of the central character as a woman. Yora's tribulations are depicted in the novel as having their origin in the pre-rational substrata of her psyche, but they receive their social form as a consequence of the distorted gender relations that prevail in the society which she inhabits at present, as well as the society from which she has fled. The same is true of the stories of almost every woman character in *Love Life*: Yora's mother, Inga, Raven, and Inga's and Raven's mothers. In their childhood, or their youth, or their adulthood, all of them experienced violence, disrespect, or exploitation at the hands of men. All of them are, in one way or another, victims of patriarchal customs, perceptions, privileges, and power.

A Novel of Education?

One approach to the interpretation of Yora's biography might pay attention to the presence in the novel of features of the *Bildungsroman*. Examples of this genre typically tell of the departure of a naïve central figure (almost always a male) from his homeland, of his life in foreign parts, and his challenging confrontations with reality, in the course of which he accumulates experience of life. Interactions with other people help him achieve maturity, acquire wisdom, and become a well-adjusted member of society capable of contributing to its weal.

Yora's history bears a number of these features, though not the chronologically narrated biography from youth to maturity: the little information we receive about Yora's early years and her departure from her homeland is not revealed until the middle of the novel. Yora emigrated because of her refusal to endure the typical circumstances of women's lives in "Eastern Europe." But escape to the New World gives her new causes for discontent. The toast to the *mundus novus* that phantasmagorical figures drink in a feverish dream of Yora's is an ironic comment on the futility of her transcontinental escape. After the unexpected turn in Yora's life caused by a love that becomes an obsession, loss of personal autonomy becomes the novel's main theme. Yora loses control over her psyche, her body, and her social situation until, beset by imminent problems of survival, she returns to her work and to dealing with other people. She is calmed by the example of Inga, who has lost her beloved Carlos but found a satisfactory replacement for him, and the advice she receives from Raven, who exemplifies the possibility of a life free of exhausting and dangerous intimate relations. A seemingly crucial moment in Yora's "education" is a dream in which she sees "the only flower she need[s], the flower of the world's wound, a part of which everyone carries inside them"; she believes herself to be heading toward a place "where she could become one with the wound of the world, collide with it and, by doing so, bring about healing, a restoration, and not just hers, Yora's, but for everyone, all the people in the world" (185). In practice, however, her "healing" not only fails to awaken her to such empathy with all humanity but takes an unexpectedly prosaic form. Yora discovers in herself the skill of treating intimacy as Sebastian had done: carelessly, as a form of consumption: "He had advised her to become like him, and up to a point, considering her recent experiences, she had done exactly that" (218–19).

But is this "happy end" the final "thesis" of the novel, the definitive statement of its worldview? Does this "novel of education" really give its approbation to an "educational outcome" where the newly "educated" person has learnt to derive satisfaction from trivial and random pleasures? The limiting expressions "up to a point" and "considering" suggest the need to proceed with caution before adopting such a conclusion.

First Reading: Tragedy

As the novel's title suggests, its theme is love, so it makes sense to examine the qualities of Yora's love for Sebastian in detail. It is love-as-eros—sexual desire in combination with a mental yearning for closeness to the beloved. The novel emphasizes two aspects of this love in particular: its existence independent of Yora's will, and the absolute, transcendental status that it attains in Yora's consciousness.

The spontaneous and uncontrolled nature of Yora's feelings for Sebastian is evident from the novel's very first sentence: "Yora could not stop looking" at Sebastian (3). She wanted to decline his invitation to see her again, "but could not bring herself to do it" (9). Anger at Sebastian when she finds out about his relationships with other women does not diminish her desire to be with him: "I can't live without him" (40), "I can't be without him" (ibid.), she confesses in the course of a conversation with Inga. Yora, it becomes clear, is not an agent in her love relationship, but rather a victim of it. Love paralyses her will, a fact of importance for reflections on its ethical status.

Yora's perception of her love as absolute (complete, all-encompassing, unsurpassable) and transcendental (located on a plane of existence beyond everyday experience) is reminiscent of the vision of love in texts of early Romanticism—in the aphorisms of Friedrich Schlegel, for example ("To deify the beloved is in the nature of those who love";[11] "Do you love at all, unless you find the world in the beloved?"),[12] or Novalis ("Love is like philosophy. It is and should be everything for everyone. Love, therefore, is the Ego: the ideal of every

LOVE LIFE XXIII

aspiration").[13] Sebastian ignites within Yora a combination of aesthetic delight, a sense of the mystical exceptionalism of the beloved, and the conviction that, in union with him, she attains an utmost and unique level of being. At their first meeting, Yora observes that he has "the body of a former dancer – (...) well-proportioned and full of quiet grace that cannot be obtained in mere weeks" and remarks that he is "very beautiful" (4), at first to herself, and then in conversation with him (6, 15). Even those of his features that are aesthetically unattractive become objects of erotic excitement: "He had hard, protruding collar bones (...). There was something almost revolting about those collar bones which made them only more desirable" (18). She is oblivious to the contrast between his pretense at intellectualism and his exaltation of food ("I love Europe. With American women, I can't even find anything to talk about. Never met a kindred soul among them... (...) By the way, I got some cheese today. It was on sale at Whole Foods... I stopped by—and the cheese was half-price" (19). Sebastian appears to Yora surrounded by various auras: "The very air around his body seemed to burn with an even flame" (10), his face is "full of mysteries and promises" (12), it seems to her that "this man knew something that others did not" (3).

Physical intimacy with Sebastian transports Yora into a mystical state in which she is convinced that she is approaching her spiritual essence—a state like that of a person on the brink of death:

> People who do hospice care, Yora had read, know a kind of total pain that is felt by the mortally ill—a pain both physical and spiritual, when everything hurts, all bodies visible and invisible, along with the soul itself, captured by the fear of death like a moth by a flame. Sebastian, elusive, now leaned down to her, now left her again—for a second,

a century. "This is dangerous, this pulling away and coming back, this can kill," Yora thought, an idea that pierced her like a needle going into a vein.

"Please," Yora begged Sebastian. "You are torturing me. I can't go on like this," and realized suddenly that she could, that she was balancing on the razor's very edge, that her very existence—and any existence at all—was now unthinkable without this edge, as the world was unthinkable without Sebastian's beauty in it, and she screamed. (16)

Yora's sensation of love for Sebastian is so nearly religious that she feels awkward when she has to descend from this high rung of consciousness to the level of the mundane. When Sebastian asks her whether she has a "dream," she replies, somewhat unwillingly, but still maintaining an eschatological tone, "I hope for an easy death" (20). Once it becomes clear that by "dream" Sebastian means "business plan," Yora's sense that the world, and she herself, are imbued with Spirit, pales somewhat: "Yora listened—somewhere in the distance, the sea raised its waves and the holy spirit, deaf from their thunder, flew above it" (21). The allusion to the opening verses of the Bible suggests a reason for Yora's deflation. Prior to the creation of the world, "the Spirit of God moved upon the face of the waters" (Genesis 1: 2). A moment ago, Yora had felt that, in her love, the presence of the divine in the universe had become palpable. But Sebastian's incapacity to feel the same points to his philistine deafness to the spiritual. For Yora, on the other hand, it is as if the Holy Spirit has become deaf to Sebastian.

Just as Yora's inner state is intense, essential, and almost mystical when she feels herself united with Sebastian in love, so terrible and agonizing is the condition into which she falls when she realizes that this love is one-sided and that Sebastian expects from her nothing more than an addition to his collection of secular pleasures—not, certainly, an intimation of the Ideal. Yora falls ill, physically and mentally. She suffers fever, apathy, and a dream full of grotesque visions. Among them are images of death, Bonnie in the form of a triumphant deity, and a man undergoing torture from whose bare feet "blood slowly seeped" (75). Later, Yora associates this suffering figure with Job of the Old Testament (133); as her own feet bleed, she begins to believe that the only "treasure" she possesses is "death, a cold little ball that grew quietly somewhere deep in [her] chest" (117).

Much in the novel is subjected to irony, but not Yora's love, nor her suffering as a result of that love's catastrophe. In the depiction of this suffering, the symbols of Yora's bleeding feet and the agony of Job play a major role. Job in the eponymous book of the Old Testament became the object of a bet: Satan believed that he could demonstrate that the righteous Job would deny God, if only he were subjected to sufficient pain. Job loses his wealth, his family, and his health (he is smitten "with sore boils from the sole of his foot unto his crown"; Job 2: 7). Job disputes with God, taking offence at his punishment, which he regards as undeserved, and demands to know for what faults he is being punished. God does not offer him the explanation he desires, reminding him that he has no right to object to what God ordains, but gives Job "twice as much as he had before" (Job 42: 10).

Job considers himself a righteous man and takes offence at the seemingly arbitrary woes that God makes him endure. The exegetic tradition agrees with him: his fate is generally regarded as a symbol of the predicament of those who innocently suffer, and the narrative as a whole is seen as an illustration of the ineluctable presence of suffering in the world. True, at the conclusion Job is compensated. But this ending is generally regarded as the work of an author different from the one who wrote the bulk of the text. Some interpreters believe that the ending cancels the tragic quality of the figure of Job and weakens the book's central argument: that, in life, there are injustices that cannot be righted.[14]

One of the possible readings of *Love Life* might point out that Yora's "happy end," like the gift to Job of twice what he had before, is not coherent with the essential content of the narrative. In the central (and also longest and emotionally most intense) part of the novel, Yora suffers through no fault of her own. In the Book of Job, God Himself ordains that Job must suffer: suffering becomes Job's destiny. Likewise, in *Love Life*, it is possible to see Yora's sufferings simply as her fate. She fell in love as a result of psychological and physiological processes over which she had no conscious control. Her obsessive love had its origin in an accidental encounter with Sebastian. Her depression and her psychosomatic wounds flow from this accident. Had events taken an even slightly different turn, none of her troubles would have arisen.

According to this reading, the contradiction between the central emotional content of the novel and its ending is the tragic "message" of the novel. The comforting epilogue—Yora's gentle erotic adventure with two charming proletarians (or, perhaps, only with one)—is not the endpoint of Yora's "education" and does not extinguish the tragedy that she has lived through. The ending merely affirms that, somehow, one must continue to be, even if this continuation of being is a sad parody of the authentic being at the edge of the abyss, where there is either the infinite joy of spiritualized love, or pain and despair. And even if the end of the novel is really the end of Yora's education, then learning to be in the world means learning to dispense with dreams and consoling oneself with small emotions and small deeds. Such an interpretation, in which philistine limitation triumphs over the Romantic ideal, would confer upon the novel the status of a tragedy, and upon Yora the dignity of a tragic heroine. This reading would

LOVE LIFE XXVII

also be in the spirit of Oksana Lutsyshyna's testimony that she was "interested in showing a woman who outwardly does everything right, but inwardly is dying of pain."[15]

Second Reading: Parable

But is it true that Yora "does everything right?" Or are there, perhaps, elements of the novel that compel us to take a more differentiated view of her acts (and failures to act), her emotions, and thoughts? After all, the fact that Yora calls forth our sympathy as a victim and as a person more spiritually active than others in her environment does not yet mean that she is endowed with virtues, or free of vices. In the tradition commenced by the fourth book of Plato's *Republic*, moderation (*temperantia*), courage (*fortitudo*), wisdom (*prudentia*), and justice (*justitia*) have been regarded as the secular virtues whose observance underpins the harmonious coexistence of human beings in society. For Christians, who hope for salvation, the theological virtues are faith, hope, and charity, of which the last (*caritas*) in the form of love for one's neighbor relates most closely to human action in the world; *caritas* is consonant with one of Kant's formulations of his categorical imperative: "Act in such a way that you treat humanity, whether in your own person or in the person of any other, never merely as a means to an end, but always at the same time as an end."[16]

Before evaluating the extent to which Yora embodies (or fails to embody) the virtues, it is worth undertaking the simpler task of subjecting Sebastian to such consideration. Sebastian believes his behavior to be justified by the fact that he is honest with himself and, as he believes, transparent and truthful in his relations with others. He does not conceal, but openly proclaims his epicurean ideology

("We should love art and all fine things, live in the moment and enjoy good food, good wine, and beautiful and wise companions like you"; 19). In contrast to Yora, whose values readers must deduce from her actions and feelings, the novel allows Sebastian to be explicit in setting out the principles by which he runs his life:

> "But you don't want," he said tenderly, "you don't want us to bore each other, do you? I'll have Bonnie, and you could have someone else too—it's refreshing (...). Do you know how boring it gets, seeing the same person all the time? (...) I learned a long time ago, it's impossible—being tied down like that. (...) No, it's not for me—this serial monogamy. [...] We hit it off right away, and I thought, here, finally, is a woman who knows what she wants. Who really gets me. You agreed to everything up till now, didn't you? [...] But we need distance to keep each other charmed. (33–4)

For him, intimate human relations are contracts about the mutual provision of physical and psychological pleasure; human freedom is the possibility of entering into a multitude of such contracts simultaneously and without limitation; and the chief aesthetic criterion that the totality of such relationships needs to fulfil is variety. "I think such economy is only reasonable" (57), is what he has to say about his termination of relationships with former lovers. The basis for such a transactional, marketlike approach to relationships between people is the fiction that the "parties" to interpersonal "contracts" are fully equal, autonomous players who agree on the idea of what is desirable. The notion of love as a commodity belongs not only to Sebastian, but also to the old lecher Tripp who invites Yora to be his mistress, and even to Inga. Inga describes herself as a marketable object with rare and therefore desirable qualities; Carlos should want to own it: "Where is he going to find another woman like me? (...) is it easy to find a woman like me?" (47).

Of course, Sebastian's speeches of self-justification are but screens for the exploitative nature of his attitude to Yora. He tells Yora about Bonnie and Mumtaz and his creed of gourmet polygamy only when it is no longer possible to explain why there are times when he cannot see her. By that time, it is impossible for Yora to discontinue her adoration of him without pain and loss. He treats humanity in the person of Yora as a means, not an end. Yora is bitter in her characterization of Sebastian's "principles," and of the neoliberal cultural context in which such principles are regarded as ethical: "everything is very civilized here. He'll tell the police he does it with multiple women and all by mutual consent, which is true, and I'm just a barbarian with no manners" (45–6).

In her dissertation, Oksana Lutsyshyna devoted attention to the collector, a figure whom Walter Benjamin regarded as one of modernity's cardinal types. "What is decisive in collecting," writes Lutsyshyna, quoting Benjamin, "is that the object is detached from its original functions in order to enter into the closest conceivable relation to things of the same kind."[17] Sebastian collects women. He values particular attributes that they possess: the piquant fact that Mumtaz is an African American ("Black girls are really something"; 33) and Bonnie's youthfulness ("Generally speaking, I like younger women. I'm very happy with younger women, they haven't had their minds and bodies spoiled yet. Very young girls with delicate bones"; 56). From this perspective, Yora, Bonnie, and Mumtaz differ in detail but, in essence, they are "things of the same kind." His attitude toward them—aside from the portions of racism and pedophilia that it contains—denies their individuality and subjecthood and reduces them to the status of commodities.

Sebastian's inability or unwillingness to treat Yora not as a means for obtaining pleasure but as a complete human being is manifest in their dialogues, which are finely drawn exercises in non-communication. Often, they are, in fact, Sebastian's monologues which Yora tries to punctuate with relevant remarks. Sebastian either does not react to these at all or replies in ways that bear no relation to what she has said, or responds with compliments that infantilize her ("You are so smart"; 26). He peppers his talk with the names of arthouse cinema actors, showing up the fact that Yora does not know them and implying thereby that she is culturally less advanced than he is. Furthermore, the refined epicurean is not averse to a little intimate partner violence: "usually so even-tempered, [he] all but shook Yora off his lap" when a remark of hers was not to his liking (34). In one of her interviews, Oksana Lutsyshyna noted that it was no accident that her novel makes mention of the actors Udo Kier, Stefania Casini, and Joe Dallesandro: "they all had roles in a film whose name is key to understanding the character of Sebastian."[18] The film, which Lutsyshyna did not name, was *Blood for Dracula* (1974), directed by Paul Morrisey; Andy Warhol was one of the five producers. The analogy between Sebastian and the vampiric count needs no explication.

One of the proofs of the formal masterliness of *Love Life* is the novel's ability simultaneously to perform several tasks that are not easily combined. By neutrally reporting on the actions, conversations, and thoughts of the characters ("I practice the principle of 'show, don't tell'—I walk behind the heroine; I don't tell the reader what she feels," Oksana Lutsyshyna explained),[19] the novel is able, on the one hand, to paint the portrait of a man devoid of respect for others and, on the other, convincingly to portray a woman who, despite the vices of this obviously unworthy man,

LOVE LIFE XXXI

loves him sincerely and unconditionally. This successful mimesis, together with the portrayal of the heroine as an innocent victim, enables the novel to invite readers to empathize with Yora.

However, empathy with Yora—deceived, humiliated, and abandoned as she is—does not automatically mean approval of all of her actions. Job thought himself innocent and unjustly punished. But that was not how his friends saw it: "God will not cast away a perfect man," said one of them (Job 8: 30). Indeed, in this rich man's certainty of his righteousness and in his willingness to dispute with God, it is difficult not to observe the vice of pride. Even as he describes the injustice that he believes is being done him, Job confesses to having had the same contempt for some of his fellow human beings that they now show toward him: "But now they that are younger than I have me in derision, whose fathers I would have disdained to have set with the dogs of my flock" (Job 30: 1). Examples of similar—if not disdain, then certainly reluctance to be with others—are to be found in Yora's life practice.

Yora is not generous in her interactions with people. She is reserved in her friendships with women. She is laconic in her dialogues with Inga and Raven, often responding to their questions with an "I don't know" and offering no information about herself in exchange for their life stories. "I don't have a story" (158), she claims. She was friends with Volodya who found and fixed an old motor car for her and his wife, and they corresponded for a while, "but then stopped, or maybe she was the one who stopped, who could remember?" (194). Yora finds it difficult to stay in touch with her mother and sister. For several weeks in her time of crisis, she "systematically declined her and their mother's Skype calls, sending a few short sentences back in response to say that everything was fine" (96). She finds different motivations for this reluctance: "my mom has called me three times already and I can't talk to her. I just can't. (...) Because I'm afraid. She'll be able to tell that I'm not okay (...). They have their own life over there. She doesn't really know anything about me, and [...] if she does understand something about me, she'll worry. I'm so far away from her" (174).

In the end, Yora admits the real reason why she can barely force herself to communicate with the women who should be closest to her: "Yora thought she had left her mother and sister when she had in order not to become like them, not to live in a world like theirs" (175). Perhaps she had chosen the autonomy that the *mundus novus* seemed to promise, but, more importantly, she had chosen not to be with her family. In the novel, Sebastian represents egotism in its extreme form, but Yora is not free of this vice either, although, in her case, it manifests itself as passivity, a refusal to act when she should have acted. Raven sees this clearly: "Do you tell your friends when you are in trouble? I had this pain inside me, and I told you, and now, see, pfft! It's gone. You have to meet people half-way. Don't take yourself so seriously, open up. Why are you so stuck up?" (139). Being "stuck up"—pride—is Yora's weak point, as it was Job's. A symptom of Yora's pride is her refusal of being-with-others. In a discussion of *Love Life*, Oksana Lutsyshyna was uncharacteristically categorical in making this point: "This book is about love (...). But also (...) about the nature of evil, which I understand as the destruction of links between people and possibilities for communication."[20]

When it comes to the question of the degree of Yora's goodness or otherwise, however, the most important evidentiary material must be the novel's main content: her love for Sebastian. The foregoing analysis of this love focused on two of its features: its involuntary nature (Yora is not a free agent when she falls in love, but is driven by irresistible psycho-physical forces) and its transcendentality (Yora's love rises above the limits of everyday experience and attains mystical status—or so she believes). If we accept that these are, indeed, genuine attributes of the love that binds Yora to Sebastian, then we confer validity on an interpretation of the novel that sees it as a Romantic tragedy about the incompatibility of the Ideal with the everyday, or about the defilement of the spiritual by its inescapable need to exist alongside the mundane.

And yet, the idea that there exist passions so strong as to be irresistible is not dominant in the European tradition. It contradicts, for example, the Christian doctrine of free will. Building on the thought of the Stoics and other predecessors, Saint Augustine and the Christian tradition that followed him saw virtue in control of the passions and their subjection to the tutelage of reason, so that they might become implements of justice in this world and salvation in the next.[21] The neutrality of the authorial voice in *Love Life*—Oksana Lutsyshyna's practice of "showing, not telling"—makes it difficult to extract from the novel an answer to the question of whether Yora should have resisted the temptation presented by her passion. Is it the case that the passion itself, and its consequences—despair and attempted suicide— are Yora's *fault*, the result of her *wrongful* refusal to control herself? Or is Yora so determined by her body and her psyche that she has no choice? If the latter, then Yora may be compared to Job. Yora's suffering, the result of Sebastian's dishonorable and egotistical behavior, is undeserved; she is innocent, and her travails are a random manifestation of the injustice that pervades a fundamentally tragic universe. If, on the other hand, Yora's love is a passion that she should have taken under rational control but did not manage to, the novel becomes a parable about how one should *not* live, and Yora—the example of an immoderate person who has culpably yielded to passion. She has sought to validate her condition of psycho-erotic excitement by weaving around it the romantic myth of her love's unique and elevated nature. What is more, immoderation is only one of Yora's imperfections; others are lack of justice and charity toward family and friends, lack of courage when she succumbs to despair, and lack of wisdom when she fails to see Sebastian for what he is. In such a reading, the ending of the narrative with a trivial love adventure *à trois*—or, perhaps, only *à deux*—does not contradict the ethos of the preceding narrative but is its logical conclusion: Yora, with no more justification than Sebastian, takes advantage of one of her fellow human beings who happens to be erotically drawn to her and uses that fellow human being as a means to her own ends.

Two Cities

Which of the two interpretations offered above better corresponds to the "evidentiary material" that is the novel? The answer to this question is that they are not simply *equally* valid; the two mutually exclusive interpretations are valid *at the same time.*

This paradoxical conclusion is supported by the role that the image of the city (conceived of as a labyrinth) plays in the novel. In her dissertation, Lutsyshyna devoted considerable attention to the labyrinth both as a motif in Schulz's prose and as a metaphor in the writings of Benjamin. The arcades of Paris, she argues, "serve as passages between the inside and outside, consciousness and space, and, most importantly, reality and myth, thus creating a labyrinth, the limits of which cannot be captured within just one of these dimensions."[22]

If one examines the novel's depiction of Yora's nervous motoring (in what is ultimately revealed to be a delirious dream) on the streets of the unnamed city, it becomes clear that this journey in its unpredictability and the anxiety that it generates resembles wanderings in a labyrinth:

> By the time she left the pharmacy and got back behind the wheel the traffic on Fletcher had thinned out a little. She merged onto Fletcher and quickly reached the highway. (...) Close to downtown, the traffic thickened; the off-ramp was down to a single lane. Yora tried to merge but could not; the cars stood bumper-to-bumper. (...) After the Kennedy exit, Interstate 275 and Interstate 4 that went to Orlando both merged into a narrow and congested portion of the highway. (...) Yora discovered that all the exits were closed, all of them—Dale Mabry, Himes Avenue, and even Armenia/Howard. The last exit was for West Shore Boulevard, from which one could take the bypass to Kennedy. But it, too, was closed. (64)

And so on; a further six roads are named before the ordeal ends. This tense but initially realistically plausible journey transitions over the next pages into a phantasmagoria replete with grotesque visions. Reality has merged into dream or hallucination. The city, both real and the product of nightmare, and its highways and streets, are places of passage between "consciousness and space," "reality and myth," and together they form the "labyrinth, the limits of which cannot be captured within just one of these dimensions." The city-as-labyrinth thus symbolizes the capacity of things to be, simultaneously, themselves and their opposites; of Yora to be, simultaneously, the heroine of a tragic drama and an ordinary human being, weak and defeated by life; and of the novel to be, simultaneously, a tragedy and a parable of human imperfection.

The idea of a city simultaneously embodying two essences is not new. In his treatise *The City of God*, Saint Augustine worked with the image of two cities, a city of God and a city of the world, which exist in the one space. The city of the world is "the society whose common aim is worldly advantage or the satisfaction of desire," whereas the City of God "lives in this world's city, as far as its human element is concerned; but it lives there as an alien sojourner."[23] It is unclear, however, who sojourns in which of the two cities. This will be known only at the Last Judgment.

It is likewise unclear which city Yora inhabits. The judgment of her life—imperfect but marked by great love and profound suffering—is suspended, deferred to some distant time in a future hinted at by the significant choice of words describing one of her moments of insight into her relationship with Sebastian: "Sebastian had caught Yora in a labyrinth, caught her and locked her in there, and she could wander there till the Second Coming" (43). The weight of the term "labyrinth" in Lutsyshyna's dissertation impels us to seek in this sentence a significance additional to its "direct" meaning, which is that Yora finds herself in a bad situation with no way out and may be trapped in it forever. The supplementary, "deeper" meaning is that the condition into which Yora has been thrust by her unplanned love life is neither clearly defined nor one-dimensional, and the task of weighing and judging it is a matter not for mortal human beings but for the judgment that will accompany Christ's Second Coming. It is to this Second Coming that the mysterious figures in Yora's hallucination raise a toast, alongside their ironic toast to the New World, prior to the appearance in that confused vision of the tortured man with bleeding feet whom readers are free to associate with both Job and Yora. In the Old Testament, Job ultimately concedes that only God may judge him. *Love Life* articulates the same principle, but from a different perspective: it is the readers who, in the end, must concede it is not for them to sit in judgment upon Yora.

LOVE LIFE   XXXVII

∗ ∗ ∗

In contrast to *Ivan and Phoebe, Love Life* is a Ukrainian novel not about being a Ukrainian in Ukraine, but about being a human being in the contemporary world. Human beings are cast, regardless their will or just deserts, into places and situations that they seldom consciously choose. Human beings may appear in the world as satiated gourmands or as disempowered migrants. Accident decides whether human beings fall victim to emotional maelstroms or not; whether they are born in "your Eastern God-damned Europe" (56) or other more (or less) salubrious places. Human beings may yearn for love-as-eros but instead find only imitations of it that neither elevate nor please, but injure. And many human beings have too little love-as-caritas for their neighbors.

In particular instances, human beings may even wish that their emotions and thoughts exist on a level of being more meaningful, "higher," than that of everyday consumption and quest for pleasure. The novel tentatively hints at yearnings for the human experience associated with apprehension of the divine—a yearning that is more directly articulated in one of the poems in Oksana Lutsyshyna's collection *Poems of Felicitas*: "Lord, hold me, for the darkness is impenetrable."[24]

Impenetrable darkness is an apposite image for the state of the world as depicted in the novel. It is not a world where evil has triumphed but an opaque world where there is no clarity as to how one should live. Augustine wrote *The City of God* at the beginning of the fifth century amidst the spiritual uncertainties of the Mediterranean world where classical Greco-Roman paganism was in retreat but maintained great cultural inertia, while Christianity, though already for a century the official religion of the weakened Roman Empire, was still in the process of establishing itself.

Augustine, who himself had experienced transition from the old to the new worldview, created in his writings a majestic apologia for his choice. *Love Life* is a novel that emerges from cultural conditions that in some respects are similar to those of Augustine's time. On the one hand, the heritage of the age of enlightenment manifests itself in the increasing secularization and despiritualization of many societies, especially Western ones, until recently Christian. On the other hand, there is in evidence a growth in various forms of religiosity and even religious fanaticism. In the midst of this "impenetrable darkness," *Love Life* refuses to advocate for any particular worldview, daring to formulate only the indistinctness of value orientations that is characteristic of contemporary experience. It records the impossibility of deciding whether we are determined by our environment and yet capable, despite this limitation, of attaining dignity, even if this dignity is tragic; or, on the other hand, whether, possessing as human beings a degree of autonomy and free will, we are incapable of exercising them with reason or to good purpose.

Into this general uncertainty, the novel inserts the particular uncertainty as to love-as-eros. It is unclear whether a human being who loves passionately, dangerously, surrendering to instinct, and perhaps selfishly, can remain innocent. With respect to love-as-caritas, the matter is clearer: one should love one's neighbor without reservation. And, furthermore, one should live not as the characters of this novel live (with the possible exception of the insightful and kind but marginal Raven), but with moderation, courage, wisdom and justice.

Notes

This text is based on an essay first published in Ukrainian as "Piv ostrova liubovi" in *Krytyka*, vol. XXV, no. 9–10 (2021), 24–32 (https://krytyka.com/ua/articles/piv-ostrova-liubovi) and vol. XXV, no. 11–12 (2021), 17–23 (https://krytyka.com/ua/articles/piv-ostrova-liubovi-zakinchennia).

[1] Oksana Lutsyshyna interviewed by Vik Kovrei, "Holovne—ne tabuiuvaty dlia sebe niiakykh tem i hovoryty pravdu" [The Main Thing is Not to Regard Any Topics as Taboo for Yourself and to Speak the Truth], *Ukraïns´kyi zhurnal*, no. 10 (2008), 48, http://ukrzurnal.eu/ukr.archive.html/529/.

[2] Oksana Lutsyshyna, *Liubovne zhyttia* (Lviv: Vydavnytstvo Staroho Leva, 2016).

[3] The novel has appeared in English as Oksana Lutsyshyna, *Ivan and Phoebe*, trans. Nina Murray (Dallas, Texas: Deep Vellum Publishing, 2023).

[4] The text of the "Key" was significantly revised and shortened by the author for this volume. For the full version in the original, with twenty-eight entries, see Lutsyshyna, *Liubovne zhyttia*, 224–37.

[5] Oksana Lutsyshyna, "The Great Phantasmagorical Season: The Prose of Bruno Schulz in the Framework of Walter Benjamin's Arcades Project" (Phd diss., University of Georgia, 2014), 32.

[6] Aristotle, *De poetica*, in *The Works of Aristotle Translated into English*, ed. W. D. Ross (Oxford: Oxford UP, 1908–52), vol. 11, IV, 1448b.

[7] Ievhen Lakins´kyi, "Roman 'Liubovne zhyttia'" [The Novel *Love Life*], *Texty.org.ua*, March 12, 2019, https://texty.org.ua/articles/98386/Roman_Lubovne_zhytta_duzhe_tochnyj_chesnyj_i-98386/.

[8] Here and henceforth, pagination refers to the translation of the novel in this volume.

9 Viktor Kovrei, "'Liubovne zhyttia': po toi bik ne zrozumilo cho-ho" [*Love Life*: On the Other Side of Who Knows What], *Chytomo*, March 16, 2016, https://archive.chytomo.com/uncategorized/lyubovne-zhittya-po-toj-bik-ne-zrozumilo-chogo.

10 Karen Underhill, "Bruno Schulz and Jewish Modernity" (PhD diss., University of Chicago, 2011), 11, quoted in Lutsyshyna, "The Great Phantasmagorical Season," 145. Emphases in the original.

11 Friedrich Schlegel, "Athenäums-Fragment 363," in *Athenäums-Fragmente und andere Schriften* (Berlin: Karl-Maria Guth, 2016), 90.

12 Friedrich Schlegel, *Über die Philosophie. An Dorothea*, in *Schriften zur kritischen Philosophie, 1795–1805* (Hamburg: Felix Meiner Verlag, 2007), 80.

13 Novalis, *Fragmente. Sophie, oder über die Frauen. Projekt Gutenberg-DE*, https://www.projekt-gutenberg.org/novalis/fragment/chap006.html.

14 See, for instance, Richard B. Sewall, "The Book of Job," in *The Book of Job: A Collection of Critical Essays* (Englewood Cliffs, N.J.: Prentice-Hall, 1968), 21–35, here 21, 32.

15 Oksana Lutsyshyna interviewed by Iryna Slavins´ka, "Oksana Lutsyshyna: Ia pysala pro zhinku, iaka vse robyt´ pravyl´no, a vseredyni vmyraie vid boliu" [Oksana Lutsyshyna: I Wrote about a Woman Who Does Everything Right but Inwardly Is Dying of Pain], *UP.Kul´tura*, January 18, 2016, https://life.pravda.com.ua/culture/2016/01/18/206459/.

16 Immanuel Kant, *Grounding for the Metaphysics of Morals*, trans. James W. Ellington, 3rd ed. (Indianapolis: Hackett, 1993), 36.

17 Lutsyshyna, "The Great Phantasmagorical Season," 77. The quotation is translated from Walter Benjamin, *Das Passagen-Werk*, in *Gesammelte Schriften*, vol. V, part 1 (Frankfurt am Main: Suhrkamp, 1994), 271.

18 "Oksana Lutsyshyna: 'Nas vykhovuvaly dlia inshykh'. Rozmova z Bohdanoiu Neborak" [Oksana Lutsyshyna: "We Were Raised for Others." Conversation with Bohdana Neborak], *Zbruč*, January 31, 2016, https://zbruc.eu/node/46970.

19 Lutsyshyna interviewed by Iryna Slavins´ka.

20 "Pys´mennytsia O. Lutsyshyna prezentuvala v Ukraïni roman 'Liubovne zhyttia'. Rozmova z Vasylem Shandrom" [Author

LOVE LIFE XLI

O. Lutsyshyna Launched the Novel *Love Life* in Ukraine. Conversation with Vasyl´ Shandro], *Media-tsentr Uzhhorods´koho natsional´noho universytetu*, https://mediacenter.uzhnu.edu.ua, quoted from *Vydavnytstvo Staroho Leva*, December 22, 2015, https://starylev.com.ua/news/pysmennycya-olucyshyna-prezentuvala-v-ukrayini-roman-lyubovne-zhyttya.

[21] Saint Augustine, *Concerning the City of God against the Pagans*, trans. Henry Bettenson (London: Penguin, 2003), 349.

[22] Lutsyshyna, "The Great Phantasmagorical Season," 117.

[23] Saint Augustine, *Concerning the City of God*, 762, 761.

[24] Oksana Lutsyshyna, *Virshi Felitsyty* (Lviv: Vydavnytstvo Staroho Leva, 2018), 5. Translation is mine.

LOVE LIFE

Back of living on little, there is the living on
nothing. These are the two chambers; the first
is dark, the second is black.
— Victor Hugo, *Les Misérables*

And those who have captured sleep in their
beds do not let go of it, and fight with it like
with an angel who tries to break free, until they
overcome it and press it into the sheets…
— Bruno Schulz, *Edzio*

The man Yora could not stop looking at was dressed with
no apparent care—he wore a gray T-shirt, with a burn
hole on the chest and faded Hindi lettering across the
shoulders, a basic pair of shorts, a bracelet made of fruit
stones on his thin wrist—but his face glowed like the face of
a saint on an icon. His entire head glowed, especially when
he leaned over the water, studying a particular bird, or peer-
ing into the thickets on the far side of the river, and fell into
the sunlight that came down in a neat cone. You could think
it was the halo of his hair that burned, in a tremulous con-
tour, a myriad tiny darts of heat. When he finally turned
so that Yora could take a better look at him, she was struck
by the clarity of his face. His features were beautiful, but
the individual features did not matter. Something more important was hidden behind them. It felt like this man knew
something that others did not.

The day was quite hot although the sun did not beat
down as hard as it had at the height of the summer. In
these latitudes, the bright greenery only thinned and yellowed a bit in winter, during the few rainless months, and
now, in September, it stood as a solid wall, impenetrable

to the sun or the still-oppressive air. The river was a clean marvel, uncommon among the tropical waterways which were frequently muddy. You could see the rocks at the bottom and the fish that weaved among them. Yora realized the man with the lambent face had noticed her and was now watching her, so she turned away. She carefully took the wooden steps, a bit rotten here and there, down to the water that smelled sharply of silt. The flatland river was slow and wide. Birds loved this place; a small white heron ambled along the bank. Yora was about to follow it, to see it find some food and to let the serenity of observation distract her when she heard a quiet voice address her. The man she had been watching—slim as a youth despite his age—stood at the top of the wet steps.

"Don't follow her," he said without a smile. "You'll frighten her."

The smell of silt went to Yora's head. She looked up at the man and said nothing. He was tall, with the body of a former dancer—not ostentatiously muscular like that of a regular gym-goer, but well-proportioned and full of quiet grace that cannot be obtained in mere weeks, or even months. Even now, when his dancing days were probably behind him, this grace inhabited him as the essence of silk persists in old, worn cloth. He was very beautiful indeed. Beautiful down to the soles of his feet caught in the worn straps of his leather sandals.

"Come up here," he said. "Don't disturb her."

He must have known what he was talking about, and spoke so softly that the sound of his voice only amplified other, ambient sounds— the flow of the river, the calls of unseen birds, and the rustle of the grass.

"Come up here," the man repeated and extended his hand with the bracelet on the wrist—a hand Yora could not have taken anyway because she was too far below him.

"Come, please, you'll disturb the birds, and they have to eat today. It's better to look from afar or to buy a pair of binoculars."

He continued to tower over her. A solar aura flamed around his hand. Yora, as if under a spell, moved toward the light, climbed the stairs, and the man took her hand.

"My name is Sebastian," he said.

"Yora," she said. Her hand burned. "It's very nice to meet you."

"I haven't seen you before. I come here every day. Have you been here before?"

"I have," Yora said. "But not often."

"Well, I'm relatively new here myself. Just moved in July."

"Where did you live before?"

"Oh," Sebastian smiled. "In Europe. Then in Minneapolis. And San Francisco for a while."

He did not say where he had moved from exactly, but Yora didn't feel like she should pry.

"Would you like to sit down?" he offered, and they sat on a bench in the shade, not far from the bank. They could see the river and the people in the picnic shelter on the other side—they looked like a family celebrating a birthday. The women were putting food out on the tables, and the men helped the children with their fishing rods.

"Divine," Sebastian sighed, making himself comfortable. "Nature heals the body and soul."

Yora didn't dare look at his face—it blinded her.

"You must be a yoga teacher," he said out of the blue. Yora gave a nervous laugh.

"I'm not. What makes you say that?"

"You are in great shape. You look like a ballerina. Short hair really goes well with your type of face."

He looked at her steadily, with attention. He was no longer smiling. Yora thanked him and felt herself blush.

"And what do you do?" she asked.

"I'm a retired actor," he said.

"What were you in?"

"I was in several very well-known films," he said evenly, not blinking, so as to make it clear that no irony was appropriate.

"Which ones?" Yora asked.

"You probably haven't seen them," he said in the same even voice.

"Could you tell me anyway? I could find them in the library or online."

"You wouldn't find them there. They were all pretty unusual projects. Some were not American. There's a whole world of underground European cinematography. Stefania Casini, Joe Dallesandro—have you heard of them?"

"No," she said. "But I'd still like you to tell me the titles of your films. I want to watch them."

"To watch my films?" he repeated with surprise that didn't seem to fit the question. "Whatever for? Hey..." He laughed—unnaturally, but in an expert, attractive way, the kind they must teach in acting school where Yora had never been—and his face, previously so otherworldly, suddenly changed into the kind of face one sees on magazine covers, with an artificial, too-wide but still handsome smile, beautiful in a very particular way. "Do you know what Udo Kier always says? Udo Kier, the actor... He and I... Never mind. Anyway, Udo Kier always says, "It is so sad to look at your young self, if I see one more time how damn good-looking I used to be, it'll make me howl!'"

"But you are—" Yora started to say but caught herself. Perhaps it still would have been appropriate to reassure him he was good-looking nonetheless, even after his Udo Kier story, but not after the way he'd laughed when he spoke. So she said nothing.

LOVE LIFE 7

"Tell you what," he said. "We could watch my films together, at my place, if you'd like. I would be happy to have you over. I live nearby."

"Thank you... I..." Yora muttered, taken aback. "You don't have to invite a perfect stranger into your home."

"It's my pleasure," he said with a charming smile—and changed once again, this time, from a glamorous imp into a kind older friend, almost a father figure. "No one is making me invite you. So, if I am, that means I genuinely want to. You must believe me. I have no particular feelings toward most of humankind and can choose who I spend my time with. And I would love to spend some time with you."

"In that case, thank you," Yora said. "I'll come by."

"Just one word of warning—I have several cats. Just tell me if you are allergic—I can lock them up in my study while you visit."

"No, I don't have any allergies," Yora answered.

"Excellent," he said, rising to his feet. "Then give me your number." He pulled out his phone.

"Only I don't know when I can make it," she said, a little stunned by the hypnotic speed at which he moved.

"No worries at all," he said with a little dismissive wave. "I get it. I'm pretty busy these days myself. We'll get together when we can find the time. There is no rush."

He had already taken down her number, and now he put his phone back into his pocket and extended his hand in parting. He was about to leave when he stopped and asked, as an afterthought, "You aren't vegetarian, are you?"

"No," she said automatically before she had a chance to take in the meaning of his question.

***

"I met a man," she told Inga once she came home to their tiny studio with its large mattress on the floor in the middle of the room where they slept together. They had no money for a bigger apartment—or a bedframe. The city had grown into a near-megalopolis over the last few years and, like all megalopolises, became expensive, so they were glad to have their relatively low-cost shelter. Inga was still a student and Yora, after losing her full-time job several months earlier, subsisted on unreliable odd jobs.

"And? What's his deal?" Inga asked, looking up from her textbooks. She sat on the mattress, propped up with pillows, reading and making pencil notes in the margins.

"I'm not sure," Yora said. She sat down on the mattress next to Inga. Her head was spinning.

"What do you mean, you're not sure? Who is he?"

"I'm not sure," Yora repeated, like a robot. She was already sorry she had mentioned the man at all.

"What's his name?"

"Sebastian."

"That's a rare name, isn't it?" Inga said.

"I'm not sure."

"Do you like him?"

"I'm not sure."

"Wait a minute." Inga put her book aside and moved closer to Yora. "I can't get anything out of you. Let's try again. How did you meet?"

"Uh, in the park."

"And what did he say?"

"He invited me over to his place."

"What kind of car does he drive?"

"I don't know, I didn't see it."

Inga laughed.

LOVE LIFE 9

"Don't forget—it's much more comfortable to cry in a BMW than on a bicycle."

"I actually think he rode his bike there. He lives somewhere nearby," Yora muttered.

"He might not have a car at all," Inga said and shook her dust-blonde hair. "And hitting on people in the park... I don't know. Seems iffy. I wouldn't go over to his place if I were you."

"If I did, it would be just to have some fun."

"Something's going on here. You are all worked up..."

"Turn on the music," Yora asked instead of answering. Inga complied. Yora got up and went to the bathroom, locked the door and, once she'd put the music and the door between herself and the world, spent a long time sitting on the bathroom floor.

Sebastian called three days later and gave her his address. Yora wanted to tell him she was busy but could not bring herself to do it. She got into her car and went where he told her to go.

"Come on in," he said, opening the door. The doormat said, "Get Lost!" Usually those things said "Welcome!"

Yora smiled.

"Quite the doormat."

"That's for other people, not for you," he said very seriously, and she stepped inside. "Here, this is my living room," he said, with a broad gesture.

The couch was black leather but antique and therefore quietly exquisite. The rug Sebastian had shipped from Iran, paying extra since it was contraband. The dining table was made of solid old wood, and so was the floor. Yora went into the kitchen; it was not so much messy as alive, in use—there were dishes in the sink, a mug with the dregs of strong black tea, a cutting board with a block of either cheese or soy, spices out on the counter, and empty cat-food cans. There was life here—his life—and Yora felt her heart squeeze: she felt like a stranger here. She left the kitchen like a sleepwalker.

"Come over here," Sebastian said softly. The very air around his body seemed to burn with an even flame. "This is my bedroom—you can take a look, I don't mind."

She did. The bed was covered with an embroidered quilt, likely another unique piece from one of the countries he had traveled to. The art on the wall was black-and-white—mostly female nudes. "I wonder how many women had been to this bed and how many more there will be once I'm out of the picture," Yora thought for some reason. She walked around his house as if it were a museum, but it was a strange museum because what it exhibited was the future, not the past—things that were certain to come. It was as though someone merciful or, perhaps, malicious opened your blind traveler's eyes and pointed: here is the road you will take back.

Back in the living room, Sebastian said, "I promised I'd take you out to lunch."

"Lunch?"

She did not think he had promised her anything—or if he had, it had been something entirely different.

"Let's go."

He stood very close and looked straight at Yora's face, that way he had, but did not touch her. Yora stood before him as if held by a spell. Eventually, he went over to the front door, opened it for her, and they left the house.

He lived in the oldest part of the city which was completely unlike the rest of it. There was no hint of showy respectability or advanced planning here; the untamed streets spread in every direction like snakes, and the houses stood in the shade of old trees whose branches drooped with bedraggled Spanish moss. Closer to the water, the touristy neighborhoods began, but there were few tourists even there, and they came for the serenity, not for glamor or

LOVE LIFE 11

parties. Everything here was imperfect, alive, spontaneous. The stores, nestled tightly along the main street, sold cute junk like little statues of Greek gods and Ganesha, mixed in with the latest Japanese toys.

The street ended at an inlet bay where the sea beat against the shores, eating away at the soil. You could not go any farther. It smelled of raw fish and bird droppings—hungry pelicans crowded above the pier, and people fed them. Fishermen called to one another out on the water. The open sea lay on the far side of this small Peninsula which itself was a bud on the trunk of a larger Peninsula.

"Look," Sebastian pointed to their right. "That little restaurant looking over the water. They have amazing shrimp. You should never order shrimp fried—it ruins the taste. They are best steamed."

Yora looked at the terrace above the water. Boats, noiseless as ghosts, glided along the bay. The wind blew napkins off the tables. For some reason, she hesitated. Sebastian, however, took her hand with a soft but compelling touch, walked on, and led her behind him.

"I knew you would be wearing a dress today," he said once they were seated. "I tried my best to match you."

He was wearing shorts, a sharp dressy pair (this also existed here, on the Peninsula), and a summer shirt with a pattern of pale-blue keys.

"I actually know very few people around here. The other day, I made friends with the owner of the bicycle store—his name is Juan. I bought a bike from him, and now I'm thinking of going back for another one, for my guests, so we could go together to the beach, or the park, you know. Do you ride a bike?"

The waitress came.

"Do you mind if I order for the both of us?" Sebastian said. "I've been here a few times."

He ordered shrimp and cornbread to go with it.

Seagulls yelped above the bay, and motorboats passed once in a while sending ripples across the water. Sebastian talked, but Yora barely heard what he was saying—she was looking at his face, so full of mysteries and promises. Sebastian's eyes glowed against his pale skin.

When she came home, Inga, of course, was asleep. The lock was tricky, and Yora made too much noise fiddling with it—even their neighbor opened his door to see what was going on but must have decided there was no threat because he slammed it shut moments later. Yora stepped into their studio, undressed, and went to bed.

"Yora, is that you?" Inga asked in a sleepy voice. The noise Yora made at the door had woken her.

"Who else could it be?"

"I don't know... The neighbors..."

Yora couldn't help but giggle. This—the giggling—happened to the two of them all the time.

"Did you sleep with him?"

Yora fell silent.

"Just don't tell me you're not sure."

Inga laughed in the dark with such gusto that Yora laughed, too.

"My raccoon," she said and stroked Inga's hair. They had pet names for each other—Yora called Inga her "Raccoon"—or Cooney—and Inga called Yora "Mom," because Yora was several years older.

"Did Carlos call?" Yora asked.

"Sure did."

Carlos and Inga had been going out for about six months. He played for a local—and fairly well-known—football team. Carlos had recently turned twenty-five—in contrast to Inga's twenty-nine and her dreams of having a family.

Carlos had stopped by their studio a few times, but normally Inga went to his place, and Yora did not know him well. He had dark hair and was of Cuban descent, but spoke English without an accent, since he'd grown up in the States. Yora thought he was shy; he seemed quite flustered when they met. He had pale, blemished skin that made him look even younger than he was, like a high-school student. Once, in the very beginning, when Inga left to go on a date with him, Yora could not resist the urge to get in the car and follow Inga. Who could tell what compelled her that day—curiosity? Jealousy? The impulse to protect Inga?

That evening, Yora spent a long time looking for parking downtown, not wanting Inga to spot her, and then walked to the fountains above the river, the very spot where Inga and Carlos had agreed to meet. It was around eight, the sun was slowly setting, but the air was still sticky and moist. Tall palm trees, imported from the Caribbean, stood around the fountains like sentinels, lit up by the bright glass squares on the ground. Inga was waiting near one of the fountains; the water reflected the lights of skyscrapers as a flickering flame. Carlos came up to Inga from behind and embraced her. She hadn't heard him approach—the fountain thundered, cars whizzed by, the downtown lived its own, near-night life. Inga turned to look at Carlos, and Yora saw their faces—lit up, like everything in this city, beautiful and full of tenderness, as if shot in slow motion. Inga ran her hand along Carlos's black hair, and he caught her fingers with his lips. Yora sighed the way a person sighs when she finally gets an answer to a very complicated question, and went home.

"So did you? Sleep with him?" Inga asked again.

"I really am not sure," Yora said, and they burst out laughing again—until they fell back, breathless.

"Now you have to tell me everything, in detail," Inga said.

"Why, are you writing an advice column—how to sleep with a man without actually sleeping with him?"

"You bet! That could make us some money..."

"Right, so we could finally buy at least one bed and use it as nature intended."

"How's that?"

"To bring men home, of course," Yora said, trying to sound serious.

"Then we could fleece them. No need to write the advice column..."

"Aha, right up until we get arrested for prostitution."

"But we won't, remember? We'll sleep with them in your special way where no one can be sure if they've actually done it. No proof."

"We'll call our bordello 'At the Raccoon's.'"

"Better, 'At Mama's.'"

"Now, that would attract customers." Yora was having fun.

"Freud himself would come..."

"..."

"Alright," Inga said eventually. "Let's go to sleep. You can tell me tomorrow."

And they fell asleep. They did so instantly, right after a fit of laughter, with no transition whatsoever—this was also something that happened to the two of them all the time.

LOVE LIFE   15

* * *

"You are very beautiful," Yora said to Sebastian when they lay on his Iranian rug in the middle of the living room.

"It's just my face. One good pastor once told me I have the face of an angel."

"Do pastors really believe in angels?"

"That one did. But actually, I have a model's face—you can write whatever you want on it."

"And do you?"

"It certainly doesn't hurt to have an actor's schooling."

Yora was finding it hard to breathe. He had put his head on her chest, pressed into her and moaned, "I love being pet like this... Exactly like this, my hair..."

She unbuttoned his shirt. He had an incredible body and perfect skin.

"How old are you?"

"I tell everyone the same lie—that I'm exactly forty," he said.

"And the truth?"

"And the truth is, forty was a long time ago. A decade, at least. I've stopped counting. Why bother?"

She kissed his shoulder.

"Come with me," Sebastian said. He rose and helped her to her feet, and they went into the bedroom.

He lay her down on her back and began kissing her; he held on to her wrists, so she could not touch him back. Then he let go. She rose toward him, but he withdrew, hovering above her. He would lean down and kiss her on the neck, then withdraw again.

"Arms along your body... Only I can touch you—you can't touch me," he whispered.

People who do hospice care, Yora had read, know a kind of total pain that is felt by the mortally ill—a pain both physical and spiritual, when everything hurts, all bodies visible and invisible, along with the soul itself, captured by the fear of death like a moth by a flame. Sebastian, elusive, now leaned down to her, now left her again—for a second, a century. "This is dangerous, this pulling away and coming back, this can kill," Yora thought, an idea that pierced her like a needle going into a vein.

"Please," Yora begged Sebastian. "You are torturing me. I can't go on like this," and realized suddenly that she could, that she was balancing on the razor's very edge, that her very existence—and any existence at all—was now unthinkable without this edge, as the world was unthinkable without Sebastian's beauty in it, and she screamed.

* * *

Later, they talked again, in the dark this time; she could not see Sebastian's face, could only hear his voice. His voice—not his words. He held her close then, and she fell asleep. She dreamed Sebastian was explaining a tabletop game to her, football, or something like it.

"Look, here's my team," he said in the dream as he lined up small plastic figures of soldiers, Native Americans, superheroes, and monsters that children collected on a piece of green cardboard without any markings or lines on it.

"But they are all different," Yora said, surprised.

"Why should they be the same?"

"Where's the other team?"

"What other team?"

"The one they'll play against."

LOVE LIFE 17

"Look closer," Sebastian said, eyes narrowed like a cat's.

"What am I supposed to look at?" The piece of cardboard was now alarmingly empty. "There's nothing here."

"Precisely," he said and smiled. "I've taken them all off the field."

"But they must still be somewhere," Yora objected in her dream—and woke up in Sebastian's bed.

Her heart was pounding as if it wanted to burst out of her chest. The digital clock showed three a.m. Yora slipped out of bed, very much afraid that she, God forbid, might touch Sebastian's naked body again, might inhale his smell—and would not be able to leave, would stay to kiss his hair and shoulders...

She picked up her things in the dark and started to get dressed.

"Where are you going?" Sebastian said. "What about breakfast?"

"I'll eat at home," she said.

He sighed, got up, muttering something, put on a pair of shorts and saw her out to her car.

"That was wonderful. We must meet again... And again," he said by means of goodbye and kissed her.

The weather turned cooler; the rainy season was almost over. Yora and Sebastian went out for walks in the city much less, now, and almost never went to the park to sit under the stars. Sebastian's living room looked out onto a small lake. There were French doors and something like a veranda. This space was enclosed, floor to ceiling, with fine metal mesh, to keep the bugs out. Sebastian put a pair of armchairs out there, and a rug he said he meditated on every morning. In the evenings, Yora and Sebastian would sit out on the veranda and look at the lake—almost every time she came, several times a week. Yora pressed herself into Sebastian's body, dying of all the affection she felt for him. He had hard, protruding collar bones—she could not even hug him without bumping against them, sometimes painfully. There was something almost revolting about those collar bones which made them only more desirable.

The lake loomed very close, like a crevasse in the Earth's mantle; fog coiled above its surface day and night. Rain fell in drops, as if not daring to let loose. It swelled with blackness and sieved, squeezed through a gauze bandage, so very close to their faces, and the black drops fell into the gaping maw of the lake, to be lost, like beads of a heavy necklace in the plants that grew along its banks.

Sitting with her back to Sebastian, Yora could not see his face, which never failed to hypnotize her, and could finally listen to what he was saying. Their conversations were odd—as soon as Yora thought she could follow his train of thought, that the two of them had finally struck that happy consonance of two people who are interested in each other, he would switch abruptly—not to a different topic, but to a different tone—and she felt lost again, but only more intrigued for being lost.

"We might as well be in the jungle here. This is the only neighborhood in this city that's still livable, although we still have our share of misadventures. Yesterday, it rained so hard the road flooded, and, to my great delight, the giant SUVs so beloved by the local middle class could not pass each other in the street without sinking into an enormous puddle. You need a small car here, like mine. My neighbor told me that, last year, the steps to a veranda collapsed when one family decided to take a photo together with all their cousins for Christmas. The skinniest cousin weighed in at three hundred and fifty pounds. They were all taken to the hospital. As a general matter, Yora, I am sorry. I am asking for your forgiveness for my misguided nation. It has become impossible to live here."

LOVE LIFE 19

"I wonder why you didn't go into politics."

"Ugh! Because I am an artist, and how could an artist ever turn into a politician?"

"They do where I'm from."

"So they do. And? Are things going well for your people?"

"For my people—no. What about other places you've lived?" she asked. "In Europe?"

"The grass is always greener on the other side."

"In the afterlife, then?"

"There is no afterlife."

"But what if there is?"

"The afterlife is a fairy-tale for neurotic people who don't know how to enjoy life. And, since most people out there are neurotic, we hear this tale regularly."

"What are we to do then?"

"We should love art and all fine things, live in the moment and enjoy good food, good wine and beautiful and wise companions like you. It's because you are from Europe. Europe is a very special place, I love Europe. With American women, I can't even find anything to talk about. Never met a kindred soul among them... I am very lonely here, terribly lonely. You can't even imagine. By the way, I got some cheese today. It was on sale at Whole Foods... I stopped by—and the cheese was half-price. I got lucky."

"Why did you come back to live here?"

"Better ask me why I left in the first place."

"Why did you?"

"Because I had to. My family was not supportive of me. I was left without anyone to fall back on when I was young," he began in an even, well-practiced voice, as if reading from a book. "Because they rejected me, I grew up very poor, couldn't even afford to go to college right away. I went through a lot. And I spent so much time and effort trying to prove to them I could do just fine without them! All that stuff about chasing your dreams and having equal opportunities is a bunch of lies. If you're poor, you have no opportunities. And then I had my wife and her lawyers to deal with..."

"You were married?" Yora asked.

"Don't ever mention it to me again... That was the last time I wanted to build something worthwhile with a woman from this country."

Another time, he threw her for a loop when he broke off his own thinking-out-loud about politics to ask her an unexpected question of the kind he seemed to despise.

"Do you have a dream?"

"A dream?" Yora asked, feeling herself shrink away from him. She did not like questions like that.

"What are you hoping for? What do you want from life? Who do you want to be? Start your business?" Sebastian kept on.

He may have been right to ask such things (it was considered all but required for being a good, close friend), but Yora got scared. She said nothing, and he kept nagging,

"Come on, tell me! I want to know."

Suddenly, Yora felt an almost childlike sense of rebellion rising inside her—she didn't know where it had come from, but she said, dropping every word hard like a piece of unworked iron, hiding behind the youth that in that moment had betrayed her so ingloriously:

"We in Eastern Europe have few hopes. We are not taught to expect much."

"But still... You personally—you must have some aspirations. Isn't it a good thing—to have a dream? How could you live without one? You can't even make any money without a dream."

"Fine," she said. "I hope for an easy death."

"Death!" he cringed. "Why hope for that? I'd rather you started your own business."

LOVE LIFE

"If I did, I would be just like everyone else," Yora said, and this made him laugh. He kissed her on the top of her head and was silent for a long time, just looking, looking at the black lake.

Then they went back into the living room and Sebastian started making tea.

"Here, drink this," he said, handing her a mug. "If you want candy or cheese—they're over there, help yourself."

He then went back out to the now-dark veranda, alone, to smoke. Yora followed him, but he did not look at her—he smoked and thought his thoughts. Or perhaps, remembered the cities where he used to live, or people he had met. These would have been actors or directors, who would have come together after the house lights went down, backstage, at night, the chosen few. She could have thought of someone, too, someone very dear to her, but Yora knew doing so would not have helped. There was nobody else; the two of them were alone on this Peninsula as if on a small far-flung planet, at the edge of the universe. Yora listened—somewhere in the distance, the sea raised its waves and the holy spirit, deaf from their thunder, flew above it. Yora glanced at Sebastian. Thick smoke curled above his head. Yora could see his hand, held to the side with his cigarette—his beautiful, artistic hand. It wasn't like he'd said something hurtful to her—and yet her heart ached. For a moment, Yora thought of just leaving his house and walking away, forever, without a goodbye, without telling him she was going. To leave, and never to come back. But she could not do it. His hand, draped over the arm of the chair on his veranda, his hand with its sensitive fingers held her there, albeit at a distance.

The following night, when Yora came home, Inga opened a bottle of wine, and the two of them had a drink.

"Carlos has canceled three dates in a row. He has a big game coming up," Inga said casually, but it was obvious she was anxious.

There were no plans, no talking. The wine went to Yora's head, felt hot inside, spread through her limbs, and she felt giddy. When she was fifteen, she got hit by a motorcycle and ended up in the hospital. The doctors had to stitch up a gash on her leg, and before doing so, under local anesthesia, injected her with a mild narcotic. It felt really great—she was still aware of everything that was happening, none of her troubles ceased to exist, but they all became separate from her. The wine made her feel the same.

"Well," Inga said, "talk to me. What's new with you, Ma? How's Sebastian? You're at his place all the time."

"It's fine," Yora said, almost defiantly.

"Has he introduced you to his friends?"

"What do I want his friends for, Cooney?"

But Inga did not laugh.

"Ma, I'm serious."

"So am I."

"What kind of family has he got?"

"I don't know."

"Where is he from, anyway?"

"From nowhere."

"What do you mean, nowhere?"

"He's lived in San Francisco. Europe. And Minneapolis."

"Why did he move?"

"I don't know."

"What's his last name?"

Yora told her.

"Did you google him?"

"I did. Got nothing."

Inga started washing the dishes. She picked up their wine glasses, not noticing Yora hadn't quite finished her

LOVE LIFE 23

wine, and held them one after another under the warm water. She moved as if she were blind, bumping into the corners of furniture. Yora realized her friend was about to cry.

"What's wrong?" she asked. "Come on, Cooney. Did I hurt your feelings?"

Inga burst out crying. She stood there, leaning on the sink, and the water ran past her, past the glasses.

"No, nothing. It's nothing, it'll pass. Carlos is very busy, he is very, very busy, and I have to remember that."

The half-darkness of their apartment suddenly oppressed Yora, and she got up and turned on all the lamps, electricity bill be damned. Inga turned off the faucet and sat down at the bar counter that served as their dining table, onto one of their two bar stools.

The light bounced off the white plastic of the kitchen scuffed by the generations of those confined to this cell of an apartment. Four walls, a mattress, a stove. It felt like there was nothing else, neither the city nor the world beyond these walls—that there were only their hopes, this plastic, and the gleaming light.

Inga kept saying, "He loves me, I know he can't live without me, where else is he going to find anyone like me? Just think—where? I am smart, I am beautiful, I have interesting things to say—where?"

Two days later, the Peninsula abruptly emerged from the rain the way a swimmer surfaces to take a breath before diving underwater again. When Yora and Inga woke up that morning, their studio was flooded with sunlight—they had left the blinds up the night before. Yora got up, made herself some coffee, and went, as she had agreed, to Sebastian's place.

He did not come to the door when she knocked—instead, he called out, "Come in!" and she went in. Sunshine flooded his apartment just like it did Yora's studio, and Yora had to shield her eyes with her hand before she could see Sebastian. He stood with his back to Yora and was hanging a painting. He stepped back, admired his work, still with his back to Yora, made a satisfied noise, and only then turned to face her.

"Today," he said, "is a big day—my paintings came."

"Where were they?" Yora asked.

"At a friend's... But she finally sent them here. She also sent some of my books—I already put them on the shelves in my office. Hip hip, hurray!"

He came up to Yora and threw his arms around her.

"See how well everything is coming together? My paintings came, and now you've come, too. Life is good."

For a while they just stood there, holding each other. Then he let go of Yora, but kept a hand on her back, touching her lightly as if to urge her to go, look at the paintings.

"These are abstract, this one, that one, and this—my friends painted these, but I won't tell you their names because they don't paint to sell. Few people know about them."

"That's a Titian!"

"I wish," he smiled. "That's a reproduction. I'm not rich enough to afford a Titian. And those are by James Ensor. He is rarely reproduced, especially these particular paintings. They are from his series about skeletons... Later, toward the end of his life, he couldn't paint like that. For his early paintings, he would dress skeletons in people's clothes, he kept them in his studio... But the most important ones are these—these are fragments from *The Temptation of St. Anthony*. Except all the temptations are modern, not medieval. Isn't that fascinating? But we have to celebrate properly, at least with juice since it's too early for wine," Sebastian declared suddenly and went to the kitchen. "We'll celebrate with wine at night, if you want," he said, and came back out, as if he had had their drinks ready and poured ahead of time. "Here!" he handed her a glass. "Tell me," he said, positioning

LOVE LIFE 25

himself so as to block the sun. "Do you believe in fate? That when people meet the way we did it is not by accident?"

Before she could manage an answer, he threw his head back and laughed.

"Really—everything's so great! I must be a lucky man! I had been waiting for this for a long time. Things rarely come together so well... And this is just the beginning... The beginning of our celebration," he added quickly, as if to correct himself, except Yora did not know what he wanted to correct. He embraced her again and spun with her around the room until she complied and laughed along with him, purely from the joy of their motion. When they stopped, he let her go and went back to his paintings. He looked very content.

They even went for a walk near the bay during the day, since it wasn't raining, and walked until the sun went down. Then they sat on the rocks near the pier. Usually, at moments like that, Sebastian would take Yora's hand, or put his arms around her, but instead he sat smoking under the darkening sky and looked into the space above him. Yora touched his shoulder—and he started, as if brought back by a sudden thought, then sighed, and turned to face her. He looked like he wanted to tell her something but could not bring himself to do it. The sky above them burned with colors that changed every minute. Yora's heart tightened, and she did not know why. By the time they got back to Sebastian's place, it was completely dark. They turned on the lights in the living room. When they left earlier, Sebastian had left the Roman blinds open on the veranda doors, and the darkness now stared at them through the gap like the void. Sebastian lowered the blinds, went to the music console, and put a CD into the player. Music poured forth like a sudden wave of pain. Sebastian made himself comfortable on the couch and now watched Yora from there, reading her face for her emotions as she was affected by the music.

For a while he was silent, and then he said, "We really ought to watch my old films some time."

"What are they about?" Yora asked.

"It's hard to explain. But I think you'll like them... Our films are very special," he went on. "Hollywood—it's so dumb—is all about stories, you know, but all their stories are so predictable by now. Life, meanwhile... Life is the opposite of predictable, it is impossible to foresee. The worst thing is, if you are constantly being shown the same thing, you risk losing your own gift for observation. When you know how to watch life, it's a hundred times more interesting than any stupid movie."

"And this—from a famous actor!"

"Udo Kier is a famous actor!" Sebastian objected, but Yora could hear in his voice that he was very pleased by the compliment. "Take love, for example... I'm picking at random, it doesn't have to be love... But since it's the first thing that came to mind... People think there must be a certain, specific 'right' love story. And keep waiting for it to happen in their lives because that's what they've seen on the screen. But this is amateur talk. It's not about life imitating art. People should just make films that are like life and live like films that don't even pretend to have any comprehensible story. It is much harder to live than to lead an existence that follows a prepared scenario."

"You say," Yora responded, in rhythm with the music that was still cutting through the space around them, with a choir singing to the screams of violins, "you say, life like a film and films like life, but how do we separate 'life' from everything we've ever seen or read? We don't lead the lives we used to have in the jungle, under the ferns."

"You are so smart," Sebastian said with affection. He laughed and called to her, "Come over here, come to me—I want to hold you."

LOVE LIFE 27

She went and sat next to him.

"Better yet, put your head on my lap," he asked.

She lay down and did as he asked. Her ear pressed against his knee, and suddenly the pain of the music equalized with her own physical pain, and she immediately felt better.

"Like that, exactly... Touch is no less essential than our daily bread... Just like that. Like that, my girl. Have you heard of Joseph Beuys? Seen any of his films?"

"No," Yora said.

Sebastian stroked her short hair, and every stroke settled in the space between them like counterpoint.

"That's alright, you will eventually. Or we can watch them together some time. I haven't watched his work in a long time, last time was in Berlin, they had a decent show at the contemporary art museum... Do you like contemporary art? Beuys is pure unpredictability. In one of the films—they are really hard to describe—he has a man doing something, but you can't tell what it is. A series of odd actions. Like, for example, he rubs cooking fat on his leg for some unknown reason. All his actions lack logic, they make no sense and have no purpose. And do you know what? That is the essence of art. Do you agree?"

"I'm not sure," Yora answered.

"You are incredible. You are my favorite person to talk to. And that's okay, I'll convince you yet. We have plenty of time. Perhaps we'll go to Berlin together one day. But here's the most important lesson—one has to construct one's life like Beuys does his films. It's an obligation that each one of us has to take. There must be an element of unpredictability in everything. The wind blowing through the scene that's being shot, so that no one—not even you as the director—knows what might happen next."

They grew silent. The choir also fell silent suddenly, and the room was still as if before a fall into the void.

"By the way," Sebastian said, seemingly out of nowhere, cheerfully, as if he'd forgotten all about art and his vision of cosmic tragedy, "do you like picnics?"

"I do."

"Let's have one sometime. Somewhere on the other side of the small inlet, say, at Pass-a-Grille. How does that sound?"

"Sure."

"Thursday then."

"I work on Thursdays."

"Until when?"

"Until five."

"That's alright, we can go in the evening. It'll be an evening picnic," he decided.

"Saturday is better. I can come over in the morning."

But Sebastian said nothing to that.

* * *

That night, Yora dreamed that she and Sebastian stood, finally, looking over the sea—perhaps it was Pass-a-Grille Beach, where she had never been. In her dream, they looked at the sea and, suddenly, a column of light, tall enough to reach, it seemed, the sky itself, rose from the water, and birds and dolphins danced around it. And then Yora looked at Sebastian and said, not quite conscious of what she was saying and listening to her own words as if they were spoken by someone else, "This won't last long." In her dream, she did not know what she meant. Also in her dream, right then, Yora realized that she could no longer see Sebastian, even though he was somewhere right there. She could only sense his

LOVE LIFE 29

ineradicable, bare presence, his very existence, stripped of anything non-essential.

She had heard about something like this from her grandmother when her grandfather died. Yora was already living abroad and could not come to the funeral. She came back for the first time three years later. For her, grandfather had remained alive—she had not seen him dead, had not gone to stand at the head of his coffin as his body sank among the roses, and now it seemed to her as if he were just about to come out of the other room and talk to her. With age, grandfather shrunk, and might have become almost a gnome in the time she hadn't seen him, losing inch after inch of his ground-down spine, but, in fact, she had no grandfather—neither tall nor short, neither alive nor dead, and only her grandmother sat before Yora, in her housecoat and socks. Yora filmed her, afraid her grandmother, too, might die before Yora's next visit. Of course, it didn't really make any difference—the film would not bring her grandmother back to life, as it would not have brought her grandfather back to life.

Last year, grandmother and Yora's uncle threw away most of the pictures from her grandfather's albums. "We no longer know who those people in the war photos are," they said. "We can't bear looking at all those strangers' faces." Sooner or later, Yora's film will also hold for someone just another stranger's face. "Did you dream of Grandfather?" she asked her grandmother from behind the camera. "No!" the old woman said, then smiled and pulled up her socks, once, and again, and then again. She rocked mechanically, the tops of her socks clasped in her hands like the ropes of an invisible swing. "Only once, but I could not see him, only knew he was there somewhere," her grandmother added. "And then he was gone again, and that's that."

Yora woke up because Sebastian had kissed her on the forehead.

"Sleepyhead," he said. "Time to get up."

Something was touching her cheek—something cool and soft. She opened her eyes. Sebastian had put a rose on the pillow next to her, red and fresh.

"Is this for me?" she asked, touched and a little surprised by the gift. He had not given her any gifts up till now.

"Yes. It is as beautiful as you are."

Yora smiled and reached her arms out toward him.

"Come lie with me," she asked.

"I was just about to make coffee," he said but lay down and squeezed her in his arms.

After a while, he pulled himself back from her and said, "The trouble is, you know, I lose my will when you hold me. If I lie here just a little longer, I'll just faint. That's no good."

His eyes were clouded. It wasn't arousal, and it wasn't passion. It was as if he had found the fountain of life itself, but could only take small sips from it, each just enough for him to survive until the next one. This upset him.

Later, they had coffee in his living room. Sebastian put the rose in a vase.

"I don't want it to wither before you go home," he said.

Yora smiled. Every so often, Sebastian would kiss her on the top of her head. Yora rose and went over to the glass doors; yesterday, everything was black, but today the silvery air glowed with an even glow—it wasn't sunny, but it wasn't raining either.

"Did you call Inga?" Sebastian asked.

"How come you keep asking about her?" Yora laughed. "Why don't you come over to our place and meet her? Then you'll know everything about her first-hand."

"I'd be glad to," Sebastian said. "But let's do it next week. Because we're going on a picnic this Thursday, remember?"

"I told you Saturday is better for me. I'll come over in the morning," she repeated what she had said the night before.

LOVE LIFE 31

"No, you can't," he said. "I'll be busy."

She did not even ask what he'd be busy doing, but he went on anyway.

"Bonnie is coming on Saturday."

Yora could not help herself.

"Who is Bonnie?" she asked. And added, not knowing why, "Another woman of yours?"

"Yep," he confirmed.

Yora laughed.

"Why are you laughing?"

"That's some way of putting it!"

"Well, I am seeing other women," he said evenly. "Don't tell me you didn't know."

Yora was stunned.

"What are you talking about? Enough with this joke, it's not funny."

"I am not trying to be funny. I am just telling you the truth. Would you rather I lied?"

"Sebastian, please, that's enough."

"I could show you a picture of her."

"Why would I want to see her picture? Are you nuts?"

"Why don't you believe me?"

"How am I supposed to believe you?"

"It's very simple, isn't it? I'll tell you about her. Bonnie is much younger than me. She's very young. Just turned eighteen a few months ago. I am her teacher."

"What do you mean? Like, a voice coach, or something?" Yora said sardonically, but he ignored her tone.

"She doesn't know anything. She is just learning how to be an adult."

Yora, still refusing to believe this catastrophe was real, confronted him.

"And what do you find to do with her, since she is so young—what do you talk about?"

"Talk?" he repeated and stretched his lips into a smile.

At that instant Yora believed him—firmly and irrevocably.

"What do you mean, what?" Sebastian shrugged. "Bonnie, she, you know, is very pretty, she has a body kind of like yours, slim, with tiny breasts. I film her often—I could show you. Everything about her is pretty, from the top of her head to her toes. She's definitely my type. I love delicate women. She does have long hair, not like yours, but there's a different charm to it. One can and must mix things up. I ask her to put her head on my lap, too, like you—I braid her hair. She loves that. Sometimes she falls asleep like that, on my lap, so young, with her hair in braids..."

There was not a hint of guilt in Sebastian's voice. Finally, he stopped talking and looked intently at Yora.

"What is it? Are you jealous? Yora? To hell with jealousy. You like being with me, don't you? So do the others. It's just an emotion, a chemical reaction, and you can't live in these bodily reactions, you should live with your mind. Bonnie comes to town once a month, and so does Mumtaz, but you are here all the time. You and I can talk about different things, we have so much in common..."

"Who the hell is Mumtaz?" Yora interrupted.

Sebastian went on.

"Do you know how they used to punish adulterers in the olden days? They would chain them to each other. Imagine what it's like to sit chained to someone! With all your physical needs. They'd sit like that until they started to hate each other. And you and I, we don't want that to happen. We want to remain a mystery for each other. And to study others. Like I study Bonnie and Mumtaz."

"And?" Yora asked. "Are you Bonnie's first?"

"Might as well be," Sebastian answered soberly. "She really doesn't know anything at all. Good sex, really good sex is not just going to bed with someone because you want to. Satisfying your lust is no more special than attending to other natural urges. Real sex is an intrigue. And it's not so easy to build up a good intrigue."

"An intrigue? But you just said it was a mere bodily reaction!"

He waved his hand as if erasing an invisible blackboard in a classroom and looked at her in silence.

"What about Mumtaz? Are you her first?" she asked after a pause, mocking him openly now, but he did not seem to notice—or pretended not to.

"With Mumtaz, yes," he said, squinting contentedly, like a cat in the sun. "I am Mumtaz's first. She hadn't been with anyone before. She's from Jacksonville, grew up in a Black neighborhood, and their church is Muslim... Black girls are really something..."

"And—did you show her new experiences? Did you film her, too?"

"I did—show her things, that is," he said, suddenly changing his tone, inappropriate as it was to this conversation, to another, still inappropriate—his dreamy lechery vanished in an instant. Looking straight ahead, Sebastian now spoke energetically, like a colonel at the front line.

"But no, I have not filmed her yet—a person has to get used to the idea of it first. Other than that, I've done everything I could. We tried a lot of different things. She trusted me completely and I didn't let her down."

For a moment, Yora was silent. Sebastian sat down in a chair and drew her onto his lap. Utterly broken, she did not resist.

"But you don't want," he said gently, "you don't want us to bore each other, do you? I'll have Bonnie, and you could have someone else, too—it's refreshing, isn't it, gives us something to talk about, right? Do you know how boring it gets, seeing the same person all the time? You'd get used to me, and I'd get used to you, and that would get boring. We'd start taking each other for granted. I learned a long time ago, it's impossible—being tied down like that. It's a boring plot-driven movie, that's what it is, and it makes a normal person sick. It kills passion, and why go on living then? No, it's not for me—this serial monogamy. I honestly didn't think that you could have missed that about me. That you didn't see it right away, honestly. I'm sorry I didn't tell you up front, but I couldn't even imagine that you had no idea! We hit it off right away and, I thought, here, finally, is a woman who knows what she wants. Who really gets me. You agreed to everything up till now, didn't you? I like you very much, I do. Please don't think that just because I have Bonnie and Mumtaz that I don't care about you. It's just that we will never live together and torment each other by being together all the time—you need to keep the mystery alive, don't you? You need to make things special. Don't you enjoy it? When you put on that special dress, it's like you are reborn, isn't it? You wouldn't want me to see you when you just rolled out of bed, unwashed and rumpled? But we need distance to keep each other charmed. You can't be Cleopatra all the time."

"But Elizabeth Taylor could," Yora said into his shoulder.

"What?" he asked. He took her chin and turned her to face him. She hit her temple on his collarbone and groaned.

"I said, Elizabeth Taylor could. She played the part and dressed like Cleopatra in real life, not just on set."

This pitiful jab that was not even intended as a jab unexpectedly found its target. Sebastian, who was usually so even-tempered, all but shook Yora off his lap, stood up abruptly, and started to pace the room.

"Elizabeth Taylor, Elizabeth Taylor!" he said. "Why'd you have to bring that philistine up? Who was she, your Elizabeth Taylor? What did *she* know about the set? Haven't you seen her movies? They're crap! You can't possibly think they are art! It's pop culture at its worst, precisely the thing that breeds legions of blinkered idiots and their wild notions of romance that have nothing in common not just with reality, but with biology itself!"

His forehead creased, his eyes glowed, having turned from gray to black; a massive dark cloud, it seemed, had come over the entire world. Even now, Sebastian was unbearably handsome.

"She'll have me believe she didn't see who *I* was!" His eyes flashed as he gave the air a savage chop with his hand. "She meets a man in the park, goes back to his place, and sleeps with him the day after she met him—and what, you expected something different from me? I might as well wear a sign! Do I need to make one? One that says, 'I sleep around and I'm not ashamed of that'? Why should I pretend to be Prince Charming from God knows what fairytale? Have you all been raised on the same stupid romance novels? How long do I have to keep convincing everyone in this idiotic puritanical country that sex—just sex—is normal, and I have all the right to have it?"

It was strange to see him so angry, and so unexpectedly—he genuinely seemed to think that Yora had just deceived him. Finally, he stopped, ran his hand across his forehead, inhaled deeply, and exhaled with a loud noise. He stood there for a moment to calm down. Then he turned his face up like a fallen angel calling back his God.

"Alright," he said, instantly in an even and kind voice, his tone and expression completely changed, as they sometimes did. "Be that as it may. Societal expectations and all that... That doesn't really matter. No need to worry about that. You're still wonderful. I love talking to you about art—and I enjoy being with you in general. Plus, you are a fantastic kisser. So, I'll see you on Thursday then?"

"No," Yora said. She sounded like someone else. "Not anymore, no."

She looked at him and said nothing, and he said nothing and looked at her—as if he had not really seen her before. Then he tried again.

"But we can still be friends, can't we?"

And the red rose in its vase did not wither, did not put out its flame, although it should have withered and died this morning, should have rotted right before their eyes, should have had worms eat out its heart and had its lifeless petals hang limp above the void where its rose essence used to be like the discarded clothes of a man about to be executed. But this stubborn flower of evil bloomed defiantly, just as Bonnie's breasts must have bloomed under Sebastian's kisses.

Yora shifted her eyes to Sebastian again, to his beautiful face, and said,

"No. I do not want to see you again. Ever."

Sebastian stood completely still. His mouth opened, his eyes grew wide. He did not move and did not look at her, but stared somewhere into the empty space, through Yora. He did not try to object, or to explain himself, did not attempt a joke, did not even act angry or stunned—because he was, in fact, stunned. If pain had not overwhelmed Yora's perceptiveness, she would have realized, perhaps, that this state was unusual for Sebastian. They did not say another word to each other.

Yora got up, went into the bedroom, gathered her things, put on her sandals, and left without saying goodbye. This was the first time he did not walk her to her car.

When she came home, Yora lay down on the mattress and closed her eyes. Inga was not there yet. She wondered what a person might feel when they fall out of a plane. Was it true that the fall was not vertical, as one would imagine, but air currents carried your body horizontally forward first, not letting it drop right away? And, for a while, you might skate across the sky, full of the illusion of flight. Did it feel cold to fly like that, or did you feel nothing because you froze instantly into an icicle? Did you have the wherewithal to admire the views? Did it last awhile—or only an instant that just seemed endless because it was your last? And when you came down to earth—did a tremble of the last premonition shake your body? Did it speed up? Or did flight turn into a fall so unmistakably that the speed itself told you that you were about to die? And when you hit the ground, did it hurt? Did you have time to feel the pain? Did the pain go out with your consciousness? Or was it too powerful even to be felt in a mortal body?

When Inga came home, Yora was still on the mattress.

"Are you asleep?" Inga asked from the doorway, fighting with the lock that would not, again, let go of the key. If anyone happened to be walking past the building, they could have seen into their cramped studio through the open door. Their apartment was on the second floor, though, so any curious onlooker was unlikely to see all that much. But they could still catch a glimpse of the unmade bed on the mattress pushed right up against the door in the tiny room, and Yora, fully dressed and in her sandals, on top of it. They might have even caught a glimpse of her pale face pressed against the pillow. It was whiter than the pillowcase.

"Yora? Ma? You don't look right," Inga said as she lay down next to Yora. "I am so tired... Stupid management class. My exam is in two weeks. What's wrong? Didn't you see Sebastian today? Did you have a fight?"

"Uh-huh," was all Yora could utter.

"Let's hear it."

Yora sat up and said in a colorless voice, "He told me he had other women, and he had to manage his time carefully to meet up with all of them. Hang on, let me finish. It's not what you think. One of them is coming on Saturday. Her name is Bonnie. He braids her hair. Her body is like mine, just as beautiful, but she, unlike me, is very young, and he is her teacher of life and sex."

Inga said nothing, shocked. Then she, too, sat down. When Yora started speaking, Inga had meant to comfort her, tell her something along the lines of lovers can say all kinds of things to each other in a fight, but they don't mean half of it, it's just a fight, and it's okay that Yora won't tell her what they actually fought about; clearly, Sebastian told her all kinds of nonsense to make himself look good, as one does, what women could he possibly have, he's like a hundred and ten!—but the mention of Bonnie's body made Inga shudder. A man could make up all kinds of stuff about other women in general, but you could not make up the part about Bonnie's body.

"Ma," Inga said slowly when Yora stopped. "Yora, you know, I didn't like him from the start, this Sebastian of yours. He was weird. Who meets a person in a park and invites them over on the spot! I told you back then, be careful, don't get involved with him, you can't tell what kind of man he is. He could have slipped something into your wine! He could have told you anything, that he was an actor, sure, that he was Udo Kier himself. Like you could prove him wrong! I'm convinced— if we'd talked to someone who knows him, we would've heard all kinds of things... You could tell he is a freak."

"No," Yora said. "He is not a freak. He has fashioned himself the kind of life he believes is appropriate. I am the freak."

It was close to noon. Inga left the apartment for a bit—she went to the store—came back, made food, read her textbooks, and Yora still lay between the sheets, not taking her sandals off and not dying. Inga called her to come eat; Yora did not come.

"At least change out of your clothes," Inga said, but Yora did not want to—she still had Sebastian's smell on her, powerful as a drug.

Behind the lowered blinds, the day passed, and only a few sparks of the sun got caught between the rectangular strips and bit into Yora's body like poisonous thorns. Inga would come and shake Yora a bit, bring her a drink of water. Yora could not remember whether she drank it or not. Then, suddenly, without any transition, it was dark, and Inga lay down on the mattress as well and instantly fell asleep—she was tired and had classes to go to in the morning. "Lucky Inga," Yora thought. "She can sleep," and realized she, too, was falling asleep, dressed and motionless. She was leaving her body, departing into a new, as yet unfamiliar kind of sleep, and whatever it turned out to be, it could not be worse than being awake.

She dreamed she was a warrior armed with a giant pair of scissors who stood facing a beast that resembled a crocodile, but with a stubby maw. The animal closed in on her, and she helplessly waved her scissors in front of its nose; she could not even close the blades, they were so heavy and hard to move, but right at the moment when the beast opened its maw, which suddenly turned out to be much bigger and capacious than it looked from outside, Yora made one last desperate lunge with the infernal scissors, and then again, and one more, and again; she heard the snap of the blades, then again and yet again, and suddenly the beast was in a shallow hole that had opened up at Yora's feet. Yora inched to the rim of the hole and, terrified, looked in. The beast lay on its back, mutely moving the stumps of its crocodile-like feet in the air, except they no longer looked like crocodile feet but like empty, severed rubber hoses. There was no blood. Yora stared at the downed beast as if charmed. The four smooth, perfectly even stumps kept moving, sucking in air, and there was something very indecent about it. "Neither man nor woman," Yora thought, for some reason, and woke up.

It felt like morning, but Inga was still asleep next to her. Yora stirred, and her body responded with sudden pain as if she had spent the night running or carrying heavy objects. Yora groaned and woke up Inga, who instantly sat up on the bed and rubbed her eyes.

"What's wrong? What happened?"

Still a little stunned by her dream, Yora looked at Inga—and burst out crying, surprising them both.

"Yora! Ma! Come on, tell me what's wrong!"

"I can't live without him," Yora muttered through tears, sobbing. "I made a huge mistake yesterday... I should have... thought about it..."

"Yora," Inga said, hugging her. "There was nothing to think about. He is sick in the head."

"You don't understand. You haven't seen him!"

"Thank God for that!"

"But I... I..."

"What are you going to do? Yora? Ma?" Inga was alarmed.

"I'm going to call him."

"And say what?"

"Nothing," Yora wailed. "I'll tell him it's okay, he can have things the way he wants. Bonnie, Mumtaz, I don't care. As long as he is with me, too. I can't be without him. I'll get him back."

Yora slipped out of Inga's arms and reached for the phone.

"Wait! What time is it?" Inga asked. She tucked her bare legs under her.

Yora looked at the window, but the dense blind was still down, and you couldn't tell by the light what time it was. Her body was no help either—it hurt as if she hadn't slept for an eternity.

LOVE LIFE

"I don't know."

"It's probably too early to call."

Yora looked at her phone.

"No, it's after seven. He gets up early."

Sebastian picked up right away—as if he had been waiting for her call.

"Yora?" he asked. He sounded very alert, as if he'd been up for hours. "Is that you?"

"Of course it is."

"I'm glad."

His voice was neither sad nor tired.

"Listen, I'd like to... We didn't quite talk things over yesterday," she said.

"About what?"

"About us."

He was silent for a moment and then laughed his beautiful actor's laugh.

"As someone with a lot of experience, I can tell you right now you can't fix things with words. Who upset whom, how, and why—I don't know why people have to talk about all that. It's no use. Usually, you can't fix anything anyway."

At this point she was probably expected to burst out crying again and tell him—tell him what? That she loved him? That she was sorry? That she wanted to see him, right then and there, that she wanted to be in his arms, forever? Forever? And to look, look at his face?

And yet, somehow, his words had made this impossible. She could no longer be okay with Bonnie.

"Yora? You're not saying anything... Okay, we can chat about something nicer. What's the weather like on your side of town?"

Yora gathered her will and lied, "That's not what I meant, Sebastian. I don't want to fix anything. I just want to understand what happened."

"Oh my God, so what *did* happen? Two people had a mis-understanding, that's what happened. It happens all the time. I wouldn't call it a remarkable thing. Nothing to be dramatic about. Trust me, it's nothing, really nothing. It's laughable to care as much as you seem to do. That's just life these days, you know? People meet, people break up—so what! There's a million people out there who can make you happy. At least..."

"But you did it on purpose. You did not tell me on purpose."

"Which part? Why do you assume people are so over-sensitive? I told you everything. And on top of that, we've already talked about this."

"No, it's wrong, it's all wrong! You acted as if I were your enemy. You actually did not tell me... You told me nothing, from the very beginning. You talked about fate. And then you were the one to get upset with me."

"Oh, here we go—"

"Just hang on a minute..."

Everything she said sounded wrong, pathetic, and trite. She wrestled with muddy masses of words (previously used, sullied by someone else, filmed over with muteness) like mountains of broken seashells and looked for a single living word among them.

Suddenly, as she wandered lost in the darkness, she found it.

"If yesterday, even for a second, you had shown that you were also hurt—if you had said, *this hurts*, this could have been an entirely different conversation."

"That it hurts? Hurts?" Sebastian repeated, lost, as if he were trying the word on his tongue—and was afraid to get physically hurt. "Oh, I see," he said, and then repeated, "I see..."

His voice turned softer—as if he had tested different intonations and had finally found the right one.

LOVE LIFE 43

"So you want me to apologize? I thought I did already, but I can do it again. It's not hard. Please forgive me, it is entirely my fault. I am just truly very bad at communicating clearly. It's just the way I am."

His apology, apparently, was supposed to stand in for his warm embrace and their nights on the veranda. But how? And how could she explain this to him? Should she tell him not to apologize, because it wouldn't change any-thing? But he already told her it wouldn't. Then what was the point of this entire conversation? Sebastian had caught Yora in a labyrinth, caught her and locked her in there, and she could wander there till the Second Coming. She had to say something in response to this, but she did not have a chance because he abruptly ended the conversation.

"Yora, I have to go. I'll call you in two hours, okay?"

"Okay," she spoke with her lips turned to stone and start-ed to wait.

Two hours passed, then three, and more; Inga had left and come back, and Yora still sat in front of the phone as if it were a magic egg that contained her own death.

Inga came into the room and asked whether Yora had eaten and showered.

"No," Yora said. "No, I haven't."

"Then come on, let's go."

"What if he calls?"

"He'll call back."

"You just don't get it!"

Inga went to the stove, put on a kettle, and made a bowl of oatmeal for Yora. The phone did not ring.

Sebastian finally called the following night.

"Yora?"

"Yes."

"I'm sorry, I had a ton to do. Got all frazzled. I meant to call you back that same morning, but it was just one thing after another. And today I got up at seven and went to the bathroom. And the cat came in and just did it on the floor. Just picture it— there I am, doing my thing, like a regular person in the morning... You know, *there*... And the cat comes in, makes himself comfortable and does his business! I gave him a good kick, but don't worry, he'll live, he's fine..."

Yora listened to this in horror. Who cared about the cat? Who cared about the floor? Did Sebastian not care about her at all? Or was he carrying on like this precisely because he *did* care?

"Sebastian," she said. "Could we meet and talk in person?"

"Yes, of course," he said instantly. "I just found a wonderful little Greek restaurant not far from my house. It has a grotto."

"When?" she asked. "When?" A small tremble ran up and down her body.

"When?" he repeated after her. "Who knows, when... Probably next week. I am so busy."

"Can you make it any sooner?"

"I can't."

He said goodbye without agreeing to anything specific—neither the date nor the place—and hung up. Twenty minutes of eternity later, she got a message from him—a picture of the lake at night, with the sky purple above it. Was he trying to mock her? Did he mean to remind her about the days and nights they had spent together, to make her desire burn even hotter, burn even more mercilessly?

Days turned into weeks, but Sebastian did not call back. "What did he even want? What did he want?" Yora asked herself in the long, unbearable evenings. Inga, herself tormented by Carlos who would cancel dates or go silent, which then prompted her to abandon all pretense to pride and call him first, consoled Yora as best she could.

"Well, Ma, what do any of them ever want?"

"What?"

"To sleep with you."

"He's got people to sleep with."

"So he must be in love. Do you think he is not hurting now? Why can't you imagine him hurting?"

Scattered fragments of different moments flickered before Yora's eyes, as in a kaleidoscope, but refused to cohere into a single picture.

"He is not hurting."

"How is that possible? Where is he going to find another woman like you? This doesn't make sense."

"He doesn't want a woman like me."

"What does he want then?"

"I'm not sure. Bonnie?"

"But he spent all those weeks with you. Didn't he act like he was in love?"

"He seemed to. But not quite."

"How could he seem to but not quite?"

"I don't know."

"You were intimate. What did his eyes tell you? His body?"

"I don't know."

"But this is wrong, this is totally wrong! What did he want from you? What?" It was Inga's turn to repeat the question.

"I don't know."

"I don't believe you! Okay, what did you want from him?"

"I don't know."

"Go to his house. You know where he lives, don't you?"

"Right, and Bonnie will be there," Yora said. In her grief, she forgot all about Mumtaz.

"Make a scene," Inga suggested.

"Are you nuts? They'll send me to jail. This is not the Soviet Union; everything is very civilized here. He'll tell the police he does it with multiple women and all by mutual consent, which is true, and I'm just a barbarian with no manners."

"But the cops aren't blind, are they? They'll see what a freak he is!"

"I'm sure they will," Yora agreed. "But they won't be able to do anything about it."

"At least he'd be on their radar."

"Gangsters, maniacs, and heroin traffickers are on their radar. The police don't give a hoot about some dude and his women, as long as he doesn't beat them, and he, as you well know, doesn't do that."

"There's got to be a way," Inga said with the determination of a person who keeps shoving the wrong key into a lock and refuses to believe that it doesn't fit. "Go and talk to him again. Or meet him as if by accident. He goes to the park, after all, goes out for walks..."

Yora remembered the souvenir shops, pelicans, and twisting old streets, and groaned out loud. It was now Bonnie who walked them. The black phone was silent. The corner of the all-seeing eye, the one that turned blue when she got a message or a missed call, had long gone out.

Dusk came sooner that day, as the tropical winter rolled up life like a scroll; here, the trees never completely lost their leaves, the greenery did not quite fade, and the bones of the earth never showed naked, but the spirit did evaporate, and things became motionless, inanimate like plastic lawn ornaments. The grass no longer smelled, late flowers hung dead here and there on the stems of bushes, and the stems themselves bent in the air in arcs that went nowhere. The birds fell silent and flew, probably, only above the sea, diving now and then after fish, because the sea remained alive even during this season.

Inga came home from classes when Yora was done with work and would lie down, exhausted, on the mattress next

LOVE LIFE 47

to Yora and say, "Carlos didn't call today either..." She would go on, "I am so tired—I can't even talk. I never thought one could be this tired. Even last semester was different. I think I know why—because I always knew I would see him. And now I can't be sure. My life has no direction. How can one live like this? It's like stepping out of a hut on a desert island in the middle of the night..."

Eventually, Inga would get up, make herself some food, and eat—and would then slowly come back to life, revived by the food, by the fact that she was finally home, by the presence of Yora who still lay on the mattress unable to move. Inga would regain some confidence.

"I can't believe it, kill me, but I can't believe that he could dump me. Where is he going to find another woman like me? But if he does want to dump me, well, to heck with him. I'll live without him, but he, oh he'll really regret it! You don't think so? I'm sure he will. Let him go, there's plenty of fish like him in the sea... I can always find someone else."

At moments like these, Inga could let Carlos go with some ease, and her own determination amplified her imagined satisfaction. The determination to let him go also bred new confidence and a new hope.

"It's impossible. Just look around—is it easy to find a woman like me? I just don't believe it. And you know what else? I know he loves me because I love him. How could someone not respond to being loved, when they are loved this much?"

At night, Yora thought she heard noises outside the front door, as if someone wanted to come in but did not dare knock and instead stood there for a while, listening in, and then walked away. On several occasions, Yora crept to the door and listened from her side, and it seemed to her she could hear someone breathing out there. "Sebastian!" would flash in her mind and she would throw the door open, but there was no one there. Just once she heard a muffled giggle (it came from the studio next door where, she and Inga had learned, a skinny Goth girl, always dressed in black, lived), but she had probably imagined it. One time, Yora leapt to her feet in the middle of the night, gasping for air, yanked the door open hard, as if tearing a shirt off her chest, and a hot sheaf of light from the streetlight burst into their studio and woke Inga.

"Ma, what are you doing?" Inga asked. "I have classes first thing in the morning."

"Nothing. I thought someone was there."

"But there isn't anyone out there," Inga groaned, bending her arm and hiding her face behind it. "Close the door!"

But Yora could not. She stood there and looked into the emptiness that seeped slowly into the studio around her.

* * *

The following day brought more bad news.

"It's Carlos," Inga said, weeping that evening.

"What happened?"

"I texted Willie."

"Who's Willie?"

"What do you mean, who? He's Carlos's coach. Did you forget already?"

Yora had.

"Anyway. Willie told me that Carlos was traded to another team. Denver. He is moving to Denver! In three days! Can you believe it?"

"Inga... Oh my... Cooney," Yora muttered, unable, at that moment, to summon an appropriate reaction.

LOVE LIFE

"But we can get through this, I know we can!" Inga said through tears. "Long-distance is not that bad, right? Plenty of couples live like that. I know what to do—I'll try to get a job over there, in Denver, it's totally doable."

She stopped crying and spoke almost calmly.

"It's nothing to beat myself up about, right? I've read that the most important thing in a long-distance relationship is to have a clear plan. A plan to see each other regularly. A plan to live together eventually. We'll have a plan like that."

"But—" Yora started to say, but Inga did not let her.

"Just don't tell me it's impossible. If both people want it, anything is possible."

Yora wanted to say that Carlos, it seemed, did not want anything of the kind, but she decided not to. Inga, she knew, could not have failed to see that. It was just like when it took time for a person to recognize they've had a limb amputated. It was no use telling Inga that her arm or leg was already gone.

"What are you going to do?" Yora asked instead.

Inga sighed.

"My mom has this fortune teller woman who comes around. They're neighbors. I'll ask mom to talk to her on Skype. See what she says. She's good, she had told mom that I'd go to the States, that I would get into college here—she had seen that."

"What has she been saying recently?"

"She hasn't been at mom's recently."

"Inga... Well, I don't know... Cooney, are you sure?"

"You don't believe these things, do you?"

"I probably don't. What do the cards have to do with us? All the way over here?" Yora looked up as if searching for the cosmic deck of cards that knew everything but refused to manifest. "But that's just me. Maybe the cards can talk to someone who believes in them."

But Inga never called the fortune teller.

Instead, she told Yora, "You are going to the airport with me. Two days from now. He is leaving in two days. We have to stop him."

"What are you talking about! You don't even know his flight number."

"I know it's a flight to Denver."

"There could be a dozen of those!"

"I know it's in the morning. Ask Mariana to let you off for a couple of hours."

"Inga, what's wrong with you? How are you going to find him? Do you know how many airlines fly to Denver?"

"I'll stand where the trains leave for the terminals. Those exits are close to each other."

"He might not even be flying direct. What if he's going through, say, Memphis? Are you going to watch all the Memphis gates, too? Or Honolulu."

"There aren't any flights like that, to Denver via Honolulu."

Yora pictured the enormous continent, the oceans around it.

"Alright. Then what?"

"What do you mean then what? I'll tell him... I'll tell him everything!"

At the airport, music was playing, the vapid and unobtrusive variety of it that was called "muzak," a string of empty musical phrases that all led to dead-ends. There were few people around—it was just after eight. Most people flew out at noon, and the airports got crowded around that time. At the moment, only airport security workers stood by themselves at the exits to the gates, connected by the trains that one could only get on with a boarding pass.

Inga and Yora circled around the four train terminals, but Carlos was not there. "What if," Yora thought, "he is not

LOVE LIFE

even coming? He could just slip away. His flight could have been rescheduled. The ticket was certain to have been paid for by the Denver team. They might not even need him for another week, they might not have anywhere to put him up yet. They might not have any volunteers, or whoever they send to pick new players up. Or do they not even send anyone? A man just gets off the plane, walks out into a new city, and starts a new life."

For lack of anything better to do, Yora studied the glass cubes of the shop windows, the alligators on the T-shirts, expensive jewelry, the boxes of signature local coconut-flavored marmalade...

"Carlos!" Inga cried out suddenly, and Yora almost cried out, too, startled by the sound of Inga's voice. She turned to look where Inga was pointing and froze in surprise. In the window of the Harley Davidson store, astride the display motorcycle, posing as if for a commercial shoot, sat Carlos, dressed in a stylish pair of track pants and a hoodie. He was saying something to his friends, flexing his arm and feeling his bicep, and his two friends who were taking pictures with their phones—one more before the flight!—shouted their approval.

"Come on now, Saint Croix, it's your turn! You sit here!"

"Oh!" Yora gasped, despite herself.

In the time it took her to find her bearings, Inga dashed to her beloved.

"Carlos!" she shouted, and he all but fell off the motorcycle.

"Inga?" was all he could say. He avoided looking her in the eye.

"It's me!" She glowed in his presence with a happy glow. "It's me! Aren't you glad to see me?"

"Well, I..."

"Carlos!"

"Hey there, I'm Tony." A quick-thinking friend of Carlos's inserted himself, a young blonde man in a baseball cap. He extended his hand to Inga, and she automatically shook it. "And what is your name?"

"Inga."

"A pleasure to meet you!" You could tell Tony had no trouble talking to women because they were usually favorably inclined toward him. His bottom lip was split, but this only added to his charm. "Uh, here's the thing, we are late for our flight, so we have to run. Bye-bye!"

Behind his back, Carlos and the third man, Saint Croix, presumably, with tattoos, retreated through another store exit. A concerned salesperson headed for the group—not only did these hooligans climb onto his motorcycle, they were now making a scene smack dab in the middle of the store.

"There! Look, they are getting away!" Yora pointed. A hunting urge had come over her. "After them!"

Tony covered the retreat. The young men ran through a row of connected stores—a Starbucks, a jewelry store, and, finally, a bookstore. They were easy to spot with Tony's blonde curls, Carlos's black hoodie, and Saint Croix's tattoos. The men ran as if they were on a football field, bursting through the opposing team's invisible line of defense with their taut, honed bodies. They ran away from the woman who stood frozen and looked around her.

"Who are you looking for?" Yora asked, but Inga did not answer.

Yora grabbed Inga's hand and tried to drag her away, anywhere, but Inga suddenly came back to life, jerked her hand, limp and lifeless only a moment ago, free, and took off so fast that Yora instantly fell behind.

For a moment, Yora felt as if she were watching a movie—a slow-motion montage, with every detail made clear—Inga running through the row of stores, past flashes of

LOVE LIFE 53

faceted glass and cubic zirconia, accompanied by the intolerable sound of "muzak," bumping into other passengers, and Carlos and his team, also running, but away from her, to the terminal where they could be lifted away into the air. The men reach a woman in uniform and rush to show her their boarding passes and IDs, Carlos first, with a *Déjame pasar! Déjame pasar!* Carlos speaks to the uniformed woman rapidly and gestures at Inga who is closing in; the quick-thinking Tony shoves Carlos from behind into safety, Carlos sprints away from the checkpoint as fast as possible, all the way to the large pane of glass through which the terminal train is already visible, and stands there, with his back to Inga, so that he would never, never again happen to look her in the eye.

Inga finally reached the checkpoint, and Yora ran up after her, just in time to grab her friend by the shoulders.

"You can't be here! Not here!" the security officer yelled at Inga. Several things happened at once—Inga wept, the officer shouted into her radio...

The train came. Inga howled. The police came running.

"I'll take her away, just a second," Yora yelled to be heard over the ruckus. "For god's sake, she is not going to do anything, I'll take her away!"

It took everything Yora had to hold Inga back; a slip—and Inga would have rammed her way into the restricted zone.

"Carlos!" Inga keened so desperately that a crowd started gathering around them. "Carlos! Just once! Look at me just once! Once!"

Meanwhile, Carlos and his now quiet friends boarded the train that would take them to a different world. The train doors closed, the train left, and the terminal was now empty.

"Miss, you can't be here, please step away," a young policeman said to Inga, blocking her way with his arm. He could have arrested them if he wanted to, but he did not want to.

"I'll take her away in just a second," Yora said again. She took Inga's suddenly limp hand and led her to the elevator, and when they got in the elevator, the expression on Inga's face froze and remained frozen for many more hours, if not days—her eyebrows came together and sort of cracked in the middle, her mouth twisted in surprise, and the light went out of her eyes. Tears ran steadily down her cheeks.

Yora pressed the button and felt an electric shock of pain in her own body: perhaps, Inga's soundless scream, locked in the molecules of air around them, looked for a way to burst out.

***

Back home, they sat on the floor, on the narrow strip left free by the mattress and stared at each other.

"No, I'm not crying," Inga said while tears kept crawling down from her eyes. "I'm not worried about me. I can cope with this, I'm strong—I'm worried about him. If only you knew what he's like! What it's going to be like for him when he realizes what he's done and wants to get me back—and I have no doubt that's exactly what will happen! I will never trust him again, never. He'll come begging at my door, he'll beg me to come back, don't think he won't. Because he loves me, oh, the fool, he is such a fool. He couldn't have lied about it, no one could lie like that, I don't believe it. He told me we would get married, that we would have children. Why, for Christ's sake, why? And I believed him! I really did."

"He said that?"

LOVE LIFE   55

"He did."

"You didn't tell me."

"Oh, what's the use now? What a fool, what a damn fool! How could he treat me like that! It's criminal. He didn't even bother to hear me out! How could he be like that?" Inga paused, and the tears rolled faster. A terrible thought just occurred to her.

"Listen, Ma," she said in a small voice, much softer than before, as if she did not dare speak her terror out loud. "Tell me honestly, do you think he'll just get away with this? God won't smite him down? He'll just have his fun here and there, and then start a family when he's an old man, and everyone will respect him? He'll just date whoever he wants, however he wants? Just like that? And promise them mountains of gold? And then abandon them? And there will be no justice? Why does everyone forgive him? Why does life forgive him—forgive him everything when it forgives nothing to me?"

Despair grew in Inga's voice.

"What about justice? Does it not even exist? Or is it asleep?"

She burst into tears with new force.

"But he loves me, he does, I know it! It can't be otherwise, it cannot! How could he eat from the same plate, sleep in the same bed, and not love me? I don't get it!" she wailed, her voice full of torment. "He loves me, he loves me, how could he not? How? Is he... just afraid to face it?"

Under the hailstorm of these unbearable words, Yora got up and, in the grip of despair herself, picked up her phone and went out onto the stairs. She dialed Sebastian's number, and this time he picked up right away.

"Yora?"

"You haven't deleted my number yet?"

"Why would I?" he said.

"Sebastian, listen, I want to ask you something very important."

"Go ahead."

"Did you... Did you really like me?"

"I did really like you."

"Did you like me a lot?"

"I liked you a lot."

"Do you still think about me sometimes?"

"Uh-huh."

"Do you think about me often?"

"Uh-huh."

"You mean it?"

He said nothing for a moment, and then said, "Has it ever occurred to you that I don't throw myself like that at every skirt, especially from your Eastern God-damned Europe?"

"Alright," she said. "Listen... Perhaps you meant... If I said something wrong to you, something that made you think I didn't have feelings for you... I meant to say that..."

"Yora, I don't have feelings for anyone. Why can't you believe a man when he's telling the truth? I believe that, if two people want each other, that is sufficient. And I am not at all lonely, if that's what you're worried about. I have plenty of people to spend time with, which is something I sincerely wish for you as well."

"Sebastian!" she exclaimed. "One more time, please, just hold me one more time! You said it yourself—touch is like our daily bread. Just one more time!"

Sebastian was silent for a moment, and then said, slowly and emphatically, "Generally speaking, I like younger women. I'm very happy with younger women, they haven't had their minds and bodies spoiled yet. Very young girls with delicate bones. You could say they're officially my fetish."

"Sebastian!"

"Yes, you're correct—girls like Bonnie."

"Sebastian!"

"Do you know what one of my directors taught me? He... Actually, his name won't mean anything to you... Anyway, he taught me this one very simple truth—there's no use investing time and effort in something that has already left you. I think such economy is only reasonable."

And he hung up.

Yora gasped for air as if someone had hit her in the solar plexus. She thought she heard a key turn in the neighbor's door. She thought she heard muffled giggling. Had someone been listening to her? Who? That Goth girl all in black?

And the following week it started to rain again. Yora woke up to a heavy drum roll—the rain, unleashed, hammered on the roof, the windows, the puddles outside; it looked like the Flood.

During hurricane season in the Atlantic, the rainstorms could be ferocious, and then muddy water filled everything—all the ponds, man-made and natural, ditches, dips in the ground, and potholes in the streets—and cars sank in their parking lots, poking their lost faces out of the water like abandoned animals. But hurricane season was over and that only added to the shock of this unexpected cataclysm. The rain was cold, colder even than in the summer when the sun would often break through a sheet of suffocating clouds. The sky changed by the hour and the clouds that had come and blanketed the horizon would grow pale and vanish above the sea. Now, blackness ruled over the Peninsula, once so welcoming, a dismal lack of visibility, an uninterrupted, days'-long gloom. The days grew shorter and shorter; the year was devouring itself. At night, the rectangle of the window would slowly flash with the otherworldly glow of lightning, each flash an omen of worse times to come. It was probably the endless rain, sticky like the sweat of a dying man, that gave Yora a fever for who knew how many days.

She and Inga barely left the apartment now, except to go to work, which sucked the life out of them as badly as men did, and rarely went grocery shopping, surviving on what they had in their pantry— cereal, canned beans, dried fruit, nuts. Sometimes they did not eat at all; Yora did not remember. They would fall onto their bed, the center of their universe, its black hole, and cry, and cry. Outside, it rained and rained. Yora no longer read books, watched movies, or listened to music because she wanted them to tell her something about herself, but they no longer did. Her fever did not abate. Fever gathered inside her and around her, and would not be chased away, and the heat of it colored everything— Yora's consciousness, people's faces, digits on the computer screen. It would not let her focus on any one thing.

"Do you have medical insurance?" asked Mariana Schneider, her supervisor at work.

"I think so," Yora said and then wondered, did she? She thought she had paid the premium that month, or was it several months ago already?

"Is something wrong?" other women at work asked when she ran, all sweaty, into the office.

"Should I get you some pills?" Inga asked.

"What are you talking about?" Yora answered. "It's purely psychosomatic."

"That's some psychosomatic reaction you've got!" Inga worried. "You're burning up!"

"Excellent—I'll burn up and there will be nothing left of me."

Yora saw Bonnie's body unfold before her eyes like a book—the young, younger than hers, powerful body she had never laid eyes on—all its magnificent curves, immune to the forces of time, all its warm hollows and dimples, all its smiles and moans, all its thin braids, and this last thing hurt the most. She, Bonnie, could be at Sebastian's right at

LOVE LIFE   59

that very moment, with her head on his lap and him playing with her hair. Bonnie would be smiling with pleasure,
closing her eyes, catching his fingers with her lips... Here's
Bonnie coming to spend the weekend with Sebastian... Yora
wondered about the details. Did she bring a little suitcase?
She must... Yora did not ask Sebastian where Bonnie was
from, and she could be from somewhere around here, within a two-hour drive. In her mind, Yora stood in the middle
of Sebastian's living room and looked around, searching for
clues like a sleepwalking Sherlock Holmes. She suddenly
remembered seeing an envelope on his desk, among other
papers—a postcard envelope, squarer than the standard
bank or insurance mail. The return address said Gainesville,
a town about two hours away from them. Within two hours,
that's right... Did Bonnie really send Sebastian cards? For
what occasion? There were no special holidays in the summer and early fall, and Sebastian wouldn't have left last
year's Christmas card on his desk, especially since he hadn't
even been living here last Christmas! His desk had been
packed and moved, and all the mail sorted, with old letters
thrown away. Did Bonnie send him a birthday card? When
was his birthday? He never told Yora and never asked about
hers. Yet, apparently, he had told Bonnie? And there she was,
Bonnie on his doorstep, with her little suitcase, fresh from
Gainesville—it's a college town, was she a student?

A freshman, if she's only eighteen; people graduated
from high school at seventeen in this country. Did her parents know about her much older lover? Did she even have
parents? It would've been her parents who bought her that
nice little wheeled suitcase, the suitcase she brought when
she came home for breaks. Here you go, they would've said,
a very grown-up suitcase for your very grown-up life. Or did
they put it under the Christmas tree as if she were still a little
girl? Or did they just put a green-and-red bow on it and place

it in Bonnie's room for her to find? Or perhaps Bonnie had no parents at all, and she was all alone in the world? And she bought that suitcase in a thrift store—someone else's suitcase, a suitcase that had belonged to a nice girl from a nice family, the kind that gave nice Christmas presents, but the nice girl already had a new suitcase, from another Christmas? Since Christmas did, if you were lucky, come every year. Be that as it may, there she was, Bonnie, on Sebastian's doorstep, with her suitcase. Bonnie looked fresh—the drive did not take long. What's two hours behind the wheel, to see the man you love! For some reason, Yora had no doubt that Sebastian was the man Bonnie loved. Sebastian would open the door and tell Bonnie, "Look, it says here, 'Get Lost!' But that's for other people, not for you." Bonnie would step into the house and Sebastian would kiss her on the top of her head, exactly the way he used to kiss Yora. And they would go sit on the veranda and watch the rain wash away the line between October and November, watch it beat down on the wet palm trees with their rotting leaves.

* * *

That night, a phone call jerked Yora out of her unconsciousness. It was Mariana Schneider.

"Yora? Don't go into the office tomorrow—go to Kennedy Street, where the conference is. Lee is sick, and we don't have anyone else to staff the booth. Paula can come but only in the afternoon, so it's you for the morning. Write it down—620 Kennedy, right at Gandhi, it's on the ground floor, to the right after you come in—you can't miss it. Did you get it?"

"Uh-huh," Yora said. She had a fit of coughing.

LOVE LIFE 61

"Are you sick?"

"No, nothing like that," Yora lied. "My tea just went down the wrong pipe."

"Oh, okay. So come in the morning. Remember—you have to be there at eight, not nine. Leave early, it's a bit far."

"I'll be there."

"Great. Call me afterwards, let me know how it goes."

The night, heavy as a wet blanket, set in right after this short conversation. Every hour, Yora woke up from the loud sound of her own heartbeat and, terrified, checked her phone with its flash of new digits to make sure she hadn't overslept. Then she would fall back onto her pillow, face down, and sink into numbness. She spent the last hour wide awake, counting the beats of her heart. Pain filled her body with a familiar wave, and rain rustled outside the window. Finally, the alarm rang—and Yora turned it off, so as not to wake Inga. She got up in the dark, dressed quietly, and left the apartment without having breakfast. When she came downstairs and got into her car, the rain suddenly started coming down harder; she heard thunder in the distance. Yora sat for some time in the car, blinded by the deluge, not starting the engine, as if this was the kind of rain she could just wait out. But the rain did not let up even for a second.

She ran into trouble as soon as she tried to turn onto Fletcher. Cars stood bumper to bumper. The cars were lining up along the center divider—the lanes on both sides of the road had been flooded. This could not happen, was not supposed to happen—roads here were built to prevent even the worst of tropical storms from doing precisely this. "It's the end of days," Yora muttered as she flipped on her turn signal. She really wanted to get where she was going as fast as possible because suddenly all her joints started to hurt so much she could've groaned out loud. Yora crawled in the line of cars through several traffic lights, only to discover that the traffic stopped almost entirely at Bruce B. Downs Boulevard.

Up till then, the cars could move, albeit at a crawl, but now they only inched forward, at long intervals. The problem soon became clear—a traffic light was out at the next intersection. It flashed helplessly yellow, while the police directed traffic. The slow stop-and-go rhythm was hard to take; Yora's joints kept hurting. When the car moved, she felt better—motion gave her hope, and Yora ached for every short interval of it. When it was Yora's turn to cross the intersection, a car from another lane suddenly sped ahead, cut her off and took what was supposed to be her place on the far side of Bruce B. Downs. Yora stepped on the gas and went through. The policeman could see these maneuvers, and he signaled for Yora to go back, but it was too late. She ended up in the middle of the intersection where the cross traffic could hit her. The policeman came up to her car and knocked on the window, and Yora had to roll it down, which was its own hazard considering the rain. The policeman was wrapped in waterproof rain gear from head to toe.

"Ma'am, you have to move out of the way," he said. "There is no room. Pull into this parking lot, and then come out back on Fletcher."

Arguing would've been useless. Yora did as she was told. The parking lot belonged to a pharmacy. Yora, in too much pain to tolerate the added delay, hesitated for a second, then parked the car, and dashed through the rain into the pharmacy. At least she could buy some ibuprofen. Given that she hadn't eaten anything that morning, it ought to kick in right away.

Just as she walked into the pharmacy, however, the building, like the traffic light, had lost power. The staff pushed open the automatic glass doors, and customers crowded there, looking out at the walls of water that were coming down outside. The uneasy darkness of the store breathed at their backs. The cash registers, of course, did not work.

"My joints are hurting a lot," Yora said to a clerk, a chubby young woman with bleached hair who stood with everyone else at the entrance. "Could you possibly sell me something? I think I have cash..."

"No, I'm sorry," the clerk shook her head. "I can't. I won't be able to reconcile it later."

"What should I do then? I'm..."

"Ask around, someone might have something," the woman suggested, and called out, "Excuse me, does anyone have anything for joint pain? This woman is not well."

People looked at each other, someone rummaged in their purse, others checked their pockets, and finally a man whose face Yora failed to register because she was faint with pain, held out a handful of pills to her.

"There's a water fountain around the corner," the same quick-thinking clerk told her.

Yora went there, but when she turned the corner, she could not see anything in the dark—there were no windows in the store. Yora pulled out her phone and used its screen as a light. Finally, she made it to the water fountain, but as soon as she pressed the lever and was about to swallow the pills, another wave of faintness rocked her. The pills fell out of her hand and rolled away in the dark. Yora got down on her knees and tried to find them. When her knees touched the cold hard floor she almost cried out loud—it hurt so much. Yora stood up. "Better take something from a shelf," she thought. She only needed a few pills; she wasn't a criminal, and she would certainly pay later. But the shelves around her were all wrong, and the store was gigantic. The pills were somewhere on the other end of it. Yora felt scared. She was alone in the dark, just her in the whole entire world—her and the rain. Yora inhaled deeply, trying to chase the fear away. She shifted her weight from one foot to another and heard something crunch underfoot. She bent over and picked up a pill, cracked, and probably unsafely dirty, but it was the only one she had. Yora swallowed it with some water and looked at her phone—it was a quarter to eight. Mariana was going to kill her.

By the time she left the pharmacy and got back behind the wheel, the traffic on Fletcher had thinned out a little. She merged onto Fletcher and quickly reached the highway. The interstate was crowded but, at least, the cars were moving. Yora was only halfway there and already running ten minutes late, and that was provided nothing else went wrong. Close to downtown, the traffic thickened; the off-ramp was down to a single lane. Yora tried to merge but could not; the cars stood bumper-to-bumper. Everyone was running late for work, everyone was in a rush, and no one had any concern for anyone else. "It's alright," Yora reasoned. "I can take one of the next exits." After the Kennedy exit, Interstate 275 and Interstate 4 that went to Orlando both merged into a narrow and congested portion of the highway. The interchange was old and always packed, especially in the morning. Yora discovered that all the exits were closed, all of them—Dale Mabry, Himes Avenue, and even Armenia/Howard. The last exit was for West Shore Boulevard, from which one could take the bypass to Kennedy. But it, too, was closed.

The only exit left was for the Franklin Howard Bridge and State Highway Sixty, where the road forked off toward Clearwater and the airport. But the Franklin Howard exit was also closed—and they closed it right before Yora's eyes, too. This meant the water was rising. Highway Sixty was considered safer in such situations, so Yora took it. It was already eight-twenty-five; Yora had to call Mariana, yet she still hoped for a miracle. "I can get off Sixty onto Nineteen,"

LOVE LIFE

she remembered. This, of course, would take a long time, going the long way around, but from Highway Nineteen she could take Gandhi, and Gandhi would take her to Kennedy. Along Sixty, which ran along a causeway, waves crashed against both sides of the road, splashing every so often right in front of the cars. This seemed insane. This was not supposed to happen. What if the road ahead were washed out? Yora shuddered. She could not turn back—275 was packed solid. It now occurred to Yora that State Highway Sixty, logically thinking, should also be closed. Was the city unaware of what was going on here? Was anyone aware? And why didn't they cancel the conference, the whole workday for that matter, if the Peninsula was experiencing such an apocalypse? Did people think this was normal—commuting through a flood? Why hadn't Mariana called her? Yora turned on the radio, but none of the stations were on air.

The levee finally ended and, a few traffic lights later, Yora could see the overpass on Nineteenth ahead of her. To her astonishment, roadwork was in full swing here, despite the rain. It was impossible to tell what the objective of it was, but a backhoe roared, pulling up shapeless fragments of naked earth, released from under concrete, as if digging a grave. Yellow clay ran down the scoop. Yora was in line to the south exit, waiting her turn, when suddenly thunder blasted overhead, and the rain came down harder.

"The southbound exit is closed! Turn around!" shouted someone dressed in a yellow slicker, probably a traffic cop. Right after this, Yora heard a strange but unmistakably menacing noise. It felt as if a wall of water was coming at her. The day turned as dark as night. The noise was coming closer. Yora bent low over the wheel, pressed her hands over her ears, and closed her eyes, but none of it helped because the noise was now inside her, inside her body where it throbbed and exploded into a million shards, displacing everything that used to be her. She heard herself scream while the alien power inside her ground her essence into dust.

She could not have said how long this lasted, but suddenly everything stopped just as abruptly as it had begun. Yora came to. She was still sitting behind the wheel of her car, but it was much brighter outside. The darkness had receded, and rain, while still going, came down in thin strings and fell without particular urgency. Everything was quiet—there was no wall of water crashing down, no noise of the moving cars, or the traffic-policeman's shouts. Yora, still not quite convinced she was alive, felt her face and neck, and moved her arms and legs. Everything was still intact, and nothing at all hurt, as if she hadn't been in pain all morning. Her body felt as if it were new. What made the pain leave—the pain that seemed impervious to entire handfuls of pills? Was it that single pill she had taken in the dark pharmacy? Yora gingerly pulled out her phone, intending to call Mariana, but the call did not go through. The internet was also down, and the GPS did not work either.

She had to find out, at least, where she was, or ask someone—if she could find anyone around. What if she was the only person who had survived the flood, or had been carried by a merciful wave to the top of Mount Ararat? "Can't be," she mocked herself. "There are no mountains on this Peninsula." If the real Flood happened, everyone here would die, and the Peninsula would revert to what it had originally been—the bottom of the sea. Yora got out of the car, looked around, and realized she was on the street where Sebastian lived. The rain fell onto the bright, unnaturally green grass in front of the houses. A poorly contained sob burst out of Yora's chest. Him, him everywhere she turned! Wherever she went, no matter how hard she tried to escape him and his house! She knew nothing, she was clueless, she had no idea how to get out of this cobweb of roads, from the net of the rain, and there was no one to give her shelter! She had nowhere else to go. There was only the sea all around her, and she felt she was about to dissolve in it like a doll carved out of salt. Would Sebastian let her in, would he take her hand, would he lead her into his bedroom the way he used to, when he would take her there right away, impatient, as soon as she came in? They would lie on his bed and entwine their bodies. They would not do anything, just lie there. It felt so good to just lie there like that with someone you loved. Lovemaking would come later, after they lay in silence for a while, after she touched his collarbones with her lips.

It took Yora an eternity to cross the wet lawn. She rang the doorbell, but no one answered. She waited for a while. The rain kept beating down on the acidic-green grass and, for a second, Yora wondered how the grass kept its color this time of year, when it never got this green even in the spring when everything in this tropical climate was fresh and new. The grass ought to have been dead by now. Instead, it seemed to bloom in the rain.

No one was coming to the door, and Yora rang again, and then, desperately, again. Could he have looked out the window, seen her, and decided not to let her in? Yora looked around—his car was gone. Which meant he wasn't home.

Who was then? Bonnie? Yora banged on the door. The neighbors should have seen her by now, or, rather, heard her, and called the police, but the weather, it seemed, had cowed everyone into inaction. Exhausted, Yora stepped away from the unyielding door. Curtains were drawn on all the windows, and she could not tell whether anyone was home. But Yora could feel someone there. Someone was breathing in there, someone took up space as pain takes up the sensation in an affected limb, and Yora flew toward this pain like a moth charmed by a flame. If only she could look into the house, even for an instant! She glanced back at the door and saw immediately it was ajar. This was impossible; who had opened it? She hadn't heard steps or the lock turning. The door had been securely locked only a minute ago.

Someone was playing tricks on her. Not someone—Bonnie. Maybe this was a game she played every day; maybe visitors like Yora came all the time, and Bonnie learned to predict their every action, even their desperation and, when she was bored, she entertained herself by luring them into the house. Or perhaps she was an enchantress who raised wild winds above the sea, so that water would wash away roads, and the narrow twisting streets, like obedient servants, would deliver yet another victim here, to Bonnie's lair. But Yora could not walk away. She slipped through the door, and found herself, not exactly aware of how she got there, in the bedroom. On the bed, covered with the familiar embroidered quilt, slept Bonnie, naked; or rather, she pretended to be asleep. Light fell on her through a window, now suddenly uncurtained. Outside, not only had the storm ended, but the sun had come out. "Right, like I'm going to believe you're asleep," Yora thought, and Bonnie, as if she heard her, rolled over onto her back and stretched with great gusto, extending her arms and legs, smiling, and tossing a long strand of her dirty blonde hair off her face. Bonnie had a perfect body, magnificently sculpted—long legs, a delicate belly, round butt, small breasts, and chiseled knees, but something about it was repulsive, too; something was off. Yora looked closer. Bonnie reminded her of someone— perhaps Inga, or, to a degree, Yora herself. That was it! Bonnie reminded her of everyone.

"Stop looking!" Yora, mortified numb, ordered herself and jerked toward the door. "You are imagining it! She is just a very young woman who doesn't know her own body yet." At that very moment, Bonnie sat up, crossing her legs, and every gesture of hers now had a new meaning—they

LOVE LIFE

were no longer spontaneous, but calculated and devastatingly beautiful. Her eyes flashed, and then again, and again, like stars with well-honed rays of light. Bonnie folded and unfolded her legs, ran her hands over her thighs, again, and again, then touched her breasts, squeezed her nipples between her fingers, tossed her head back, and ran her tongue around her lips. She fondled herself with growing passion, she bent back on the bed, she drank up her own—or was it someone else's?—beauty; she stroked her smooth, perfect skin as if she were kneading the dough of her body, rolling it out to make sure it could feed more hungry pilgrims; her fingers drew paths into the very mystery of luxury and awe, and she moaned out loud with the sweet torture of it all.

Yora's body, on the contrary, did not exist. Yora was invisible. She raised her hands before her eyes, but she had neither hands nor eyes. How did this happen? Could Bonnie have somehow, by magic, taken her body from her—robbed her, like she robbed other women like her? What other explanation could there be? A new idea stung Yora. What if she, Yora, had died? She had read about this—people died and did not notice it. But, if that were true, where was her body? Who was watching over it? Or had she already been buried and failed to notice that, too? And was she now stuck in-between worlds, doomed to haunt Bonnie for the rest of her life? Was this her penance? Yora fled from the room, looking for the way out, but the house suddenly multiplied, unfolding in every direction, sprouting endless hallways. There were no windows in these hallways, and they seemed to lead exactly to the heart of nowhere—or into other hallways, locked into one closed circulatory system. Yora flew up, but either she did it too quickly for her incipient flying skills, or the space where she was did not obey the rules of mechanics, but the hallway seemed to flip over, and things that used to be above her head were now to her left, and then beneath her, and then Yora lost her bearings. She spun in this house like an astronaut in zero gravity and flew somewhere, no longer in the horizontal or vertical plane, instantly and fully aware that, yes, she had no idea how to be in this world where everything responded to her every motion a hundred times more powerfully than in everyday life, and there were more dimensions of existence than she had once thought possible. She could move here not up or down but in, into the depth of depths, only to find countless more depths beyond. She had no control over these whatsoever, so the best thing to do was to give herself up to their will. So Yora did.

The insane motion stopped. Yora floated in one spot under the ceiling of one of the hallways which now had regular Newtonian characteristics. After a while, she saw a faint light up ahead, like candlelight, and carefully floated toward it. The light came from a rather large, terribly messy room full of people; the floor was littered with scraps of multicolored ribbons, shards of masks and similar detritus. The people in the room were kind of shuffling in place; some had their faces hidden by masks. Right in front of Yora was an interesting group—four older men, a bit heavy, one of them holding a baby. The baby slept, dressed in a colorful onesie with what Yora thought was a pattern of parrots. She looked closer and realized she had been wrong—those were not parrots, but flowers, white lilies and red, and crimson roses. The men stood before Yora a little tense, as if before a photographer. Someone invisible said, "Ready!" and the men nodded their heads, smiling—yes, of course, they were ready—they came out of their rehearsed pose and began making their way toward the center of the room. One of them bent down and picked up two plaster masks with capricious mouths bent in a cry, handed one of them to the man next to him and put on the other one. The other two,

LOVE LIFE

including the man holding the baby, stayed unmasked, giving Yora something else to puzzle over—despite the fact that she could see them perfectly, she could not, for some reason, quite see their faces. "I wonder why," she thought. One of the men looked over his shoulder, as if he had just now noticed her, and yelled into the space in front of him, "Because we've got god-damned multiculturalism here, and quit asking stupid questions!" Yora, still airborne, followed on the men's heels.

There was a line to exit the room. Yora's new acquaintances, however, unceremoniously shoved their way to the front, holding out the baby in its colorful onesie and exclaiming, "We've got a baby, let us through!" Everyone let them through, right up until the door that opened into the next room, but they had to stop there. People were packed into this room so tightly that there was no way to squeeze in. Yora studied the crowd, but she doubted she would've recognized any of these people if she met them on the street—provided there was a world with streets they could walk. Nearly everyone wore a mask. One man with a mask on kept his eyes on Yora as if he could see her—not only sense that she was there like the man who just yelled at her, but as if he could see her in the flesh and clearly visible. His mask was no different from others—a white face without any particular expression, with a sharp nose and a slit for the mouth. He must have seen or heard Yora because he turned his head to follow her every movement, so much so it made her uncomfortable. She had, however, nowhere to escape and nowhere to hide, so she did the only thing she could do—float as high as she could to the ceiling and stay there. From above, the large room looked even stranger than from the usual angle—she could only see the backs of people's heads with the white protrusions of masks; only the baby in the man's arms lay with its face up and, for an instant, it seemed to Yora that the eyes of this baby in its colorful onesie were crushed and dead. Yora looked again at the man who seemed to have seen her. He—there was no doubt about it now!—waved at her pleasantly, as if inviting her to fly in closer, and then, after glancing about him cautiously, freed up his other arm from the long sleeve of his shirt sleeve—the arm was bandaged, and he started to unwrap the bandages. It was a little funny—no one in this mass of people paid any attention to him. He would have been more conspicuous in a less crowded place.

He continued to unwrap the bandage that covered his arm up to his elbow while gesticulating non-stop, as if he were intent on explaining something to Yora very clearly. There was something very comforting, even grand in his action—there he was, wounded, showing his body to her who had no body of her own, as if he wanted to cheer her up or help her somehow. But then other people started to push past him, the line moved, the crowd stirred, and the man got swept up in it. He threw his head back—his masked face, that is—trying to see Yora, perhaps, to shrug ironically at her, as if to say, see what's going on here, I can only wish I could stay and show you my boils, but I can't even feel my own shoulders in this crowd. For a long time, Yora, from her suspended position under the ceiling, watched this sea of people and the man's white mask that bobbed on its surface like a lost coastguard boat. She never did see his face. Eventually, the crowd thinned out a bit, and the man himself was no longer there; his discarded mask lay on the floor. Yora flew to the entrance to the other room, where all these people wanted to go so badly, and saw an empty gallows inside.

Next to the gallows stood the executioner—a very amiable skeleton. A few men and women, no more than a dozen, hurried into the room, and the door into the messy hall was shut behind them so abruptly it almost cut off countless

LOVE LIFE 73

fingers that reached in-between the door and its frame like the tentacles of tiny octopuses.

"Is everyone here?" asked a man whose face, like those of the others, was hidden under a mask.

"Yes, everyone is," the men and women confirmed, once they looked around.

Yora, hanging very quietly under the ceiling, wondered how these people knew they were supposed to be together. What if there was someone who didn't belong hidden by one of the masks? Perhaps they could identify each other by the sound of their voices.

One of the men looked up, and Yora, terrified, stopped thinking—it appeared that many people in this universe could overhear her thoughts.

"What is it?" a masked woman asked. She was dressed in an evening gown and carried a fan.

"Nothing," the man snorted. "They think it's the land of milk and honey here, but they won't even be able to hide. Especially, if they won't stop thinking of *Her*." He emphasized the last word.

"You should stop talking about it, before you jinx us all," another man interrupted. "So what if they found you in a bathtub filled with salt? That's in the past now."

"The salt was solid with blood," the first man responded. He uttered his words with great weight, as if he were revealing a great secret, but no one even noticed.

"Alright, let's get started," a third man said. He was the tallest and the skinniest and wore a broad lace collar like men in Velasquez's paintings.

"If only they knew what we're talking about here," another man sighed and went to a pale-green, rustic-looking sideboard that stood deeper in the room. On top of it was a tray that held glasses and, apparently, wine. The man poured wine for everyone, and everyone reached for their drink.

Yora looked around again. The room seemed large, and its corners sank into deep shadows; only the section where the dozen or so people stood was illuminated. There were no windows. Had she somehow fallen into hell? Yora looked at the ceiling, then at the floor, and heard the woman in the evening gown laugh.

"As above, so below," she said, running her finger around the base of her glass, speaking to no one in particular.

Sebastian's home had to be here, somewhere among these rooms, but it had gone deep into the folds of existence and hid there.

"Ready?" a man asked.

Yora wondered how the people were going to drink through their masks. Would they take them off, or pour wine down their throats through the openings of the masks' twisted mouths? This small thought flitted through Yora's mind.

"Mundus Novus?"

"Mundus Novus."

"To the Second Coming?"

"To the Second Coming."

No one took off their masks, but magically, the wine vanished from the glasses. There was no atmosphere of ceremony or celebration; all these people were carrying out a ritual—if this was a ritual at all—as if they'd grown bored with it a hundred times over.

They put their glasses back on the tray and turned to look at the gallows. Only now did Yora notice that another person had been standing by the gallows this whole time, someone wrapped entirely in a cloak. Then the cloak was taken off. Underneath was the very same man who had unwrapped his bandage to show Yora his wounds. He was no longer wearing a mask, but he looked down, so that Yora could not see his face. The man climbed the low platform, and two other men climbed behind him.

The skeleton helped the men adjust the rope—the noose was too high. Yora stared at his spine, at the shifting of his vertebrae, so mobile and at the same time so strong, and had the urgent thought that she had never seen a person quite so naked before—if this were, in fact, a person. In pictures, death looked like this—a skeleton, usually with a scythe. But this guy hanged people—so he had no need of the scythe. A scythe would've been absurd here. It's not like he needed it to cut the rope—that would defeat the point of his being here.

Finally, the men adjusted the rope—it now hung down low, almost touching the platform. The man with bandages put one foot in the noose, lay on the platform, and tucked the other leg under him. The executioner and his assistants started to raise him—first the foot, then his entire body that instantly became heavy and lifeless. They took the protective mesh of bandages off the executed man's legs like a layer off an onion. The platform creaked, the red wood of the boards strained under the weight. The skeleton's spine crackled with exertion. Tight under the weight of the body, the noose now cut into the flesh of the man's ankle. The man's head jerked and hung loose, his fingers brushed the platform, and Yora finally saw his face—round and young, almost child-like, it showed no shadow of suffering. Blood slowly seeped from the man's bare feet and dripped down. The people in the room became ecstatic. Instantly, they were transformed from bored guests at a tedious party into real priests of mystery. They raised their arms, and a great shared "A-ah!" escaped from their chests. They had all their attention focused on the gallows, all of them charged with a new force, as if connected to an invisible source of energy, and it seemed to Yora that she could see their exalted faces even through the plaster of their masks. Blood dripped onto the tousled hair of the hanged man and from there onto the platform.

He swayed a little at first, then hung still, and the rope cut deeper into his ankle.

Yora flew closer to the hanged man; when she was next to his face, she flew past him, like a ghost. Suddenly, the heavy smell of blood overcame her, bodiless, and something dragged her irresistibly down, as if the weight of this entire world pressed upon her shoulders. "Gravity," she realized, surprised at herself. It smelled sharply of blood, and there was no escaping this smell, as if every vein and artery on the planet had ripped and exploded around her. Gravity pulled her down, pressed her against the ground, and Yora resisted with everything she had, with her entire being, because she had nothing else. "But I don't have a body!" flashed in her mind and, at the same instant, the force pressing her down let go—she flew up to the ceiling, launched like a cork from a bottle. It felt as if the force of gravity had abruptly reversed its vector, and the ceiling now drew Yora up like a magnet. This was a powerful force, much greater than Yora's own and, again, she had to resist it. Yora looked down at the hanged man, his quiet body, his blood. The woman in the evening gown came up to him and gave him a little shove—the body swayed like a pendulum, just like Yora's essence had a moment ago, between up and down. "Where am I?" thought Yora, terrified. "And *what* am I?" At that moment, more than anything in the world, she yearned to be touched, the way Sebastian used to touch her, the way he made her body manifest to her. Then the tallest man in the room waved his hand, and Yora found herself outside, without realizing how she had gotten there.

This was a street of a different city, an intersection before an entrance to a shopping arcade. The store windows glowed from inside, bright against the dark sky. Yora, without hesitation, lurched into the arcade, flew through it, and emerged suddenly in a square where a great number of people were

LOVE LIFE

milling. The people here did not wear masks, but all their faces seemed to be washed-out and stretched, as if seen on a broken monitor. Yora flew high above the square, so she could see everything. In the heart of the crowd, a woman sat astride an animal—Yora thought it was a goat, but she could have been mistaken, because, for a goat, the creature was impressively large. The woman was wrapped in purple silk. She sat magnificently, as if on a throne. This, of course, was Bonnie—the resplendent, powerful Bonnie; her skin looked to be embellished everywhere with jewels, and Yora did not find this the least bit surprising. Bonnie's shoulders and stomach were bare, and an enormous diadem adorned her forehead; the diadem sent out rays of hot light, bright in the surrounding dusk. Yora took the precaution of making herself as small as possible as she hovered right above Bonnie, but Bonnie could not see her.

People around Bonnie held their breath. Bonnie, queenlike, still sat on the goat's back. The light from her diadem dazzled like a magical searchlight aimed at the crowd. A stolid man with a light-colored beard came up to Bonnie and said something to her; she tipped her glorious head like a chalice filled with a potion. The diadem flashed so brightly that Yora had to look away, and Bonnie laughed. The man gently squeezed Bonnie's wrist, giving her a signal, and the spectacle everyone had been waiting for began. Bonnie raised her arms like a pair of wings, and a long sigh rolled through the crowd. She waved her arms again and again, until it seemed like she had a hundred arms, so quickly did they flit through the air, waving a yet-invisible pattern. Finally, Bonnie stopped. She did, in fact, have more than two arms! Rather, more arms now grew from her original arms like smaller branches from the boughs of a tree. But no, those were not arms—they were strange bulbous growths, like giant buds ready to burst into leaves. They weighed Bonnie's arms down but could not bend them to the ground—her arms swayed above the crowd like pendulums. Another moment—and the buds really began to burst, turning pockets of flesh into new Bonnies, exact copies of the Bonnie who sat on the goat's back. She brought forth new women, as beautiful as herself. She sprouted new growths like a plant. The new Bonnies grew before Yora's eyes; they separated from the trunk of the original Bonnie's body and fell into the crowd like ripe fruit, like gifts for the faithful.

The crowd was no longer quiet; it swirled. People picked up Bonnie's daughters and carried them; everyone shouted, rejoiced, and praised their mistress. Anyone could commune with Beauty, anyone could touch her body. "Sebastian!" Yora suddenly shouted, forgetting that she had no voice. It was, in fact, him—he was just receiving a copy of Bonnie from Bonnie's own hand, and he was just another starved pilgrim among thousands of others—the regal Bonnie on her goat did not even recognize him. "Sebastian!" Yora, abandoning the main Bonnie, flew after him, through the entire bacchanal. Sebastian stopped, with one of the many Bonnies in his arms; she was, like her mother, dressed in silk. He stopped next to a large device reminiscent of a first-generation computer, and Yora understood without being told that this was a mirror cinema projector.

Cheerful music came out of the machine, as if someone inside of it were playing a shameless piano. Sebastian and a few others undressed their Bonnies—their copies of Bonnie—and placed them in the mouth of the machine. A moving picture flashed to life from the machine's other end, a kaleidoscopic vision—first Bonnie's face, and then her body—arms separate from her legs, stomach separate from her breasts. Sometimes the projected body came together, and then twisted, danced, changed clothes, or undressed altogether; at other times, the magic lantern produced many bodies that were actually all the same—and all this happened while the real (was she, though?) Bonnie lay in the guts of the machine. After some time, Sebastian and his helpers pulled their Bonnie out of the machine—she was old, wrinkled, and apparently dead, but the machine did not care. Only young Bonnies danced and pranced on the many screens. The machine could run for a long time—even, perhaps, until the next budding. Yora flew high above the square. She saw projectors everywhere, and each burned, like fuel, its own copy of Bonnie, and each projected or manufactured something. Sebastian's machine was merely one of many. Yora shuddered—not with her body, which she did not have, but with her entire being—she was about to learn the truth; the order of things would be revealed to her now, she would understand everything, the hanged man, and the many priests. Never before had Yora lived such a full, extraordinary life as she did for those few moments.

But Yora did not get the chance to learn what exactly she was supposed to know, because she heard someone's insistent shouting. Someone was calling her, Yora, by name, and the calling pulled Yora away from Bonnie, Sebastian, and the many machines with a transparent but impenetrable membrane, and Yora beat her fists against it, forgetting that she did not have fists—and everything grew distant.

It was Inga. Inga knew nothing yet. Inga kept calling, and Yora thought she should fly over to Inga for a few minutes and calm her down, tell her she would come back in a little bit and that there was nothing to worry about. Yora hurried over to her friend. She focused—and went through the arcade. "Yora, Yora!" Inga called again. Yora made the final effort—and returned to her body.

A bright light shone into her eyes—Inga had turned on a lamp. Up on the ceiling, Yora saw a large wet stain. The stain was spreading—the roof was leaking. Yora lay on her back, drenched in sweat, and racked by pain in her muscles and joints. A feeling of not being finished haunted her, too—she was on the cusp of learning something important, but she didn't.

"Water," Yora said, pointing to the stain above.

"What are you talking about? Yora! You scared me, you slept so deeply! I called you—I thought you were dreaming something."

"Dreaming? Oh yeah. You won't believe it." Yora smiled weakly and was just about to tell Inga about Bonnie, Sebastian, the movies he made, and the man in the crowd, but Inga said, "Hey, do you want me to take you to the doctor? Something's not right with you."

"Okay," Yora said. "In the morning."

"Sure, in the morning. Can I bring you anything?"

"No."

"Then try to go back to sleep, but maybe without those dreams of yours, alright?"

"But what about the stain?"

"What stain?"

"The roof is leaking."

"I'll call them tomorrow, they should fix it."

After this, it was suddenly evening, without there first being day or morning. Inga, in a beautiful sequined dress Yora had not seen before, stood in the bathroom applying lipstick.

"Where did this come from?" Yora asked.

"I bought it," Inga said with a mysterious smile.

This was almost the old Inga, smiling and happy, confident. But her smile did not make Yora feel better, quite the opposite—it made her anxious.

"You and I are going out to a bar tonight," Inga said.

They were chronically short of money.

LOVE LIFE 81

"Whatever for?"

"You'll see," Inga said, mysterious again. "It's a special place."

"What's special about it?"

"Get dressed," Inga said by way of an answer, and Yora obeyed.

When they got to this very special bar, they learned it was a members-only club on the outskirts of town. It was dark, cars sped past them. People milled around in front of the entrance.

"What are you doing? Why did we come here?" Yora asked Inga, because the place was making her uncomfortable, but her friend did not even look at her; instead, she focused on the people in line to get in.

Yora studied her face and thought she knew what was going on.

"Is Carlos back in town? Are you hoping to run into him here?"

Inga shook her hair and laughed. Her laugh was very resonant and loud, not like hers at all, but Yora had forgotten the way Inga used to laugh—before, when she was herself.

"But this is wrong," she said, trying to reason with Inga. "You know he's not..."

"I know. But you have to give me credit—at least I'm looking for closure. If not for myself," Inga added for emphasis, "then at least for you."

"What are you talking about? What closure?" Yora asked. "I want to go home, do you hear me, don't take me in there, I want to—"

She did not get a chance to finish, because a man with a light beard (where had she seen him before?) stepped out of the line, called their names, and waved for them to follow him in. This seemed strange—someone ought to have come out from inside the club, while the man appeared to be just one of the people wanting to get in just like everyone else, but they had to follow him. They were immediately let in.

The club was half-dark; there was music playing. They could not see anything special about it— there was the bar, dining tables, a dance floor, and a film of invisible grime on every surface as is always the case in less-than-reputable establishments. Next to the bar, it smelled of spilled beer. They perched on bar stools, and Inga ordered them drinks.

They sat and sipped their red cocktails—not particularly enjoyable and made with cheap vodka that left an unpleasant aftertaste—and did not get drunk. The sequins on Inga's dress sparkled, and Yora could not stop looking at it. To entertain herself, she turned to watch other patrons—there weren't actually that many. Yora wondered why whoever was in charge wouldn't let the people standing in line outside in—there was plenty of room for everyone. But perhaps the owners knew something Yora did not. Perhaps the line was not for the bar, but for an underground cinema that showed rare censored films.

Yora's attention was drawn to a woman in a wide-sleeved black dress who sat alone at a table not far from them. Everything was beautiful about her: her shoulders, short hair, dark eyes. Here was someone Sebastian wouldn't have dumped for a Bonnie—although, to be fair, Sebastian did not dump anyone. Yora was the one who walked out on him, but it was easier to think of herself as the one who had been dumped. This woman was not as young as Bonnie, she had crow's feet at the corners of her eyes, and her face had that fragility that awakens in a body abruptly, when one's skin suddenly becomes tight, only to crack and collapse under this tension. But this woman still had time with her beauty. Yora looked at the woman as if mesmerized, greedy for every movement and sway of her wide sleeves. The woman's eyes shone with a feverish gleam when she caught Yora's eye. Why did she

LOVE LIFE

have eyes like that? Could she be on drugs? No, that wasn't it—drugs would've ruined her beauty. This was something different, something unique to her, natural, inseparable from her. If Sebastian, Yora thought, had wanted to sleep with this woman, she, Yora, would have had no choice but to consent, because this woman was really worth it.

Yora turned to Inga. Inga looked at her with understanding.

"I told you, if not for me, then at least for you," she said, mocking a little.

"What do you mean, for me?"

"You know what I mean."

"I have no idea."

Inga giggled, then changed her tone abruptly and wiped the smile off her face.

"I can see the way you're staring at her," she said. "But that's great, that's why I brought you here. Stare all you want!"

"Inga, what are you talking about?"

"You know."

Yora did not know. She wondered if there was a conspiracy afoot—between the owners of this bar or club, the man in line, Inga, and now this woman. Better to pretend she understood and see what happened next. Except that all of this scared her more than the priests, the hanged man, and the Bonnie from her recent dream. In the dream, at least, she knew to expect the unexpected—but here... What was going to happen?

"Alright," Yora said. "I do. And what am I supposed to do about it?"

"You want her, don't you?"

"Who?"

"You know who."

"Why would I want her?"

"Because you see how beautiful she is. How beautiful everything about her is. How special she is."

"I don't know if she is special. She might be as common as it gets. It might just be the alcohol."

"There's only one way to find out."

"Which is?"

"Ma, do I have to spell everything out? Go over to her. Talk to her. Introduce yourself. Kiss her."

"Why do I have to kiss her?"

"You don't. But it might be a good idea. It'll put your mind at ease. Come on. This night is for you."

Yora looked at the woman; the woman returned her gaze, rose, and went deeper into the hall, into the darkness. Music—rock, too heavy for this kind of space and this kind of club—was playing louder, so loud Yora could no longer hear anything except the thumping of her own heart. She glimpsed the woman's dress up ahead. The woman turned into a side hallway, of which, Yora noticed, there were many. This reminded Yora of something. Yora went down the same hallway. A young woman in very short shorts, with bleached blonde hair, heavy eye-liner, and sparkling-white teeth stopped her.

"Where are you going?" she asked.

"There," Yora answered concisely, pointing ahead.

She wanted to follow the woman in the black dress, but the young woman would not let her pass.

"Are you looking for someone?" the young woman asked, too casually.

"Hey, bug off," Yora snapped. "I have no time for chatting."

"Oh, really," the woman scoffed. "You have all the time in the world to chat, come on! Tell me about yourself. Who are you?"

"None of your business."

LOVE LIFE 85

"Okay, fine, I already know that anyway."

"What do you know?" Yora asked. She went cold inside.

"I know what I need to know."

"Tell me what you know."

"I won't. Because you are a liar." The young woman laughed harder, showing all her sharp white teeth, her mouthful of sharp teeth. "And that, by the way, is hard work! But no worries—they'll tell you the truth here, just like you wanted. You ran away too early, though, like a fool. You should really take a moment here and rest."

The young woman was standing very close to Yora and breathed alcohol fumes right in her face. From up close, her face, with a thick layer of foundation on it, looked like a mask that was cracking, threatening the entire painted facade to collapse and reveal something terrible inside.

Somewhere ahead, Yora heard door hinges creak. She pushed the young woman aside and ran toward the sound. In the hellish light—a single light bulb hanging from the ceiling, the yellowish haze of inevitable blindness—Yora saw a scarlet door that led, it appeared, to the bathroom. Yora was surprised—were they supposed to meet in there? After a moment's hesitation, she pushed the door, and the door yielded. The woman who had come in here first did not lock it. Yora stood for another moment in the hallway, with her hand on the doorknob, not daring to go in, and then went in—only to stop, utterly stunned, in the doorway. Under the same dim light that lit the hallway, Yora saw the woman she had followed—the woman sat, with her underwear around her knees, and blood ran down her white thighs. She did not bother to wipe it off; the blood was on the floor, and on her underwear—the woman's period had started, and she seemed not to care at all whether anyone knew about it. She could spray her blood over the entire surface of this planet—without shame, without fear... In her hand, she held a stick of lipstick which she had just put on, exactly as Inga had earlier in their bathroom, except that Inga had done it perfectly, like an artist, and this woman applied it haphazardly, all over the contours, laying on the lipstick thick and vulgar. The woman slowly parted her thighs to let Yora see the shaved bloody space between her legs—the hole where the blood was coming from, and said in a hoarse voice, smiling with her red mouth and flashing her eyes, "Which of my flowers do you want to kiss?"—and, in the same instant, Yora recognized herself in the woman—her own face, her own body. Yora stepped back in shock—and regained her consciousness.

Her bladder spasmed. Yora got up and walked into the bathroom, despite the pain on the bottom of her feet. She had a fever. As she walked back across the room to the mattress, she realized she was walking as if the floor was wet. Had the roof leaked so much that their apartment was filled with puddles? She looked for the light switch and could not find it, while the pain in her feet grew intolerable. Finally, Inga woke up and turned the light on.

"What are you doing?" she asked, turning her face, puffy with sleep toward Yora, and in the next instant shouted, "What happened? What's wrong?" pointing to the floor under Yora's feet.

Yora looked and froze in shock—she was indeed standing in a puddle, but it was a puddle of blood. Tracks of blood stretched across the room. Yora's feet were covered in burst boils like angry bleeding flowers. Her skin burned like fire. The mattress was all stained red—you could have thought a solicitous lover had scattered rose petals on it to romance his date. Yora gasped and slid down onto the floor, where she sat, with her head in her arms. She wondered if this was yet another dream, if she were still sleeping.

"I'm asleep, I'm asleep," she said, and the fever racked her body with shivers. "I'm asleep, wake me up, I'm asleep..."

LOVE LIFE   87

***

At the hospital, they got lucky—there was almost no wait. A hospital room followed, the IV drip, and finally—dreamless sleep. When Yora woke up, it was evening, but she did not know what day it was. It was dark outside her window, and the noise of Fletcher Avenue throbbed somewhere down below—the street itself was invisible. No one had closed the curtains on the windows, and the black glass, like a mirror, reflected the room and their faces—Inga's—tired, and Yora's—waned, as if someone else's.

"Did you... Have you been here the whole time?" Yora asked.

"Oh, you are awake! No, not the whole time. I got here an hour ago. You were asleep."

"In a coma?"

"Good God, what are you talking about? No, just asleep."

"What's wrong with me? Did they say?"

"Not to me."

"How long have I been here?"

"It's the second day."

"Are you sure they did not amputate anything?"

"Yora, come on..."

"Maybe it's scarlet fever."

"I doubt it."

"What does the doctor think?"

"He'll be back in the morning."

"Well, I can't just lie here like this—I have to go to work. I've already missed two days."

"Yora, you are ill."

Yora forced herself to sit up in bed and looked at her feet. They were bandaged. An IV line went to her arm, so she had to stay in bed as if tethered—if she wanted to get up, she'd have to move the entire wheeled apparatus with her.

"Now what?" she asked, either Inga or herself, that part of herself that knew the future. She did not hear an answer, however, and fell back into a deep sleep.

Every so often, nurses would wake her up for new manipulations—someone drew blood from her vein, another person took her temperature. Yora looked at them, half-conscious. When she finally woke up, her entire body ached. A dark-eyed woman stood at Yora's bedside; the woman's hair was hidden under a Muslim headscarf. The name tag on her doctor's uniform said "Dr. Neya Fernandes." She had wide open eyes and a wide smile, and her mouth and eyes gaped like openings behind which lay the void.

"Good morning," she said, not closing her mouth or shedding her smile.

"Hello," Yora answered.

"My name is Neya Fernandes. I have come to check on you. I am your doctor."

The woman stood before Yora completely still, and if she had not spoken, you could think someone had just painted her dark head on the white wall as a prank.

Yora ran her hand across her face and asked, "What's wrong with me?"

Still smiling, the motionless Neya Fernandes said, "We can't quite understand that. You have an infection of unknown origin. We will give you some medication."

"Could you also give me some painkillers?"

"I doubt that is necessary," Neya Fernandes answered slowly. "Just avoid stepping on your wounds for the time being. You can stay in bed. Once your feet start healing, they'll hurt less. Nothing hurts while you're lying down, does it?"

"My joints hurt."

"That's different. Tylenol will do the trick."

"How am I supposed to walk? I need to go to work."

LOVE LIFE 89

"You won't be able to walk for some time. Take some sick leave," the doctor suggested.

"Who's going to give it to me? I'm on a grant. My insurance is not with my employer either."

Neya Fernandes said nothing and kept smiling. The void shone out of her right at Yora.

"I heard there are flesh-eating bacteria in the local water," Yora said after a pause. "Is that what I have?"

"No, not at all. Yours is a little-known infection. I can't tell you where you got it, but everything depends on your immune system, and yours is weak."

"Do people die of this infection?"

"Oh!" For the first time, Neya Fernandes moved. Her smile faded for a moment. "This is a hospital, you know. Not a funeral home."

"I'm sorry."

"Don't worry about it." Neya Fernandes smiled again. "I completely understand. You are exhausted."

"I dream very strange dreams."

"Dreams are just a sign that you are unwell. A healthy person sleeps without dreaming. I'll be honest, you have bigger problems than your dreams. Your lymph nodes are enlarged. We found the right medication for you, but the recovery will be slow. Your wounds will heal, but you should be prepared for them to open up again. At any time. There will be relapses. What you have is a virus, and it lives in the ganglia. It is impossible to remove fragments of viral DNA from your nerve cells. Besides, to be honest, we don't know whether this virus can affect your internal organs, and what might happen if it does. You must be very careful from now on. Your immune system," Neya Fernandes said, bending over Yora and lowering her voice to a whisper, "will never get rid of this virus. And please pay attention to your circulation," she added. "Especially in your feet. Here's my card. Get well."

After this visit, Yora dialed Mariana Schneider.

"I'm ill," Yora said.

"That's bad, and I'm very sorry to hear it," Mariana said in her usual even and stern voice. "I asked if you were okay, you looked unwell. But if you don't come back soon, what am I supposed to do?"

"I don't know, but..."

"I can give you three days, tops, Yora. If you don't come back in three days, I'll have to look for someone else."

"This won't take three days. It looks like—" Yora wanted to say more, but Mariana interrupted her.

"That is just not possible, Yora. You understand, don't you? I'll give you a call as soon as I hear about another grant."

"But wait! You don't know what happened!"

"*I* don't know what happened? I know *perfectly well* what is happening—we are holding up the entire university. I have to finish the reports, or they'll throw me out of here, and the entire department with me. You aren't the only person who works for me."

"But I have a virus! I'm in the hospital!"

"Are you contagious? I am truly very sorry. Let me tell the girls, and someone will stop by your place when you come home. Get better!"

Yora didn't even have a chance to explain her misadventure before Mariana hung up. In the evening, Inga came, just as tired and tearful as the previous time.

"You look better," she told Yora. "Because you were a fright before."

"I don't feel better," Yora objected, looking again into the black window as if into a mirror's abyss.

"What about your fever?"

"Still here. But it's going to last for a while."

"Does it hurt?"

"It does, but it's tolerable. Mostly my body and my joints."

LOVE LIFE 91

Yora turned away to wipe away a tear that budded in her eye. Even now, in a hospital bed, probably deep in debt, sick, and no longer employed, she was thinking about Sebastian. It didn't take Inga long to figure that out.

"So call him, or text him. Text him that you're ill. He's not a monster, he must have something for a heart! Let him come visit you. Bonnie or no Bonnie, he can come see you just as a friend."

"He won't come."

"So text him—and then you'll know for sure. Then you can tell him to go to hell and feel like you've done your duty. You will have done everything you could."

"I have already done everything I could."

"But you are still thinking about him. You are wondering, what if... So text him, and there will be no what ifs. I have no one to text anymore, but if I did..."

Inga was right. Or, perhaps, she was not, but her words lit a fire in Yora's chest. She could no longer think of anything else—except that the universe was giving her permission to reach out and touch Sebastian, if only with words. Her heart skipped several beats.

"Alright," she said. "But I won't call him."

She wrote what Inga and the searing feeling inside her heart suggested—"I'm ill and I'm in the hospital. They're letting me go home tomorrow. Come visit, I'll be at home." After she hit send, she and Inga spent several minutes hovering over the phone, waiting. The screen lit up, and both women, with a groan, leaned in. But instead of a response from Sebastian, the message was from the mobile operator—"This user has blocked your number."

Inga put a hand on Yora's shoulder.

"Yora, he didn't know you would get sick, did he? So he blocked you like a real dick. Don't give it another thought... I wish I'd never suggested this. I'm sorry... Do you want me to go see him? I could tell him everything. He's not a total—"

"Nah," Yora said. "It's nothing."

She smiled and thought about her message, the handful of words lost halfway between her and Sebastian, and wondered if they needed phones at all. Perhaps words traveled the world on their own, without the aid of any technology. They may be at his house now, milling under the windows and, later, when Sebastian and Bonnie fall asleep, her, Yora's, words will glide quietly into Sebastian's dreams like snowflakes. And he will hear Yora. He will.

Inga, seeing Yora's smile, became worried.

"What are you thinking about?"

"Nothing," Yora said very softly, with her lips only. She could no longer see Inga—she saw only her words, small and rustling, the way they seeped into Sebastian's mind, how they burrowed in his blondish hair. Later, she seemed to have a dream about a red room where Yora and Sebastian were supposed to go immediately after—it seemed—their wedding. Yora was still seeing off the last guests. When she locked the door after the last person, she saw that Sebastian was already waiting for her in the red room, and this anticipation of being in his arms felt so good, even better than actually being held. Yora still stood in the doorway, while he called for her, and this was a moment of utter bliss. And, once Yora had had her fill of anticipation and was ready to go join Sebastian, who was now her, Yora's husband, she suddenly woke up, even though no one had disturbed her— woke up alone, in the middle of the night, with her roommate breathing behind the partition, and she lay there for a while, listening to the feeling of happiness inside her that quickened like a baby who was just about to die inside her.

LOVE LIFE 93

***

The following day, they sent Yora home from the hospital. Inga picked her up and drove her home. Yora was still in the throes of a smothering fever.

"We got the meds," Inga said. "And that powder she mentioned, the one you put in a bowl of water and let dissolve. Alright, you've got it. I have to go to work."

"Of course. Thank you so much."

Inga left. Yora woke up to a quiet knock at the door.

"It's Sebastian!" she thought, instantly awake; her words—they had found him! Through the heavy cloud of fever that enveloped her, a new fever rose—the fog that fills your mind and makes you weak in the knees when you see or hear someone you were expecting for a long time. This fever was like the sweet, intoxicating molasses of hope. Yora's heart throbbed, but who cared about her heart? Did she even have a heart? Yora got up and walked the few steps to the door. Their studio was so small that this effort was negligible. She rubbed her eyes, pulled down on her T-shirt. She did not even ask who it was. She opened the door—and stood dead still. It was not him, but the girls from her office. So, Mariana Schneider did tell the other women what had happened and even bothered to find her job application to look up her address.

Despite rubbing her eyes and pulling down on her T-shirt, she must still have presented a terrifying sight, because fear clearly registered on Mel and Cynthia's faces, and Cynthia, the younger of the two, even took a step back. Mel took Cynthia's hand and stepped closer to Yora. Yora knew Mel a little—they used to run into each other in the cafeteria, and Mel had told Yora that her sister from Cuba had just moved in with her, undocumented for now, without a driver's license, and unable to work. The sister had a child with her.

"How long are you staying at the office?" Yora asked on that occasion.

"Until six," Mel sighed and smiled.

"Wow. Since nine?"

"Since eight. We'd leave earlier, but it doesn't work that way. We get paid for what we get done, not hourly."

Yora didn't know Cynthia as well—Cynthia walked the hallways always nicely dressed, slim, in high-heeled shoes. She was very young and tried to appear very serious. It had felt very awkward to approach her, so perfect—the way Yora felt about those girls in first grade, with gigantic bows in their hair, dressed in lacy aprons their parents had bought abroad. As a child, Yora only wore what was available in the stores; her mom could barely afford that.

But here they were. Mel and Cynthia had come to see her.

"What happened, Yora? We've come to see you—could you let us in."

Yora said nothing. How could this be— these two— instead of Sebastian. She was certain it was him—and it turned out not to be him?

"We brought you chicken noodle soup," Mel said, unable to tolerate the awkward silence. "Here it is. Why don't you let us in? We'll put it in the fridge."

"Girls, you shouldn't have..." Yora finally squeezed out.

Mel let go of Cynthia's hand and came even closer to the door.

"Come on, Yora, let us in—tell us what happened..."

Mel craned her neck trying to see into the studio behind Yora's back.

"Listen, it's not a good time, come back later..." Yora muttered.

"That's enough!" Mel interrupted and started forward.

"Girls," Yora suddenly got an idea. She lowered her voice as people do when they don't want someone else, an invisible third party, to overhear. "Thing is, my boyfriend's here. We were... you know... It's not a good time. I'm not alone, that's why I'm not letting anyone in."

"Boyfriend?" Mel and Cynthia looked at each other.

Cynthia believed her, but Mel, apparently, did not, considering the way Yora looked—a person that sick would not be interested in lovemaking, but then again, Mel couldn't quite force her way into someone else's apartment where someone else's naked man might be lying in bed.

"Well, in that case..."

"I'll call you when... when you can come see me, another time, if you want."

Cynthia rocked a little on her heels, came up to Yora, and handed her the pot of soup.

"Here. This is for you. Eat up and get better soon."

"Thank you."

Yora slammed the door shut behind the girls and fell onto the bed. A hot wave of missing Sebastian seared through her. Why, why didn't she talk to him then, didn't tell him, didn't try to explain everything to him? He would have understood, he had to! Yora was still convinced that, by some mystical means, Sebastian had read her message and had almost come to see her, but, because she'd sent a signal of doubt into the cosmos, at the last moment, Sebastian dematerialized and sent Mel and Cynthia in his stead. Where was he? Who was looking at his sublime face at this very moment? Why didn't she go to see him, as Inga had suggested? If only she could talk to him about anything, in any way! And now she could not even call him, or text him!

Yora grabbed her laptop and opened it, not quite aware of what she was going to do—check, in vain, her email again? Stare mindlessly at a parade of websites? In the next instant, Yora startled—the laptop responded. Someone was calling on Skype.

She should have known it could not be Sebastian, because they had never used Skype, but she still automatically pressed the green button.

It was Yora's sister. For the last several weeks, Yora systematically declined her and their mother's Skype calls, sending a few short sentences back in response to say that everything was fine. She knew they would ask their simple questions—how's life, how's work, any hope for a better job soon... And Yora wouldn't have been able to tell them anything. Mother would have noticed something, and would try, just in case, to convince Yora that everything was fine, that Yora had a great life, much better than those of most of their family and friends, and that Yora should appreciate what she had. Their mother never had much in terms of resources, neither for herself nor for her daughters, but she firmly believed you had to be able to support yourself, at the very least, and depend on no one. She managed everything on her own without asking Yora's father, and then her younger sister's father, for money when they abandoned her with yet another child and left for parts unknown. She worked like a horse, no matter how exhausting her life already was. "No," Yora's mother used to say. "I'm not about to haggle with them."

"Hey there, old girl!" her sister said. That's what she called Yora. She was younger than Yora, but people often thought she was actually the older one, so authoritative was her voice, and so much unhurried deliberation was in her every movement. Outside of the frame, in another room, a child started to cry. "Come on, come on now, bunny," Yora's sister sang over her shoulder, and then turned again to face Yora. "You've disappeared on us, gone silent..."

"Well... I'm sorry, I just..." Yora muttered.

LOVE LIFE 97

"Mom's worried sick. Hang on a second, let me call her, so she can join..."

"Oh no, don't do that," Yora interjected, terrified. "Anything but that. I can't talk to Mom right now."

"Turn on your video."

"I can't," Yora said, recalling Mel and Cynthia's faces when they saw her. "I'm at work, there are people here..."

Her sister was silent for a moment, and then asked, "Is everything alright?"

"Everything's fine," Yora said, making an effort not to shake with fever. She lay down flat; only her voice was alive. Her voice clung to the past, to the acacia blooming in the parks, the smell of lindens along the river, to the fall when the line of the horizon changed and the cold flashed somewhere behind it like air catching on fire behind a screen. Her voice clung to her sister.

"You don't sound very good, you know," her sister said.

"Well, you know," Yora said. "It's just stuff."

"What stuff? What happened?"

"It's this man. My love life. Don't say anything to Mom. Just tell her everything is fine," Yora asked.

"Of course, I won't."

Yora had to tell at least part of the truth, to prevent her sister from interrogating her. Let her think that Yora was an immature idiot who chased after men. Which she basically was.

"Actually, why don't you tell me how *you* are doing."

"Everything's the same. The kids are good. Myshko is good."

Her sister took some time sharing the news—which child was starting school, which had a runny nose, what they wanted for Christmas, what the weather was like, and Yora listened, happy that she was not being made to talk. But then her sister finished and asked what she really wanted to know.

"So what about that man? Your love life?"

"He broke up with me. You know how it is."

"What happened?"

"Actually, you could say nothing happened. It was nothing serious. You know how it is sometimes."

"I guess, I do," her sister said, and, typically very chatty, fell silent. She was no longer laughing. The two were not close, but, at this moment, her sister could sense what was going on with Yora, and this was intolerable. This had happened before and, every time, her sister's clairvoyance scared Yora. What could her sister know about life? She lived in the same city she grew up in, raised her children, didn't go out much, didn't travel, and didn't read sophisticated books. But her sister knew.

"Well, I have to go," Yora said. "I'm at work, like I said. Don't worry about that man. That was just a... Just a fling... It meant nothing."

Her sister waited in anxious silence.

"Alright, I'm going now. Tell everybody I said hi!" Yora tried again.

Her sister said nothing.

"Can you hear me?" Yora asked, filled with an alarming premonition that her sister was about to say *something*, and then...

"I can," her sister said. "You know, don't think your thing meant nothing... What happened with that man. Don't downplay it. Don't, okay?" she repeated, and then said something that made Yora shudder. "You know what they say—love can only be found on the other side of sex."

Yora ended the call and stood up. Her head throbbed, her joints hurt, and the tension of it all made sweat roll down her back. But none of this was important, as it hadn't been before, because Sebastian was still the most important thing.

LOVE LIFE 99

She felt him the way one feels pain. He hurt like a burn, so badly she wanted to scream, but she could not let herself scream, because if she did, people would come for her, they would send for an ambulance for her, and this would be a very cruel ambulance indeed, the kind that sends you straight to the loony bin, for several days, but those several days are enough to ruin a person's life. Plus, the loony bin had to be paid for. You could only go there with a light heart either if you were certain that you were about to die, or if you were sure you would live a long and happy life, and there weren't many who could claim to possess such knowledge.

No, this all had to be finished and dealt with. She had to tell herself frankly that he was not coming, was never coming, because this waiting, this hope was going to kill her. She couldn't very well keep thinking that every person at the door was a messenger from him, that every knock was a message, and someone's random text was a reply to the words she sent to him.

...He was not coming!!!

Inga and Yora put out their knickknacks on the shelf next to the closet; Yora's included a few small prints framed under glass, a pair of Christmas ornaments, and a clay woman's figurine from an artisanal market. In a fit of fury, Yora knocked them all down, swept them off the shelf onto the floor. Now they lay there like ill-fitting periods at the ends of confusing sentences. One of the prints had flown at the wall, hit it, and glass sprayed across the room in shards. Yora lay down on the bed, covered in small sharp bits of glass and wept. How hopeless this was—destroying things in her own room, how impotent! It would change nothing, nothing!

***

Days passed. Inga got up early and came home late, when Yora had already surrendered to an unhealthy kind of sleep. With each day, Yora seemed to have less and less energy to resist, as if someone had cut triangles of light out of her. Sometimes, at night, she'd grow feverish again. The fever wrapped its hot, seaweed-like tentacles around her so tightly that she would dream of a river that she was trying to swim across, a tropical river of dark water. The Peninsula was rich in rivers that gravitated to the bottom of it, as rivers do, and crawled to the evergreen jungles at the southern tip of the Peninsula, to mix with sea water there and wash the roots of the mangrove trees. All the roads, too, crawled south, into nothing, into the sea itself that breathed there like a living thing. Yora would push as hard as she could away from the river's bank trying to reach the other side, but she couldn't. The seaweed held her by the ankles. Yora fought it, the water grew hotter, almost boiling, and then Yora would wake up in her bed, soaked with sweat and exhausted, and every muscle in her body would ache desperately, and her heart would ache, too.

"Let something happen," Yora whispered with her dry, hot lips. "Anything at all, I can't go on like this!"

She yearned for anything that could bring her relief, a drop of coolness and peace. Finally, one day, she discovered she had a sharp and titillating desire to die, as if she had found a honed frosted blade with her tongue. Death alone, like a great wizard, could help here—reward and console, punish the guilty and restore justice. Yora even grasped at her chest—it was in there, deep at the bottom that death, all-powerful, and yet obedient to her, Yora, was biding its time, ripening—her death, her payback, her final letter to Sebastian who would, of course, find out eventually,

LOVE LIFE 101

and would then realize what he had done and regret it all. What would be left for him to do? Stand an eternal vigil at Yora's grave, his grieving head low—that's all he could do.

"Grow now, grow," Yora whispered to the death inside her. "Grow big and strong and protect me!"

Death would make her invulnerable, or even more—death could make the future itself change its course and permit Yora to enter it, not as an exile but as its one and only queen. Resentment swirled in Yora's mind, refusing to cohere into a larger picture, and eventually it exhausted her. Unable to grasp the most important thing in all this, she fell asleep.

***

Finally, one morning, Yora woke up without this now-familiar heavy feeling in her body, without a fever.

"Are you awake?" Inga asked from somewhere beside her. Yora turned to face the voice and looked at Inga as if seeing her for the first time. It was light in the room—Inga had raised the blinds.

"School break, finally."

Which meant it was mid-December already. Inga was sitting on the floor, cross-legged, her head sunk deep between her shoulders. Her face had changed imperceptibly over the last few weeks—as if it had swollen with the great weight of tears inside her and now looked unhealthily puffy. She now spoke slowly; she never used to talk like that before, and sometimes repeated phrases as if she could not quite believe she could speak and had to hold on to the rope of the most familiar words that was supposed to help her out of her labyrinths of silence. Some of the words resisted her, and she would half-swallow them and move on to other, simpler ones.

"Mom talked to me—her fortune-teller came and told her that the dark-haired man would break up with me, but I would meet a light-haired man instead. But I almost don't even think about Carlos anymore. I'm surprised myself— that I think of him so little, but I just don't have the time. I wake up and then it's evening before I know it. I have no energy for anything. I don't want anything. I still have head- aches... So much pain, so much pain. I had thought I would want him forever, at least that I would want something, but there's nothing left, not even cin... cidr.. cinders. Yora? Are you listening?"

"I am."

"I thought I would want him forever," Inga said, still shrinking, as if someone were about to hit her—another mannerism she didn't use to have. "But I don't want any- thing. These are supposed to be my best years, but I don't want anything. I don't even want to wash the dishes, I don't care... Yesterday, I went shopping, just to go somewhere, I have no money, but I had this urge to buy something, you know, just to... buy it. So I did. I don't know why, I got a little thing of skin oil, you know, the scented kind—really expen- sive. With herbs. Clarins, you know the brand. I had this idea while I was walking in the mall—what an idiot!—that Carlos would come back, and I would put this oil on. But when I brought it home, I realized... It's all wrong, the smell of it makes me sick, I hate it, I showered three times yester- day while you slept—here, try it."

The smell was too strong, indeed, completely wrong for Inga.

"I'll put it away, in the bathroom cabinet, use it if you want because I won't. I don't know why I bought it. I must have thought I was buying happiness... and Carlos—I really

LOVE LIFE

think very little about him, very little. I do think about other things. I was just thinking about things while you lay there, sleeping. But not about him. I wake up and I just lie there, I don't want to get up. What for? If I don't have to go to class, there's no reason at all. You know, he told me he loved me, that he wanted to be with me, forever. What am I supposed to do with his words? Everything is gone now, his body is gone, but these words are still here, and what am I supposed to do with them? But I haven't been thinking about him. Even when I want to think about him, I can't. I just want to sleep. I had this dream, just now—are you listening, Yora?—that I was at his mother's house..."

"Have you," Yora asked, "ever been there? I thought you guys only went to his apartment."

"I have, I just didn't tell you... He brought me over once for a barb... babre... barbecue."

"Why didn't you tell me?"

"When was I supposed to tell you? You were at Sebastian's all the time... So we went there—this house is in the suburbs, a very nice house, tall, and basically in the woods. Carlos has a sister. Still a teenager. There's woods all around. And they had this swing in the yard, you could go swing on it, and the house on the hill, the forest around it, the palmettos... It was like flying. There were other people there, and Carlos introduced me to his family. And since then..." Inga shook her head ruefully and lowered her puffy face that, it seemed, would just run with tears, be washed away entirely and vanish, as if painted on. Inga would look up then, and...

But she no longer cried.

"Do you know what his mother called me? She thought I didn't hear it, but I did. 'Natasha.' As in, 'what do you want with this Natasha!' Like we are all greedy whores who just want to marry their sons. But what if I have my own Mom and Dad at home, you know, I'm not desperate. My dream was that I'm at Carlos's mother's again, and I'm hiding from everyone, I'm afraid they will find me and throw me out, you know? Like they won't kill me, or call the police, or send me to jail—they'll just throw me out of the house, but, in my dream, this was the worst thing possible. I'm hiding in the closet, hiding from everyone, and I can hear Carlos's mom in the kitchen, can hear his little sister, can hear the swing creak outside, can hear Carlos's car pull up, but I'm standing there neither dead nor alive, because if they find me—they'll throw me out, and it will be the absolute worst thing that can happen. Then I hear someone coming up the stairs, and I bolt out of the closet because I realize they are about to find me in there, and run into the bathroom, and it's very quiet in there, and the tile is very cold, blue, and I'm standing on this tile thinking they're about to find me, how can I get out of here, they would still know I was here, even if I manage to slip away unseen. They would smell me. And that's when I realize I am bleeding. It's my period, and the blood's dripping all over these clean tiles, and it smells so sharply—just picture it—someone else's bathroom, everything's so clean, all these shampoos and things, and suddenly—blood. I grab toilet paper and go to wipe it, and it runs and runs, so heavy, and I realize there's no way I can get out of there unseen, they'll be able to track me..."

From that day on, Inga talked all the time. She filled the space with her voice, as if she knew that Yora had nothing left besides her, Inga's, voice and her words. Or, perhaps, it was the other way around—perhaps it was Inga who clung on to Yora, the last person in the world who could hear her. She would wake up in the morning, raise the blinds to make their room light, and talk the entire time until the pale winter sun set, until it was time to go to bed again.

"You and I, Ma, have lived together for such a long time, and seem to have talked about so much, and have had all

LOVE LIFE 105

kinds of adventures, but actually we haven't really told each other things, and all these adventures of ours are wrong, the wrong kind... This, now, is our biggest adventure yet—what I am telling you and what you will tell me, right? Listen, listen." She took Yora's hand, and spoke fast, letting her words bump into each other because her words were just like the little electric cars at an amusement park. "I have gotten so disgusting, cellulite everywhere, I don't do anything, I haven't been to the gym in a hundred years... And I used to do gymnastics, but then I stopped, when my stepfather took our apartment away from us—have I not told you how he took our apartment away? I remember the day well, no, not the day you are thinking about, but the day he first came to our place. He was sitting there, at the table, when I came home from school (I went to school by myself and came home by myself, at night, I had the second shift and, in the mornings, I had the gymnastics studio—my mom would still be asleep—I got up in the dark, and went to bed in the dark), so I came home from school, and there he was, sitting at the table wearing his short leather jacket, missing half his teeth, and there's a half-empty bottle of cognac in front of him. He brought it to celebrate our meeting each other, but what was he thinking—I was twelve, and my mom..."

"...My mom did not drink. He polished it off himself and then moved in with us. He slept with my mom in her room, I mean, in the bedroom, and they moved me out into the living room, and you know how small those rooms were, how thin the walls were, I slept on the pull-out couch every night, and they'd spend half the night screaming over in the bedroom. I didn't even have a Walkman to drown them out. And then he started to steal. One day I wake up and see there's only one earring on my bedside table, the other one is gone, and lots of other things started disappearing. My mom was not stupid, she graduated from a good college as a sales specialist, it was the best job for earning a living back then, and she knew that bad times were coming, because people in sales knew more about the market than all the professors of Marxism-Leninism at that college, and she had bought gold jewelry, and then, in the nineties, we sold it piece by piece—that's how we survived when there was no heat, or electricity, and nothing in the stores, and it was so cold you wanted to cry—and we cried, but we survived. And he stole everything we still had, took it all to pay for his mistresses. And then he threw us out of the apartment—Mom divorced him, but he'd still come over, drunk, and he'd do things—I don't even want to tell you what—and she hit him one time, picked up a hammer, and hit him, and then we lost the apartment. She cried so much—I have a child, she said to him, don't you have a mother, and he then pulled out this little book he carried in his pocket, and it was full of poems about mothers, mother this and mother that, how I love my dear mother, he kissed the pages and sobbed all over that little book—but he never went to visit his own mother where she lived in the country, and his mother, people said, was fine with that, that she was rid of him, the plague, she called her own son the plague, and that's what he was. He'd cry over his little book and once he started his hysterics like that you couldn't talk to him about anything, I'm a poor son of poor parents, he'd wail, and was I brought into this world only so that people would wish me ill, people can be so evil, evil—and he meant my mom and me. And that's how we ended up on the streets..."

"...it was spring, and we got on a bus, the roads were all muddy, and we had nowhere to go, we rode the bus to my aunt's, my mom's sister, to the village, just picture it—from the city to the village, we couldn't have known he would take our apartment from us, we didn't realize what was going on until the very end, my mom's lawyer kept telling her

LOVE LIFE 107

everything would be fine, and she believed him, she trusted him and didn't listen to anyone else, so we went to this aunt of mine. We got off at the bus station in that village, walked over to the street where she supposedly lived, but there wasn't even a house with that number. Our feet were wet, there was mud like you'd never seen all around, I certainly hadn't before, and haven't since, and we had our city shoes on. This man came up to us, wearing rubber boots, like everyone there, and asked, like, who are you looking for? We told him, and he scratched his head and said, I can't tell you where your sister lives, but I can take you to some people who might know. And we're standing there, shivering like wet dogs, Mom with her suitcase in hand, and our feet all wet. And we're supposed to go somewhere. It was so cold, I was absolutely freezing, couldn't feel my body, couldn't even tell if anything hurt or if it was already all over and I no longer had a body, I did gymnastics, you know, I know what pain is, and there were these houses on both sides, with no electricity, and I was walking—I didn't know where, or who that man was, just following his back. Things were just getting worse, only worse, and it was dark, so dark all the time... Just like now..."

"And where did he take you?"

"Nowhere, we didn't stay with him. Who knows what kind of person he was. We got as far as the paved road, and there was a bus coming—the last bus for the day—and my mom jumped out in front of it, shouted at the driver, waved her arms, and he stopped and let us on. We got on, soaking wet, people started asking, what happened, where are you going, and we couldn't even say anything. We got back to the city and spent that night at the railway station. And a few more nights..."

"Why didn't you ever tell me about this before?"

Inga looked up at Yora. She looked scared.

"I don't know," she said.

But really, when would she have? Up until then they were either running to work or going on dates, taking turns in the bathroom (*Oh, I'm sorry, I didn't know you were in here—no problem, go shower, I don't mind—Oh, do you need the sink right now, I haven't brushed my teeth yet—How's this dress? Do you think he'll like it?*), or sleeping in their bed together. Or crying.

"...and then I left. Because Mom had found another man. And kept saying, 'I love him, I love him.' But I didn't believe her. I didn't believe anyone or anything anymore."

"Where did you live?"

"I was in my first year in college by then, and I had this boyfriend, I've mentioned him, Edyk, remember? Well, so, there I was, seventeen, and I moved in with him."

"What about his parents?"

"They didn't mind. They got used to me. Plus, I never told you this, but he felt guilty because back when we'd just started sort of dating... I say 'sort of,' but that's because... Anyway, we went to his place that time, though he had been helping me for weeks, feeding me sandwiches he brought from home, and other things. And I was too embarrassed to say no to him. And, on top of that, I had no idea how it worked, but he went beet-red all over, he looked like he was about to be sick, he shook, he just had to have me. I sat down in front of him in this chair, and he knelt before me, he'd taken off his pants, and was all beet-red and shaking. And I let him. And then he announced that we were getting married and that I would move in with him. His parents said, no need to get married just yet, go ahead and live together a bit, see what you think. I remember I thought then—and later kept thinking—they were wise and kind, but now I see they may have been wise, but, if there was any kindness there, it wasn't for me. But they let us do it, no problem—to live together, play house. So we did."

LOVE LIFE 109

Inga got up and went to get some water. Where she stood, the light from the window fell on her legs so that it looked like a short skirt was being remade into a floor-length one, long as a monk's robe.

"What about you?" Inga asked, sitting back down. "What happened to you?"

Yora thought about it for a moment, gathered her courage, filled her lungs with air, and determined to tell Inga about her mom, thin and forever preoccupied with something else, and about their street of newly constructed apartment buildings that didn't even have any roads or sidewalks for the first two years they lived there. One time, in the fall, the city turned off the water and electricity in the apartments for two days straight. The women came out into the street, into the darkness, and started to scream. They could not really call for anyone in particular—there was one functional phone in the entire neighborhood, and that night it wasn't working. Everyone had forgotten about them. The authorities were busy divvying up whatever spoils there were still to divvy up; the gangsters were busy killing each other for what they had done; and the women screamed. They screamed because they could no longer stay inside the small cages of their apartments where the men had fled and children cried. They screamed without hope, and their screams echoed off the tall buildings, dark against the dark sky. That was something Yora remembered. She would tell Inga.

Yora all but opened her mouth to begin when she noticed that Inga had lain down on the edge of the bed and dozed off. And that's when Yora realized that Inga would not be able to hear her no matter how much telling her these things would have cost Yora, because she, like Inga, was not used to talking—only to fighting for her life. Inga would not be able to hear her because she was overflowing with her own stories, and the stories were heavy, almost unbearable. She couldn't possibly manage someone else's, too. It was better to listen to her, listen to her for as long as Yora could.

"My mom doesn't talk to me much these days," Inga spoke again as soon as she woke up. "Only when her husband is not at home, because she says he gets jealous, says to her, 'Why are you talking to your daughter for so long,' and I said to her, 'You should tell him it's important,' but she didn't listen to me. Who does he think he is? How dare he feel jealous, what does he know about us? But she doesn't want to hear it. Then she sent me some nonsense about a digital flower farm, asked me to join her... And what about me? I have to graduate in the spring, and there are no jobs, if only she knew what it's like for me here! What it's *like!* Another six months, and I have to start paying off my student loan—but how? With what money? I'm already afraid of opening the mailbox—it's either all bills in there or a fine because I went through a yellow light, I swear to God it was yellow, but the camera caught it and it shows the light was red, so I have to go to court, but I don't have the time, which means I have to pay. But how? I haven't been to a doctor in two years, maybe I'll just die here, it'll be the easiest way out, right?" And she sighed as if the idea of it brought her relief.

"It's terrifying to go on living, terrifying!" Inga went on. She opened her eyes wide in the face of her fear, but then glanced at Yora's face and remembered something. "Ma, you're ill, are you tired? Am I wearing you out? You should get some rest. I'll tell you more later," she would say, but then wouldn't be able to stop, and Yora still heard her voice while she slept, heard the fragments of her stories. "Are you tired? Are you?"

"I am. But I'm listening."

LOVE LIFE

"You'll tell me about yourself, too. Promise?"

"I promise," Yora said, knowing she would not. "As soon as I'm a little better."

"Don't worry, this will pass," Inga said by way of cheering her up. "You just started to get better."

She wrapped Yora like light. She held her.

"I don't want anything anymore," she said. "I'm happy just the way I am, do you believe me? We are finally talking, and this makes me happy. We have time for everything. I'm happy right now, I've been looking for happiness all my life, and right now, here, I'm happy. I don't give a hoot about the rest of the world. Thank you, thank you for just being there for me. I want things to stay the way they are now, let those men all vanish from the face of the earth, you can't find a single decent one out there."

"Don't say that, Cooney," Yora said, hoping to comfort Inga. "There are all kinds of men out there."

But Inga got angry.

"So what do I want with them? Just to get laid? I don't care about that, might not ever care again. Do you think I want anything, after Carlos, after your getting so sick, after all this? What decent men, huh? They don't exist, never did." And she hugged Yora tighter.

Advent came. Yora still wasn't leaving the house. Inga would run out to the grocery store and come right back, unable to stand the festive bacchanal out there. A classmate of Inga's called and invited her to a Christmas party.

"I won't go," Inga said, sitting down on the floor, as was her custom. She sniffled.

"What's wrong?" Yora asked. "Why?"

"I won't go without you. I don't want to. What am I going to talk to them about? What do they know about me?"

"But it's no fun being stuck around me either," Yora smiled.

"And on top of that," Inga added after a pause, in a slightly different voice, "I've got nothing to wear. There's so much cellulite on me, nothing fits."

"Don't say that," Yora objected. "Just try some things on."

Inga got up and went over to the small built-in closet that was stuffed full of clothes, hers and Yora's. From its depths, she pulled out one thing after another.

"Take something of mine," Yora suggested, and Inga obediently put on an item, then took it off, and tried on the next one. In this manner, together, they chose a dress, yellow-and-brown, not really right for the season. Yora had bought it the year before, and the colors were not at all Christmassy, but the winter was tropical anyway, despite the unusual amount of rain, and no one was going to pay attention to the colors.

"You can have it," Yora said. "You can have it—for good. I never wear it anyway."

* * *

"That's it," Inga said on the day of the party. She was nicely dressed and wearing make-up. She had spent nearly an hour in front of the bathroom mirror, humming a song and working magic on her face, and now it no longer looked puffy, as if all her yet-unshed tears had hidden somewhere deep inside her body, at least for a few hours. It had to be said—Inga looked stunning.

"You know, Yora, you should come with me. I'll lend you one of my dresses if yours are all too big. I'm a size smaller... I'll do your make-up. I have everything. It'll look great if I do it like this, with the pencil... Come! Why not?"

LOVE LIFE   113

But Yora was afraid to even look at herself in the mirror. She thought about Sebastian—and shook her head. What would he be doing tonight? Going to see his family? Or did he not have a real family—only the women with whom he shared his warm bed at night?

"Nah," Yora said. "I'm feeling kind of dizzy."

"You'll see, everything will be just fine," Inga reassured her. "You are already feeling better. You are just weak, but soon, everything will be different. Right?" And Inga laughed, because, at that moment, she sincerely wished everything would be just fine for her and her friend, for everyone in the world. And, most importantly, at that moment, she believed things would, indeed, be just fine. Her make-up looked so beautiful, so natural...

"Soon you'll be going to all kinds of parties," Inga said to Yora. "Don't mope. I'll come back and tell you everything—how it was, who I talked to, and what we talked about. And I'll be thinking about you. A lot."

"Don't!" Yora smiled. "Think about the party instead. You'll have plenty to think about without me."

"No, I don't want to do anything without you anymore. You are my strength. You are my talisman..."

It was after midnight when Inga returned. Yora woke up to the noise of Inga's fussing with the lock—the lock, as always, was jammed, and no matter how hard Inga tried to be quiet, Yora heard the grinding of the key. Finally, the key turned, and Inga tiptoed into the studio. She avoided turning on the light, so as not to wake Yora up completely.

"Yora? Are you asleep?" she called through the dark in a suggestive whisper.

"No."

"Oh, you have to hear what happened! What happened!" Inga giggled, and the sound of it told Yora that Inga was intoxicated.

"So, what happened?"

"This thing! This... You won't believe it!" Inga sat down on the bed.

"Tell me already!"

"Okay," Inga said, but instead of telling Yora anything, she lay down on her back and laughed happily. She smelled of perfume, alcohol, and festivities. After a while, Inga spoke.

"Yora? I met a man."

"What's his name?"

"Donald."

"What car does he drive? A BMW? Or did he bike there?"

"N-no," Inga smiled. "Just an old Toyota, nothing special. I mean, does a man have to have a nice car? Am I going to live with his car? Come on, tell me—what's the car for? Do you want to live with someone's car?"

"What does he do?"

"He has his own business."

"Do you like him?"

"Uh-huh. We agreed to meet for New Year's Eve... To celebrate... Together. Don't be mad at me, okay, you don't really get up these days, what am I supposed to do? But if you'd like to come along, I'll ask Donald, and we—"

"Don't be silly! Of course, you should go celebrate however you want!"

"I do... And he..."

"I was thinking you might—"

"It's not like that... He kissed my hands, you know, just held my hands and kissed them, and told me I was the best in the world, and no, he was not drunk, and he..."

"Just be careful, okay?"

"I know! But we can't live like that."

"Of course, we can't, but that's not what I..."

"You have to get up! Come over here, let me take off your dress, and you can put it on, and you'll see how—"

LOVE LIFE 115

"Inga! Don't... It's your dress now. I gave it to you. Let go of me! I don't want to!"

"Why not, it's fun to try on a dress... Okay, it's mine, so you can try on my dress..."

"What do you want from me? Let go..."

"What if I don't..."

"What are you doing?"

Inga was struggling to pull off the dress in the dark and simultaneously put it on Yora. Yora fought her—the half-naked Inga was breathing in her face, and she smelled of wine.

"What's wrong with you? You just said you can't live your life like that, and now..."

"Nothing, I just..."

"I'm not doing this because of that, but because..."

* * *

After that evening, their conversations stopped. Inga no longer told Yora stories from her life. Both women, in silent agreement, no longer finished their sentences and abandoned them half-formed; the sentences were not even worth starting, but they, Yora and Inga, started them just out of habit. The fragments were like the roads of this city that ended abruptly and inevitably at the sea. And the sea was louder than language. Perhaps those sentences of theirs went on living for a while, somewhere out there, in the water, like those salt dolls that went to measure the depth of the sea, but they never came back to the shore—neither to this one nor to the other, distant one.

Inga transformed; even her gait changed. She did not sit cross-legged on the floor anymore and did not hunch. On the contrary, Inga's bearing was almost regal, her laugh sounded like the laugh of a very young woman, and her cheekbones emerged sharp and beautiful. Her eyes flashed at Yora who lay like a defeated giant and had to look up from below at this parade of beauty.

Inga wore a different dress every time she went out with Donald. At first, she would ask Yora's advice—which one was better for the evening, which one looked better on her—but then she stopped and would change right there in the middle of the studio into whatever she wanted, humming her little tunes, smoothing her hose and adjusting her bra straps. Her entire body radiated a powerful light. Suddenly, it turned out that Inga had an entire closet of her own dresses that fit her just fine. She would shave her legs in the bathroom and not bother to close the door, draw smooth lines with her eyeliner, and grab the purse Donald had given her as a present, making the sequins flash in the light of their lamp, just like her eyes.

As with Carlos, she never brought Donald home. However, while she at least introduced Yora to Carlos, Inga was keeping Donald at a safe distance from their cheap apartment and Yora's tubs of bloody water, powders, and pills. Inga no longer called Yora "Ma"—and Yora did not dare call Inga "Cooney." There was something about Inga now that reminded Yora of the Bonnie from her dreams—she was just as beautiful, queen-like, with the same mysterious look on her face and her light-colored hair arranged into an up-do.

Inga would step into her high heels, give Yora one last foxy look over her shoulder, and blow her a kiss before running out of the studio. Yora could hear her laughing on the stairs.

Inga now stepped through life proudly, like an actor walking down the red carpet. Could she possibly have thought that Yora was jealous of her—because why would Yora be jealous? Inga had everything—her beauty, her

LOVE LIFE 117

youth, her health, and a man who would go crazy at the mere touch of her hand, who was prepared to do anything, go anywhere for her. And Yora? Yora had her body which had betrayed her, and her loneliness. But Yora was not jealous, because Yora had a treasure whose existence Inga could never guess—death, a cold little ball that grew quietly somewhere deep in Yora's chest.

Inga entered the world like an exotic peacock, but Yora had no desire to do the same; she wouldn't have wanted to, even if she had the energy for it. What was the point? To show yourself to the world? That was, for this new Yora, too petty a dream, too simple. "Anyone can do that," she thought, smiling, and her mind promptly summoned visions of hellish machines with the old, wrinkled Bonnies being tossed out and replaced right away with new ones. This picture was followed by another one—of a grave (her own, Yora's), at which Sebastian stood in mourning, his head bent low. He was going to stand there as long as he lived, until the end of times, Yora realized suddenly, and shivered with excitement. He was going to grieve for her alone, only her, and he would never have another woman. That was it! Only now did she dare watch the sequence of pictures in her mind until the end, and this is what was revealed to her—Sebastian would nurse his memory of Yora like a mother would nurse her heart's most cherished child, and nurture it, and raise it—this fruit of their love, yet unknown to generations to come. He would bequeath them this love—and they would weep with gratitude. *This* was worth dying for. And life's red carpet? *That* was just a boring, unnecessary spectacle. Why should Yora parade in front of gawkers whose faces she couldn't even see? What did she want their faces for? She only needed one face—*his* face—sublime and sorrowful.

On the infrequent evenings when Donald did not come to pick her up, Inga now sang. She did not have a good pitch, or a decent voice, but neither prevented her from taking up one song after another. The songs were in English, from old American movies, most often from *The Sound of Music* which Inga and Yora did not finish watching two years ago—it seemed too kitschy; Inga had watched it with Donald and now trilled like a nightingale, carefully enunciating foreign words with rolled *R*s.

The past retreated and hid somewhere, an entire continent of the past sank under water, and only the Peninsula was left, the Peninsula, where one could live as if a child again, happily and peacefully. Clocks ticked in beach-town antique stores; housewives baked chocolate-chip cookies; farmers put on their denim overalls in the mornings; and roadside diners cooked fluffy cheese omelets, while their customers waited over cups of weak coffee. This was a different country, a different planet, a place where one had to sing precisely like this—happily, loudly, with an ineradicable belief in oneself.

Weeks passed like this. The reborn, singing Inga ran in and out of the apartment. She took her things.

"I need to grab some clothes," she said. "It's easier to keep them at Donald's. Donald wants me to bring my textbooks and study at his place. He likes having me around. Donald asked me to get my suitcase—we're going to visit his parents in North Carolina. I packed my make-up. I'll just go to class straight from his place."

"Are you coming back?" Yora asked when Inga ran in to collect the last things that were left—the few trinkets of hers that were still on the mantle—a small icon, a China cat, and three large yellow shells from Sanibel Island, where they had gone together in Yora's rickety Honda. The resort there was expensive, but one could stay the night next door in Fort Myers and drive over to Sanibel just to go to the beach—one of the island's nearly wild beaches with dry white sand and

LOVE LIFE 119

shells famous over the entire coastline. Yora and Inga had spent hours just lying by the sea, on the shore of the lazy Gulf of Mexico whose turquoise water nudged against the similarly turquoise sky on the horizon. Birds would come down to the water and levitate, hovering above the waves.

"What do you mean, am I coming back?" Inga asked in surprise, but she did not sound sincere. She was not coming back, Yora realized.

"Just tell me, so I know."

"And what if I'm not?" Inga made a face. "Do you think it's easy being here with you?"

"Of course not," Yora said.

"You know... It seems to me," Inga continued, "that you *would prefer I didn't...* That you... like it here."

"I can take care of myself."

"I know. But I can't just look at you and do nothing. It's like this—you come home, and there's a body there. And I can't help you in any way because you won't let me."

Yora said nothing. This was hard to deny.

Then Inga suggested, "You should find someone, too."

"Who?" Yora asked.

"Someone. Anyone. I don't know. You are almost healthy now. You're just scared. Time to come out of your shell."

"I don't want to be with anybody," Yora said.

Inga was right—her body lay on the bed, and that was the way she had come to think of herself—a *body* on the bed. Even a little while ago, she would have said, *I am lying on the bed.*

"You don't?" Inga asked, and Yora suddenly heard a threat in her voice. "You don't? I'm the only bitch here who does, is that right?" Inga exclaimed, now in tears. "I'm the bitch, aren't I? Bitch!" she exclaimed again, enjoying the word on her tongue—the familiar, menacing, deep word, so unlike the smooth, rounded words she had been uttering as she sang. This was frightening, and all the more so because it seemed completely unexpected.

"What's wrong with you?" Yora said, scared. "What are you saying, Inga? A bitch?"

"I know what you would like, I've been watching you and I finally got it... I didn't get it right away, you can laugh at me, how dumb I was... But now I get it. You would like," Inga said very slowly, "the two of us to lock ourselves in this madhouse, forever, until we die, and for us to suffer, suffer until our skin cracks!"

"Well, mine did crack."

"Stop it! It's just a disease. It'll go away."

"This one won't."

"Still, it'll get better! But you want us to be like a pair of jilted brides from Dickens—I read those books, too, when I was a kid. Rotting in our white dresses, next to our white wedding cakes. But a woman cannot be alone. Who are you without a man? I've tried it—but because life had me on the ropes! And I can't stand it! I refuse to live like that! It's not normal. I need support, a man's shoulder, can you understand that? How can you go so long—without being touched? Do you not remember what it feels like when blood runs faster in your veins, and you bloom? Have you not felt that?"

Yora sighed. In her native city, everything was in bloom in the spring, and the cemeteries she used to walk by smelled of fresh flowers.

"No," she said, obstinately. "I have not felt that."

She lay there in half-darkness while Inga stood above her.

"Then why don't you—"

"Why don't I what?"

"Why don't you find yourself a man? A different one, not like that guy." Inga did not want to utter Sebastian's name. "You know he's not coming back."

LOVE LIFE

"Oh," Yora said. "Of course I do. And I'm not—"

"...waiting for him?"

"I'm not waiting for him and I'm not—"

"Then why don't you get up?"

"Not because I—"

"Why then? Why are you letting him hold your life hostage?"

Yora shrugged, searching inside for the death that should have stirred right at that moment, should have stirred and in that way showed her that it was still there, that Yora hadn't lost it, and it was the reason Yora remained in bed. She wanted it to confirm that everything would be fine, that she, Yora, was just biding her time, until the hour of retribution, because she would not consent to anything less than retribution upon Sebastian. But death was silent; it lay hidden and quiet somewhere as if it weren't there at all—neither inside Yora, nor in the rest of the world.

"Yora," Inga said. "I can't imagine why things had to go this way. I don't know what's happening to you and how to... But call me. I've left you money—my half of the rent and a little more... And... Donald gave it to me... But I've left you half of it. It's probably better this way. It's right here, okay?"

Inga picked up her sunglasses off the kitchen counter, put them on inside the apartment, sniffled, and turned the doorknob. The door closed behind her.

***

When Yora woke up the next morning, the sky was just turning gray.

"Go ahead, leave, I won't stop you," she muttered into the empty space, surprising herself with her own energy—as if Inga's departure had unlocked a previously sealed reservoir of strength inside her. "I'm not *so* helpless without you."

She felt like being brave. She was brave! She was, actually, brave. Why not? Was it so hard, being brave? Yora got up—her feet did hurt less; she made herself some oatmeal that was, thankfully, still there. She needed to make a budget, take stock of the pantry, and pay the bills. Once, before everything had happened, she and Inga used to crunch the numbers in the evenings—how much for the electric bill, how much for the water, the internet, when the rent was due; whether they would have enough money. It used to be a regular thing, a ritual they used to keep but had recently abandoned, being late on their bills, crying, being sick. Each of them used to then account for their own expenses, out loud— how much for insurance—health and car, the phone... Together, they were less scared.

Yora opened her bank's web page; her heart skipped a beat. Her account, as she had suspected, was almost empty. She had spent weeks, if not months, buying medications at the hospital, and giving her debit card to Inga to pay for groceries, each time spinning the roulette—was there still money in the account, or would the card be returned to her as having insufficient funds? One could say she had been lucky. But her luck was over now.

Yora dialed the phone company; they were threatening to turn off her phone, and she could not allow that. Her internet service was about to get canceled, too; she had to keep

LOVE LIFE 123

what she had through her phone. After long negotiations, the phone company agreed to take the last of Yora's money as a payment against her debt and to wait for two more weeks for the rest, but if she did not pay the balance then... Yora read out her card number. That was it. She might as well not call anywhere else—she was out of money, and Inga's—meaning, Donald's—cash had to cover the rent. She wondered, still, if she could get extensions on her other payments.

"Blue Cross, Blue Shield," said the voice on the phone. "How can I help you?"

"I'm calling about paying my premiums."

"What's your policy number?"

Yora read out her number.

"You've got two weeks until the final deadline."

"What happens then?"

"Then we will stop your coverage."

Without insurance, she would not be able to buy medication at a reasonable price and would simply die.

"Did you lose your job?"

"Me? No, I..."

"Then please give me your credit card number."

That would have been pointless.

"Yes, I lost my job," Yora blurted out.

"I am very sorry to hear that, but our rules..."

"I will pay you by check." Yora suddenly had an idea. "Please make a note in the file. Except it won't reach you within two weeks, because I am ill and almost never leave home, I'm dependent on others for everything..."

"Alright," the woman on the phone said doubtfully. "I will make a note here not to cancel your insurance."

Yora had no money in her account, but she had time while the check traveled to the insurance company and however long it would take for it to bounce...

Next, she had to call the hospital. Yora owed them almost a thousand dollars. Most of it—for the emergency room visit in the middle of the night. The hospital stay had been covered by her insurance, but the emergency room visit was not.

Such were the rules in this country. Still, emergency rooms were crowded with poor people who had nowhere else to go and had no insurance of any kind.

Yora thought of the hospital and shuddered. She called the finance department.

"Good afternoon," she said confidently. "I am confused as to why you sent a bill to me instead of my insurance company."

"Your name please? Your case number?" the voice on the other end of the line asked.

The voice did not sound tired. That was bad news—in the mornings, it was said, people were more likely to do their jobs properly, and in this case, doing the job properly meant telling Yora to pay the bill and not bother the hospital with her phone calls. The woman on the other end checked something, and then told Yora there had been no mistake, that her insurance did not cover the amount of the bill.

"Please check again," Yora insisted.

"Is this the only policy you have?"

"No, I have another one," Yora lied.

That was a thought. She told the woman on the other end of the line the number of her policy from two years ago.

"Okay," the woman said. "We will contact them."

Of course they would, and the company would tell them the truth. But Yora had won herself some time.

Next was the car insurance policy. Yora could not do without it either. She would be arrested if she were stopped anywhere. This company, however, was stuffed with tougher people—they only laughed at Yora's offer to pay by check.

LOVE LIFE   125

"Oh, sorry," they said politely. "That's only an option with companies that are unable to take direct card payments over the phone and do bank withdrawals. We accept Visa cards. There's a note here that says you have a Visa. If you'd like, we could set up automatic payments for you? It'll give you peace of mind and you won't need to call us in the future."

"Thank you," Yora said. "I'll think about it."

So, now she would have to risk it and drive without insurance, or not drive at all.

Yora sighed and checked her list—what's next? Food was next. She had no money left for food. Yora opened the pantry to see what was left in there. Not a lot, but there was still canned tuna, in oil and in water. She could subsist on that for a while.

What to do? Yora looked around the studio like a hunted animal—there was the mattress on the floor, and their crockery in the kitchen—Inga hadn't taken any of it. Donald probably had a French-chef-equipped kitchen with an espresso machine on top. Could she sell anything? But what? Her tuna? And who would buy it? The pots and pans in their kitchen cabinets were basic, most of them bought used at thrift stores; they weren't worth anything. Yora opened her closet—her dresses drooped there like bodies of the hanged. That's how it will end! She'll just end up on the streets like millions before her—without money, and without a home. How long could she last? She was lucky she wasn't homeless yet. If she couldn't find a way out... What did she have? What?

Still, Yora felt like the girl from the fairytale who had a magic fishbone—she just had to pull it out at the right moment. What was it? What was her fishbone? Suddenly, Yora remembered—death! She still had death. Yora searched for it inside her, and even asked, are you still there? But death, just like it did with Inga, betrayed her again. It was silent.

"Where are you?" Yora thought. "Where? Now you can come, I've done everything, I was wrong about everything, it's your turn. Come!"

But death did not answer.

Yora was so sad and tired that she fell asleep, and when she woke up, it was already evening. The day had passed, and she didn't even notice. Yora got up with a heavy head and a heavy heart and went to the bathroom. In the corners, transparent clumps of their thin tangled hair, hers and Inga's, lay like lacy doilies on the tiles—they hadn't bothered to clean in forever. Yora stood there and stared at their hair, entwined like people in an embrace. They had lived together for a while, they lost their hair here, but now it seemed like someone had come and pulled their hair out in handfuls, chasing them like a frightful lion over forests and ravines, reaching out for them with claws, and they left bits of their skin and strands of blonde hair in the predator's grip. Except that Inga had tamed her lion, and he obediently let her put him on a leash, and the two of them, Inga and the lion, went on their own merry way somewhere.

Yora opened the medicine cabinet. There was a gaping void where Inga used to keep her things, and only one last little jar cowed deep inside it.

Yora pulled the jar out into the light of day as if it were a precious gem. This was the herbed oil that Inga had bought to attract Carlos. She did not like the scent and did not take the oil with her when she moved out. Yora slowly opened the jar, dripped out half a spoonful of oil, mechanically rubbed it into her chest, and all but cried out with longing, "Oh, Inga, Inga!" The smell wasn't even Inga's; it was a strange, sharp smell, but why did it hurt so much?

Then everything went suddenly dark. A thunderstorm began outside. Yora could hear the water run down the streets, turning them into canals.

LOVE LIFE

A wet stain spread across the ceiling again; no one had even thought of getting the roof fixed. Water dripped onto the floor, and Yora had to put a bowl there; the drops hammered the bottom of the bowl. Soon, the ceiling would give. That would be the peak of destruction of this emptied home, where there was no longer any money or hope. Thunder clapped against the walls and the windows; lightning flashed momentarily to light the room, and then it was dark again. After several flashes and thunderclaps that made the entire building shudder like it had been hit by an artillery barrage, the electricity cut out. Or was it turned off? No, there was still the deposit that Inga and Yora had put down when they signed the lease; maybe the company now just took it as payment for the month. So it wasn't them this time—it was the storm. And who could tell when the power would come back on? No electrician would go fix the wires in the rain. Did that mean it would stay this pitch-black and scary until the next day?

Yora thought it was the darkness that made it hard for her to breathe, so she went to the kitchen counter, felt for a candle and a lighter in one of the drawers, clicked on the light and lit the wick.

The candle produced a tremulous spot of uncertain light that made the surrounding darkness even denser. Rain continued to drip into the bowl, where the drops now splashed in the accumulated water.

Yora looked around the studio; she had done it so many times over the last few months! Everything here reminded her of herself; she would never be able to forget anything here, this studio was her memory. An iconostasis of sorrow looked at her from the walls, the kitchen counter, the ceiling, from everywhere: Sebastian, Bonnie, and Inga. How could she ever have hoped to be brave here? How? She stood in the middle of this dark church like an archaeologist in the middle of a secret dig. Should she have agreed to Sebastian's conditions, to Bonnie, all the Bonnies with whom she'd have to share him? Sharing, after all, meant owning, just not entirely, but what was so bad about that? Maybe everyone had arrangements like that—how would she know? Sebastian would've just made a schedule, and she would've had her days, not every day of the week, of course, and perhaps not even every week, but so what; when her turn came, she would've had him to herself, and he would've busied himself in the kitchen, humming, to make her dinner, as he always did, and then later Yora could've put her head on his chest and cried as much as she wished, about anything, Bonnie or something else, and he would've comforted her...

And Inga! Inga would not have left her, wouldn't have left her like this! Oh, Inga! Yora wept. Of all her losses, this was the worst, the one that hurt the most. Without Inga, everything was flat and unreal, because the real only lived in her voice, in her presence. What wouldn't Yora have given just then for the promise—offered by anyone at all—that Inga would come back, that, tomorrow, Yora would wake up to the sound of Inga's voice, to the telling of stories, even the ones she had already heard? Those stories, those tangled hairs on the bathroom tiles... Never had Yora cherished anyone so much. Why had she not appreciated her friend more, why had she made her leave? It was she, Yora, who was to blame for everything. The entire world rolled past her window like a fiery wheel, but the world was innocent, and she—she was guilty. She even let Inga leave her money—as if she could not do without this last sign of her own incompetence and approaching bankruptcy that was, as it turned out, always closer than one thought. Where was Inga now? Did she really not miss Yora? Could Donald have replaced Yora, her friend? Could Inga have gotten used to him, in all his manifestations, so hopelessly quickly that everything

LOVE LIFE 129

that had come before him—and everyone who had been in her life before him—no longer mattered and vanished from her memory, from her very soul? But that could not be! What if Yora called and asked her? But would Inga pick up? She could just ignore the call. And she would not come back.

Unless Yora died. Then Inga would have to come back. Yora called death again. Death still did not answer. Yora closed her eyes. She looked for death inside of her, angry now, irked, but could only see the bare walls of her essence, an emptiness that stared, mocking, back at her.

And that's when Yora had a kind of epiphany. There was no mystery in death; nothing was growing ripe inside Yora; the promises of a later reward were worthless. Nothing would be born of death. No one would come and stand, thoughtful and sorrowful, at Yora's grave. Sebastian had forgotten all about her, and Inga had left to be with Donald. They wouldn't want anything to do with a grave! They were plenty happy with Donald and Bonnie and, if that weren't enough, there would be new, fresh Donalds and Bonnies. Who would even notice if Yora died—so quietly, so confined to these four prison-like walls? A bad thing had happened— Yora had fallen in love with death and was now ashamed of it more than of any other sin she'd ever committed. This mistake, her gravest, tormented her, and it was impossible to go on living with its consequences.

A long time ago, when Yora was young, her friends used to have this joke when something unpleasant happened or when life required superhuman effort (getting up at seven a.m. to go to class, waiting in line at the store, working the night shift)—how long 'till we get to the next world, they used to say, where we can get our rest, we'll rest in the morgue; with a life like this, I wouldn't be sorry to die. They tossed death generously in front of themselves like a magical tablecloth that could become a bridge above an abyss, like a trump card in a game that had to go on after death. But the death Yora used to joke about, the one she waited for and tried to summon, the one that was supposed to humble Sebastian forever into submission was not real. Real death was not a tablecloth or a card, not even the other shore, but a concrete-walled hole rooted in the innards of the earth, a Gray Rose at the bottom of which sat Sebastian who was not a Sorrowful Knight but a low common servant who held a thread in his fingers—and Yora's soul was tied to the other end of this thread. Death was in no hurry to yank on the thread too often, but it made Sebastian smile seductively to lure Yora toward him, to get her to descend into this concrete dungeon of her own will. Because Death wanted neither Yora's soul nor her body; it only desired her will. It did not mean to cut her heart out of her body; it wanted to take the spine out of it, like a flute it could play with its toothless mouth.

There was an iron pipe that stretched the length of the room from the stove to the window. It might have been intended as a pull-up bar, but it seemed too thin for that. The designers of this space must not have known exactly what they were doing and why.

Yora got a length of rope from a kitchen drawer, climbed onto a chair, and tied the end of the rope to the pipe. She made a noose on the other end. She sat on the floor and unwound the bandages on her feet. She got up, shifted her weight from one foot to another, and saw the bloody prints her feet left on the floor. Carefully, she put her head into the noose, as if trying on a new garment. She entered death slowly, because she was accustomed to considering the consequences, but what was all this thinking, really? An atavism. People worried about every step they took, but to die, it turned out, you had to quit thinking. You just had to jump. What would happen next? Yora imagined a transition,

LOVE LIFE 131

a total darkness she now tried on just like the noose. There would be a great blackness which she would have to traverse alone. Here, Yora smiled ironically. People were wrong to ask their family and loved ones to be with them in the hour of their death, wrong to hope that it would be easier either in a hospice or at home. They were really alone, and that meant both those that are inconsolable and who have been consoled. And no one could really be *with* them. They would still have to traverse the blackness alone. Now, after Yora had tried the noose on, the only thing left to do was to jump off the chair, but Yora hesitated. She rubbed her feet on the seat of the chair, opening the myriad small wounds on her soles until they started to bleed slowly. Maybe she didn't have to jump—she would just bleed out, little by little?

Yora was shaking all over.

"Come on," she told herself. "Come on!" Yet, for some reason, she did not jump.

"It's the candle—that's what's distracting me," Yora thought. She took off the noose and climbed down from the chair.

The candle had to be blown out; the candle was not letting her die. Yora went over to the mattress, sat down on it, and looked at the candle. The narrow flame burned evenly and sharply, making a circle of light—a circle as solid and powerful as the one the noose had just drawn around Yora's neck. The candle reminded her about life. It *was* life; there was a reason people spoke of someone burning up like a candle. The rain kept whipping at the roof and splashing into the bowl. Yora drew a full chest of air and blew as hard as she could at the candle—let there be no more life. The candle went out, and darkness fell on everything. The candle had gone out, but life had not; it still beat, like a fish, deep inside Yora's chest. It had not gone anywhere, and it filled everything now—precisely because it was so dark, and life was so lonely and vast. It required no body, it needed no face; it was life that created them, and not the other way around. Bodies and faces lied, like actors wearing poorly made masks. They only distracted one from what mattered, the heart of the issue, and being alone, face-to-face with it was intolerable. This, this heart, was everywhere, just like Yora herself.

This was indeed the darkest of all times—the Hour of Self.

In the dark, Yora went over to the wall, barely able to support the burden of her life, climbed onto the chair, and put the noose around her neck. She had blown out the wrong candle, but, fortunately, she could still fix that. Did she imagine it, or did someone actually knock at the door? Just to think, a few weeks ago she wouldn't have been ready to believe it was Sebastian. Now she no longer waited for him; she had told Inga the truth. Do those committing suicide always think they heard someone knocking on their doors? Yora jumped. The pipe broke under her weight and fell, and Yora fell with it. "Die, die!" she whispered, cradling her head in her arms, but she did not die, or, perhaps, after all, she did, perhaps the fall was a phantom of her dying consciousness, its way of protecting itself against the horror; perhaps the other world had already begun; the non-being had begun.

Yora lay, unmoving, with the noose around her neck, in the dark, and did not know if she were dead or alive. No one knocked at the door. It was very quiet; the rain had stopped dripping into the bowl, and even the thunderstorm outside seemed to have ended. Or was it just that Yora could no longer hear it? She couldn't hear anything, not a sound. But no—there was a sound, and it was her ineradicable breathing. There was nothing, but there was her breath. Her breath filled her body and her bitterness-racked face. She'd make quite the picture now, Yora thought, next to the beautiful Bonnie. Her breath, meanwhile, filled her, and was not

LOVE LIFE 133

stopping. Yora closed her eyes, and a bright light flashed under her eyelids. That's who that man from her dreams was, the man who signaled at her and undid his bandages to show her his wounds; it was Job. He was looking at her now, too, and his face was the face of a very young man. His wounds had not healed, but he was not at all ashamed of them.

"It's me," he seemed to be saying to Yora—or not saying exactly, because she could not hear individual words. "It's me, do not be afraid. The real machine of being is not what you thought. To be with another means something, it might mean everything, because we have nothing without another. But, at the same time, to be with another means nothing because we exist regardless. It's like a pair of scissors, with the human body between the blades. The body takes up space on earth, the body breathes. It's me, it's me, do not be afraid..." Job said nothing more—if he had said anything at all; in the next instant, he disappeared, and everything went dark again.

***

That evening, Yora, newly awakened to life, showered in the dark and cried the entire time with angry, hungry tears, the way young children cry. She cried and said, "Idiot! What an idiot!" She scrubbed her skin until it hurt. She washed off Inga's oil, washed the blood off her feet, and then took her time to dry them carefully, so as not to stain the towel, before applying fresh bandages.

She lit the candle again and studied herself in the mirror—for the first time in a very long time. "What have I done? What have I done? There's my face, it's just a face, a little drawn, the cheekbones are sharper, and there are new wrinkles around the eyes—but so what? It's my face! It's mine!" She rubbed cream into her face, and another— all over her body so thoroughly as if she were doing it for the first time in her life. She touched her face and her body deliberately, not the way she did before, like someone who was ill. She carried the candle into the room and opened the wardrobe with her dresses again. Just to think, she wanted to hang herself! It was very late, but Yora picked out a dress and put it on, found her eyeliner—she had almost no make-up left, and Inga had taken all of hers—and did her eyes, in front of the mirror, in the light of the candle. It would make sense to do her lashes, too, but she had run out of mascara. Delicately, she ran lipstick along her lips, put on her shoes, and sat, dressed and made-up on the bed, as if she were ready to go out, until she fell asleep.

* * *

The following evening, someone did knock on the door. The knocking was not menacing, but calm and confident, as if the visitor knew he or she would be welcome. Yora, just out of the shower, with her hair done, and dressed again as if she were going out (because she had decided that was the only way to live), opened the door. There she found the Goth girl, her neighbor. She had the kind of face that did not surprise with beauty—bony and tapered at the chin— but also did not age. She had a sharp chin and a mocking mouth, but her forehead was high, and her eyes were large and serene, although savagely outlined in black.

"Hello," the young woman said. "My name is Raven."

Of course, Yora thought. What else could it be? Girls like that were always called Raven, or Morticia...

LOVE LIFE   135

"So," she went on. "Our place seems to be falling apart."

"Place? What place?"

"The roof." Raven pointed up. "Your roof is leaking too, isn't it?"

"It is. So what?"

"Nothing. I called them, but so far, *nada*."

"I called, too. They said it would be a few weeks."

"Yep, same here. But they said the electricity is back on—like we wouldn't have noticed without them. They've got one toothless meth-head who does all the maintenance work, and I'm guessing he's really not in good shape at the moment. Everything's just going to fall apart around us, and we'll have to live under the blue sky."

Yora looked up and tried to imagine what that might be like. They would look at the stars and call out to each other. But no, there were no stars—only rain. The rain would fill their homes with water, and they would live as if in giant fish tanks. They would learn to swim like fish, and to blow bubbles.

"Are you going to keep me on the stairs?" Raven asked.

Yora opened the door wide and stepped aside, but Raven did not go in.

"I changed my mind," she said. "I'd rather you come to my place."

Yora picked up the key, locked her door, and limped after Raven. She actually had to walk only a few steps—to the next door over, the same one from behind which she had occasionally, at moments of high passion, such as her last conversation with Sebastian, heard giggling. So it was Raven.

"Come on in," Raven said.

She also had a studio. The bed, pushed into the corner as far away from the stain on the ceiling as possible, was hidden under a mountain of pillows and stuffed animals that would've been more appropriate in a child's bedroom—not on the bed of a woman like Raven. But then, Yora knew nothing about Raven—perhaps she was, in fact, a child.

"Take a seat," Raven said, and sat down on her bed. "Let's watch TV—I know you don't have one."

"I don't really need one," Yora said, sitting down next to her. "I don't like television."

"That's a shame."

Yora looked at Raven more closely. She was, in fact, very thin, unnaturally so—Yora wondered if she were anorexic or a drug addict. Under the wide cuffs of her sweater, Yora could see another pair of cuffs, a striped long-sleeve shirt. Raven's legs were clothed in thick black stockings; you could tell they were stockings because a band of bare skin showed between their tops and the bottom of Raven's miniskirt. She had sharp knees. Her legs were very thin. How did her stockings stay up? Yora thought she knew where Raven got her clothes. There was a store not far from their apartment complex, on Fifty-Sixth Street—it was called The Anarchist's Closet. They sold second-hand underwear, corsets, and other stuff for Goths and progressive hipsters.

Yora never went in there, only saw their window displays; instead, she frequented the store next door, a Middle Eastern one. The owners were from Jordan. Yora bought the tahini for her hummus there and, sometimes, figs. For some reason, the Jordanians always thought she was one of their own, and would speak to her in Arabic first, before switching to English. Yora was surprised every time—did she look like a woman from those parts? Then, again, the young man at the check-out had blue eyes, but the way he spoke, with his guttural G's and K's, left no doubt about his origins. On the TV, Bill Maher interrogated some unfortunate pastor:

"So, what good have you done for other people, Mr. So-and-So?"

Two men in armchairs and the slow scroll of captions underneath, repeating what they said. Mr. So-and-So looked like he wished he weren't on air anymore, caught as he was in the clutches of the host, whose face, after all his plastic surgeries, looked like the face of someone resurrected from a deep freeze, but he answered obediently:

"I recently saved a man from killing himself. He wanted to end his life because he was unhappy in love."

"And what did you tell him, Mr. So-and-So?"

"I said, put the passion you feel into God, dedicate yourself to God and listen for His will."

Bill Maher laughed at this and went on tormenting him.

"Mr. So-and-So, could you please tell our viewers—was it also God who wanted you to buy this two-thousand-dollar suit? Were you following God's will when you purchased it?"

The embarrassed pastor said nothing; he glanced at his suit but didn't deny it—this Bill Maher had an eye as sharp as the rest of him. He knew his haberdashery. Yora wondered how he knew. Why didn't the pastor ask him how he knew? This was a dead screen, with a dead Bill Maher, a dead pastor, and dead words on it. Only one word was alive—passion.

"I've been eavesdropping on you for a long time," Raven said. "You and your very serious-looking friend."

"She moved out."

Yora found something about this woman really annoying. Why did she even agree to go over to her place? What was she doing there? She thought that it might be more interesting, or fun, but now...

"I know. Do you think I would've missed such an epic development? Actually, if you had just asked me, I could have told you a month ago that she would move out."

"What do you mean, if I had just asked you?"

"Just like that! If you had knocked on my door and asked, 'Excuse me, would you happen to know if my very serious-looking friend is planning to hit the road?'" Raven looked at Yora with her big eyes. She was very good at making them look innocent. "Alright, don't get mad," she said. "You can stay the night if you'd like. That would be more fun."

"But, if I stay, how will you eavesdrop?" Yora had a strong urge to taunt Raven.

"Well, we could just talk then, couldn't we?" Raven replied, ignoring Yora's sarcasm. "I think it's time we became friends. You wouldn't be so sad about your friend all the time if we did."

"Are you trying to replace her?" Yora said, inflamed.

"What if I do? Do you have people banging on your door wanting to be friends with you?" Raven squinted. "Oh, come on, don't be mad, you'll like me… Don't make that face. Why don't you tell me about yourself."

"There's nothing to tell."

"Then should I tell you about myself?"

"Sure, go ahead."

Raven laughed and fell back onto her multitude of pillows.

"Oh, I can't even! 'Go ahead' she says! Oh, help me…"

"What's wrong with you?" Yora asked, angry, but her anger only made Raven laugh harder.

"What's wrong! I can't even! 'Go ahead'! And it's coming from you!"

"So what?"

"You should be the one telling me things, but you want me to… Alright," she went on, once she caught her breath and calmed down a little. "I will, since you want me to. I'll tell you how I cured myself of love. We went to Albuquerque together, Tom, Samir, and I. They are good guys, you don't know them, but that's okay, doesn't matter. And, at the time, I was totally in love with Greg."

LOVE LIFE 139

"Wait... But Greg didn't go with you," Yora noted.

"No, he didn't. But I was in love with him. He stayed home. And I wanted to... You know... Take some pills. Women, when they try to kill themselves, always go for pills. Did you know that? You didn't know that? Few can manage anything else. You know, cutting your veins hurts, jumping off a sky-scraper hurts even more... Or, like, hanging yourself, you know." She glanced at Yora sideways. "Greg was a biker. So, I got the pills and was all set to take them. And then the guys came in and opened the window, and there was music outside, it was a nice neighborhood. "Bésame mucho" was playing. And we went dancing instead."

Raven stopped talking.

"And then what?" Yora asked. Everything inside her rebelled against this story. She felt a terrible urge to cry. She was being forced to listen to this... This... Instead of Inga.

"Nothing."

"That's not a story!"

"What do you mean, not a story?"

"You didn't tell me anything. About how you cured yourself of love. How did you do it?"

"Of love?" Raven asked and frowned as if taken by surprise. "Love? Oh yeah... Love. I don't remember. I danced for a while—and then I was cured. I just wanted to tell you about it. Take you, for instance," Raven said, squinting again. "Do you tell your friends when you are in trouble? I had this pain inside me, and I told you, and now, see, pfft! It's gone. You have to meet people half-way. Don't take yourself so seriously, open up. Why are you so stuck up? It's not good for you. This hurt..."

"You're lying. That didn't hurt you."

"Look who's talking! She comes in here and tells me I'm a liar," Raven scoffed.

"I'm going home," Yora said.

"Suit yourself," Raven said with a shrug. "You are welcome to stay and sleep here. Or to tell me a story. I told you one, didn't I?"

"I'll come back tomorrow, and tell you one then," Yora promised politely. Anything just to get rid of this apparently crazy woman.

At home, she lay down on her bed and sighed with relief. She could just lie there and breathe in and out. She did not owe anybody anything, had no obligations to anyone at all, and least of all to this vagrant in black, this spy with her wily eyes. Yora listened—she thought she heard a rustle on the other side of the wall. Was Raven eavesdropping again? But what could she hear? Yora's breathing. Yora pictured Raven's focused face—and surprised herself by laughing out loud. Then she reached out and knocked on the wall. She heard a knock back. Yora knocked again, and again Raven answered.

"So are you going to tell me what happened to you?"

"You've been listening in on us for months. How do you not know already?"

"I do, but not everything," Raven confessed another night, when they sat together, like the previous time, on Raven's bed, and turned on the TV that flickered soothingly. They turned down the sound, and Raven turned off the captions that had annoyed Yora so much the last time. It was cozy even.

"Well, then tell me what you already know, and I'll tell you what you don't know."

"I know next to nothing."

"That's hard to believe! I remember you heard me screaming on the phone one day. I was out here, on the stairs."

"And I was watching a movie. I only heard you when you stopped," Raven said, squinting.

LOVE LIFE 141

"Was that why you were giggling?"

"Yep. That's it. I also know that you were super worried about your insurance." Raven laughed and continued, "Are you new here?"

"No, I've been here a while."

"Then you should know by now how this glorious country brainwashes you. Everything here is backwards. A shaman I know told me it's because we don't listen to the earth anymore, we've covered it with concrete…"

"What does that have to do with—"

"Your serious-looking friend didn't know any of this, did she? What's she doing when she isn't singing—studying management, right? How to sit in an office and go to shopping malls? She'll never get it, as long as she lives. She'll just keep singing. And thank God for that! And other people have to learn how to live in the dark, and on the streets, and without insurance—like you at the moment."

"But I thought—"

"You thought it was your own fault. That's the message in this Babylon, isn't it? Make something of yourself! Succeed! But now you are really one of us. You are one of Those Who Know the Truth about This Country. Finally."

Raven jumped off the bed, dance-walked to the kitchen counter and poured two mugs—she was not, evidently, the kind of person who had wine glasses—of the sweet, pale-pink, very low alcohol wine that was made here on the Peninsula. She offered one to Yora.

"We have to celebrate! Welcome to the club!"

They clinked the mugs and, in the light of the TV's mute flickering, downed the contents.

"I actually love you," Raven said. "I've gotten used to you."

"That's not how it works."

"When you live alone, it is."

Yora felt her eyes fill with tears.

"What's wrong?" Raven asked. They said nothing for a moment, and then she said, "Will you ever tell me what that idiot did to you? You'll feel better, I promise."

"That's not why," Yora muttered.

"Then why? Your insurance? That's nothing to cry about. I'll give you mine, I have a PDF of it, will move it into Word, change what we need to, and you'll be set. You can go to the DMV then, and they'll extend your registration at the window. It'll be months before the system shows them you don't actually have insurance—I know from experience. It's a sure thing. It's like your check—takes time to get there, takes time to bounce... Don't even worry about it. I don't have a car at the moment. Emmanuel promised to give me his, soon..."

"Take mine," Yora suggested.

"Thank you, that would be great! The red Honda, right?"

"Yep. Only there's this thing... With the car insurance. Did they ever catch you?"

"Not me! Of course not. Although my insurance is not really mine, either... A... friend let me borrow his... PDF," Raven said, laughing.

It was clear no one had let her borrow anything, but she got her hands on the certificate anyway.

"More generally," she said seriously after a while and sat back down on the bed, "I can see that you are really naive and don't know how to take care of yourself."

"Well, I..."

"Well, you. Do you even know where to go shopping properly?"

"What do you mean?"

"I mean, where the rich people shop. You dress all nice... Don't look at me like that—I have a special outfit for that, very nice... I'm skinny, and that makes sense—poor people here are never skinny like that, they eat badly—cheap bread, potato chips, soda... If you are skinny, you must be rich... So, you

LOVE LIFE 143

dress up, and march in there, pick what you want from the shelves, and then go out—but, you should know, their alarm only works at the exit, and you go out through the entrance. It's no problem to go through the entrance, everyone trusts everyone, they all behave like they know each other. Whole Foods is like that, and a few other places. And you drive all the way over to Aldi like an idiot. Don't cover your face, I can still see you. Because Aldi is cheap. It's true that it's cheap, but you cannot exit through the entrance doors at that very respectable establishment. Pretty basic stuff. But you didn't know that, did you? That's alright, you'll try some day, there's a first time for everything." Raven was almost giddy. Then she got up and pulled a flash-drive out from under the bed.

"Here's your PDF. Download it, and I'll give you the date next time. If you have a laptop, bring it over. Mine broke about six months ago, and so I go to a church nearby—I know the pastor."

"Thank you," Yora said automatically.

"Sorry I can't help you with your medical insurance—I don't have any."

"Well, I..."

"It's just that no one has ever taught you how to survive in this system."

"But this is..."

"You want to say, stealing? Nope. Because you know what?"

"What?"

"They've stolen much more from me than I could ever steal from them. And they'll steal more."

They were quiet for a while.

"Oh, hey," Raven said. "I've been meaning to ask you—would you like to go visit Obike? I don't mean, like, today, whenever you feel like it. He's at that church every day. The one I go to... When I need to use a computer."

"Who's Obike?"

"He'll do a Tarot reading for you."

"I don't believe in those things."

"You don't have to."

"I'll think about it."

"There's nothing to think about, just go."

"I don't have any money to pay him."

"You don't have to pay him," Raven laughed. "He and I have our own accounting."

"What kind of accounting?"

"A special kind," Raven said, squinting again. Her eyes were laughing. Yora understood it wasn't worth asking more questions and changed the subject.

"I mean, how can anyone know what will happen?"

"Exactly!" Raven exclaimed. "But I have one question. Do you think you can know what is?"

"What do you mean?"

"Nothing." Raven lay back down on the bed, skinny, black. She opened her arms into the shape of a cross. "There's no future you say. But the present exists! Right?"

"But," Yora said. "How can there be no future?"

"If you don't understand anything about it—there isn't one."

Yora said nothing.

"If you tell me what happened, you'll feel better," Raven spoke either for herself or on behalf of Obike. "And you could bring a donation to church—clothes you don't wear, or shoes. There's always someone who needs them."

LOVE LIFE 145

***

The church was half-dark. The black faces of the congregation blended into the black pews. The pastor shouted something from the pulpit and pointed a red-tipped electronic pencil at the slides that glowed above his head.

"This is the only true church of our Redeemer," he repeated every so often, and the congregation nodded and said in unison, "It truly is, it truly is…"

Yora did not dare sit down; people turned to look at her—white women didn't come here every day. It was difficult for Yora to imagine what ties Raven had to this church and these pious people—except, of course, God's mysterious ways.

Yora backed away deeper into the church, to the water fountain. She could have pretended she had come in to get a drink of water—it's not like anyone would chase her, a thirsty soul, out from the House of the Lord. But then again, they could have thought she was tormented by a terrible thirst, and who knows what they would do then? What did they need this white woman for, though? Everyone here had known each other since they were kids. Went to each other's baptisms and funerals. They had picnics by the river—and the gods spoke to them from the river waters in Yoruba, a language most of them had forgotten.

Someone took her hand, and Yora shuddered. How did this man sneak up on her so quietly, especially given that she kept turning her head and looking around?

"Are you Obike?" she asked.

The man—not particularly tall, a bit heavy, but energetic—smiled a very wide smile but said nothing.

"I'm Yora."

"I figured," the man said in a conspiratorial tone. "Who else could you be?"

Yora shrugged. She felt like an exile in this church.

"Could we go somewhere else?" she asked.

"If you want," he said, smiling. "Do you not like it here?"

"No, that's not what I mean, I like it here. But you couldn't..." She was about to say "do a Tarot reading here" but then wondered if she ought to avoid polluting the space with the mention of such worldly matters.

"Are you in a hurry?" Obike inquired, and his smile grew even wider, even though that had not seemed possible.

"Me? No, not really."

"Great. They are about to sing the hymns. Do you like hymns?"

Yora did not have a chance to answer, because suddenly everyone jumped to their feet and started to sing. Talking became impossible. The singing was quite loud; it should have been deafening in the small building but somehow was not—the walls, it seemed, pulled apart to make room for the voices. The slides had long been turned off, and the pastor's voice blended with the others. One man led, everyone else followed. The man had a slightly hoarse voice, deep like the purgatory of the Atlantic where the captives who had died in the Middle Passage called out from the bottom of the sea.

When the hymn was over, Obike looked at Yora and said, "You see? Now we can go."

They did not wait for the second hymn. Obike went toward the exit, and Yora followed. He crossed the churchyard and the parking lot and turned onto a narrow street where he lived in a small, almost toy-like house, with a porch painted blue and equipped with a single derelict cane chair. He opened the door and invited Yora in.

"Wait for me here," he said, leaving her in the tiny living room that barely accommodated a small couch, a coffee table, and two faded armchairs. A very dusty air conditioner hummed in the window. It smelled damp, as it always did

LOVE LIFE 147

in old houses on the Peninsula, where the sea slowly washed away their foundations.

A cat with a ribbon tied in a bow on his neck entered from another room. He marched right up to Yora—solemnly, yet trustingly, like an old aristocrat at a reception; Yora felt tears in her eyes. The ribbon on the cat's neck was not even a collar—just an adornment, and the cat wore it proudly. He had a great sense of his own dignity. He came up and rubbed against Yora's leg, then raised his head and meowed, once, and then again.

It had been a very long time since Yora saw cats, or any animals, or touched their innocent fur. Her fingertips tingled with tenderness. Sebastian's cats would not come close to her; all they did was eat and sleep, or jump onto the dining table, if allowed. Neither one of them would have consented to wearing a ribbon like that. They would have bit at it and torn it off as a sign of subjugation. Yora crouched next to the cat and stroked him. She could barely hold back tears. Obike, who had the gift of materializing suddenly, might see her like this, but perhaps he ought to. Perhaps he had intended for her to meet his friend. Plus, he already seemed to know everything about her, and there was nothing wrong about tears.

"This is Alistair," she heard a voice say above her ear.

Obike was already there. Yora stood up and studied Obike's face the way she hadn't dared study it in the church. He really did have a very wide smile and very full lips, but his ears, by contrast, were petite, disproportionately small for the rest of his large face. Still, she did not get the impression that he talked more than he listened.

"Please, take a seat," Obike invited, and Yora sat where he pointed, in the armchair upholstered in faded flowers. Obike made himself comfortable on the couch.

"Would you like a piece of candy? Please, help yourself." He pushed the candy bowl toward her, but Yora shook her head. Obike took a piece of candy and ate it with a sorrowful expression, licking his lips.

"You shouldn't deny yourself simple joys. It's good to be alive."

Then he put a tea towel on the table, and on the towel—a deck of cards.

"Here they are. We'll start in a moment... By the way, thank you for your donation."

"Are you a..."

"Depends. There was one woman who came here—I helped her marry the man she loved."

"Did the man love the woman back?"

"Of course," Obike smiled beatifically.

"Did you... put a spell on him?"

"We don't do that. Some people here play a little with hoodoo. Not to be confused with voodoo."

"I know," she said.

"But you don't believe in such things, do you?" Obike asked.

"I don't."

"Good. I wouldn't encourage you to. You must come to people like me quite seldom."

"I never have."

"That's what I thought."

"But what about you—are you married to the woman you love?" Yora asked and instantly regretted it.

Obike sighed.

"A sensitive man has a hard time finding his path in life," he said. "About the only thing he can be is a Tarot reader..."

"Have you ever been," Yora went on—Alistair had curled up in her lap—"have you ever been wrong about absolutely everything?"

"I have," Obike answered, not at all surprised by her question.

LOVE LIFE 149

"Does it happen often?"

"Not often, but it does happen."

"What does it mean, then? That there is no such thing as fate? Because there's no way to read it?"

"Why should it mean that? It's like the planets: some have a round orbit, others—an elliptical one. I am only human, I get things wrong. I might try to recognize a circle and then be surprised not to find it where I think it's supposed to be. But the reason it's not there is the fact that it's not a circle."

Yora pictured Obike feeling blindly in outer space for slippery orbits strung between the stars like a laundry line stretched between trees in the summer. The lines slowly slip from his fingers until he gives up and flies somewhere into the vast emptiness of space, arms raised in a helpless gesture.

"What's the point then?"

"Of what?"

"Of everything. If no one knows anything?"

"And you would like me to know everything, wouldn't you?" Obike smiled again.

"I'd like someone to know something."

"You see," Obike sighed, "most people are interested in one of two things—love or money."

Yora remembered the virus, and asked, "What about health?"

"Oh, no," Obike sighed, "if they have any health problems, they go to a doctor."

"Don't people ever come to you to ask if they'll survive or something like that?"

"They do. But I never talk to people like that."

"Then how could you know—perhaps I've come here to ask about my illness?"

Obike looked at her and raised his eyebrows.

"Oh, no! You already know everything there is to know about your illness. You didn't even come to ask me about money, although money is very tight at the moment. You aren't worried about money. And that's good! You'll soon have enough to get by."

"Then why have I come here?"

"Scratch him behind the ear... Like that. You? You have come to ask me about a man. Am I right?"

"That's not hard to guess," Yora snapped. "You just said you know everything anyway."

"Do you want to know if he'll come back to you?" Obike asked. Suddenly, his narrowed eyes seemed to pierce her.

"He won't come back."

"Shuffle the deck."

Yora picked up the cards, heavy and larger than usual.

"When should I stop? Will you tell me?"

"No, you'll tell me. You'll know."

"But how?"

Obike giggled.

"You'll see."

Yora did as she was told—and, in the next instant, her hands became completely empty, more empty than she had ever experienced them, as if a wind had blown between them and swept everything clear out.

She shuffled the cards, but it felt as if they were not in her hands. She did not feel their weight. "What is this space?" Yora wondered and suddenly felt a scorching pain near her heart; she knew then—this was the space of her pain. Now she went on shuffling the cards knowing that the cards were not the point; it was her pain that knew the answer and would crack prophecies from every shell in the world, peeling off protective layers one by one, as a conservationist peels layers of paint off a canvas. Rivers ran through her hands; had she touched trees—they would bloom, had she brushed wounds with her fingertips—they would heal. "It's a life-giving pain," she realized. This meant being close to

LOVE LIFE 151

everything, to the very mystery of life, if it were a mystery at all. Did a mystery remain a mystery when you became part of it? "There is no future," she thought, not exactly in those words, but words were what she could remember, the words in which her thought had to take shape, like a bad translation. And then there was a black screen between what was now, and specifically this room, Yora herself, Obike, and Alistair on her lap—and everything that could yet happen. She could not see anything, and this was comforting; it did not matter at all what would happen next. Only being mattered.

"Take them," she said, handing the deck back to Obike.

***

"What did he tell you?" Raven asked that night.

Yora let her into her studio, where they lay down on the bed and turned off the lights.

"He said I'd find a job soon," Yora said.

"Right... Like I believe that. Did you really ask him about a job?"

"What if I did? I don't like the idea of starving to death. And I don't have anyone to borrow from."

"Ha! I'd let you borrow money from me," Raven said with a smile. "You'd never dare not to pay me back, you are too conscientious. But I don't have any. Tell me what he said about that special man of yours."

"I don't have any special man."

"Okay, you don't now, but you did before. So tell me!"

"There's nothing to tell. I didn't ask Obike about that."

"What do you mean you didn't ask him? I don't believe you."

"Okay, I did. He wanted to tell me, but I stopped him."

"Hey," Raven said. "Why do you think I don't understand you? I really do. And you would feel better. I'm not as stupid as other people."

"Other people are not stupid either."

"Right, because they took out a mortgage on a nice little house in Temple Terrace, put a white picket fence around their neat little lawn to keep death out, had themselves a bunch of kids and are now sitting pretty, waiting for the whole world to come bring them thanks and blessings," Raven said, but she sounded neither angry nor bitter. She just seemed to be reciting a text she had memorized, intending, perhaps, to annoy her listener.

"Aren't we waiting, too?" Yora asked.

"That wasn't worth your going to see Obike."

"Why not?"

"Because if that was it, he wouldn't have taken the time to talk to you. He doesn't talk to everybody."

"Who does he talk to?"

"People like you."

"What's so special about me?"

"Tell me what happened, you'll feel better."

"I fail to see the logic in this."

"What's logic got to do with anything?"

***

"Did your mom want you?" Raven asked a while later, apparently bored.

Dear God, Yora thought, she's gonna launch into some psychoanalytic babble; she'll say, as they do here, your mom didn't want you and that's why you don't love yourself.

LOVE LIFE 153

"I don't know," she said out loud. "She had me, and that was that."

"I know about mine."

"Good for you," Yora muttered.

"My mother," Raven carried on, "got pregnant from... Well, his name won't mean anything to you. But he was, believe you me, a very powerful man."

"So you are the daughter of a very powerful man?"

"Yep," Raven smiled in the dark. "Only we don't know each other. What about you? Do you have a father?"

"Somewhere," Yora answered reluctantly. She could have told Raven what she had heard from her mother about her father, whom she never met, but she didn't feel like it.

Raven, meanwhile, appeared to have been waiting for this very answer.

"So, your father did not want to have a child?" Yora asked to distract her.

"Worse. When my mom got pregnant, she was, like: 'Honey, here's the deal... I'm pregnant.'"

"And he?"

"And he was married and had his own kids, so what do you think he said? My mom was very young. So, he thought about it for a very long time, and then said, go ahead and have the baby, and we'll figure something out afterwards. And she asked, 'Figure what out?'"

"And then what happened?" Yora asked, not exactly sure why—she had no interest in Raven's story and, in fact, found it irritating. Raven, she thought, was just jealous of her and Inga, of *what* they *had*, and wanted the same for herself. But she had no one to talk to, so she stuck to Yora like a burr to a dog's tail.

It was very dark in the room.

"You won't believe it... He told my mom... He says,' I'm running—for office,' he was in politics, went all the way to

Washington... Basically, he comes to see my mom (he rented an apartment for her) and says, 'Let's hand this baby over to these people I know. They can do a Black Mass. They'll do their thing, and we'll live better. I'll get elected President, and things might turn around for you, too.'"

"You read that in some Goth book of yours and you're clearly lying to me," Yora blurted out.

But Raven did not take offense.

"Wait. I know what book you're thinking, but that's not it. This isn't from that book, and it isn't that story. I'm telling you nothing but the truth. And my mom was small and skinny, she didn't even show, and her neighbors didn't give a hoot. It was a big city. She went ahead with the pregnancy, and he would come over every so often and tell her how great everything would be for her. But my mom thought, 'Maybe, or maybe not, or things might turn out completely different...' That's what she thought..."

"Wait... How do you know this? Did she tell you?"

Raven did not answer. But she went on.

"And then my mom got bored and asked him to buy her a ticket to the movies, or a concert, or something. He thought about it a bit, and bought it for her, because he was rich."

"Wait, you're all over the place. You want me to believe that your mom didn't have the money to go to the movies? You are making this up!"

"Don't interrupt. So, he bought her a ticket to a classical music concert, and those are expensive, not like some stupid movies, and bought her a dress—she took her time trying it on, and he sat there and admired her, how beautiful she was. He held her face with his hands and said, 'But you are my girl, aren't you?' And mom said, 'Of course, how could I not be, after all this?' Well, she did feel like she was his girl—I don't know if you ever felt like that. It's like when

LOVE LIFE

everything—the entire world—everything around you—is him."

"Jesus, what nonsense! Do you really think I'm going to believe this?"

"Don't get mad, let me finish."

"I don't want to hear it! Or do you think I'll believe it's all true? Did you climb into your mother's mind? No one ever tells anyone things like that."

"I'm not saying she told me. I'm just saying I know. Okay. Don't interrupt. I can't think straight today. It's because I had bad dreams... Turn the lights on... The little lamp, right. That's better. Now I can see you. I dreamed of the street I grew up on, except someone had built a giant water park right in the middle of it. Normal people dream of angels, or demons. I dream of water parks. It's depressing. It really depressed me today. What was I saying? Oh yes, so he had me put on this dress and was admiring me."

"Wait," Yora said, startled. "What do you mean, *you?* Wasn't it your mom?"

"Oh yeah, my mom... The following night..."

"What happened the following night?" Yora asked, seeing in the light of the nightlight that Raven was smiling a sleepwalker's smile, apparently lost in thought.

"If you don't like my story, then why are you asking?" She squinted slyly.

"Just go on," Yora sighed.

Against her will, she was captivated by the crazy narrative.

Raven made a gesture that could have meant anything and went on.

"Mom went to the concert hall and took her seat, and it was close to the front. He got her a good ticket, but he didn't do it just to be generous. He knew that, if she sat close to the front, fewer people would be able to see her face, because you know how it is, what if her neighbors were there, the ones who had seen him with her. The musicians started to play, and there was this violinist..."

"Good grief, Raven!" Yora blurted out again. "First it was all Goth, now it's romance, can you at least lie in one genre?"

"And this violinist," Raven went on, inspired, as if she had not heard Yora interrupt her, "he was not exactly handsome and, in fact, not handsome at all. He looked rugged, and these huge shoulders, he didn't even look like a violin player, more like a gym rat from a bad neighborhood—you do know where those guys from the hood work out, right?"

"I have no idea."

"Gosh, in jail! Where else? They've got nothing to do in there, just lifting weights. It's boring in there. Next time, when you go out, pay attention—when you see some ripped dudes, all draped in gold chains and tattooed—you'll know they've done time."

"So, what, that violin player had done time?"

"Of course not!"

Raven pretended not to pick up on the irony in Yora's voice and carried on.

"So he started to play. He played with such ease! And she saw his face, and it was completely transformed! It was sublime. Have you ever... Ever looked at a man's face and known..."

"Have I known what?" Yora asked after a short pause. For some reason, this turn of the story stunned her more than the mention of a Black Mass. Because she could choose not to believe in a Black Mass; but a beloved face was a different story.

"She started to dream of his face. It happens—it's not love, it couldn't be—she'd only seen him that one time, and they had never even spoken. She only heard his violin—and you could love a violin by itself, without a face... So there my

LOVE LIFE

mom was, at night, in bed, sleeping and dreaming of that musician and his violin. He seemed to say something to her, but she forgot... At first, she forgot her dreams, too..."

Yora gave up on interrupting Raven and pointing out the utter improbabilities in her narrative—if her mother had forgotten the fact of having those dreams, how could she have told her daughter later?

"...Just his face before her, and it was as if he were talking to her with his face—not even with his music. She could see his face so clearly, could see him focus before he started to play, and then start to play—and his face changed. And no music—she didn't need it. And my father—that's a big word for him—the guy who'd gotten her pregnant—he started to notice that she was sort of absent. She's like this, she seems meek and spineless at first, reminds me of you a little, no offense, because there's strength in such people, too—it just takes time for it to show..."

"But you were talking about your mom..." Yora interrupted.

"Yes, my mom. So there she was one night, sitting in her armchair, wrapped in a blanket; that guy liked to sort of protect her, and bought her all this stupid shit he thought women liked: blankets, coffee-mugs, socks with little deer on them. Because she wasn't just anyone—she had his hopes in her belly. The devil would give him power..."

Raven fell silent... Yora was just about to ask, sarcastically, and did he? But resisted, afraid that the question would send Raven down a rabbit hole of apocalypse, already predicted by a numerology-practicing priest of some underground church. The end of the world was coming for sure. Because when the only person close to you turns out to be insane, that's the end of the world.

"So," Raven started up again. "There my mom was, in her chair, and all she could see before her was that violin player's face. She fell asleep. And she dreamed of my life, how I would grow up, no, actually, how little and helpless I would be at first, and then how I would grow big, and, truth be told, just as helpless... You know what I mean. And my mom woke up and knew beyond any shadow of a doubt what she had to do. She packed her suitcase and went outside. It was cold—couldn't even tell you how cold it was. A kind of a damp cold, because the lake is nearby, and you know how deep it is, over two hundred feet. The subway above her head...The subway there ran on elevated tracks, you'd ride the train and look into people's windows. Rattle, hum. Lights. She got into a cab and went to the bus station, because it's not as easy to disappear in an airport. I hate airports—they're the worst. You?"

Yora thought of Carlos and Inga's weeping. Raven looked at her steadily, as if picking up fragments of thoughts and feelings from Yora's face, and then went on.

"And she didn't have the money for a plane ticket anyway. He wasn't *that* generous, that man. And she left. Don't ask where she went. Away. Where else? To the White House, to file a complaint? My married lover wants to give my child up for a Black Mass? Oh no. She was young and uneducated, but she had never been stupid. So, I was born. And how about you? Now you tell me your story."

"I don't have a story," Yora said and reached for the lamp switch. "Sweet dreams."

LOVE LIFE 159

***

A week or two later, on a Thursday morning, Yora woke up to her phone ringing.

"Yora?" asked Mariana Schneider on the other end. Then she added, reproachfully, "Were you asleep?"

"I've got a sore throat," Yora lied.

It was nine o'clock.

"I see. Can you come to N** today?" She named a small private university located downtown, right above the river.

"I can!" came out of Yora's mouth before she even had a chance to think if she actually could. Up until then she had only driven to the grocery store, the Aldi Raven had advised her not to go to, then once—to the hospital, and another time to Obike's, but those were all democratic places, full of disabled people, the poor, and the homeless. Downtown was a different thing altogether.

"What's there?" Yora asked.

"You were born under a lucky star. They got the same grant we had last fall. I recommended you to them. No one's promising you a permanent job, but at least you won't starve until the end of summer. Come on, get into your car, ask for Yingru Li when you get there. Barnett Hall, second floor, room two-oh-two. Got it? Yingru Li. I suggest you go right now, because they have lunch at noon, and after lunch they have meetings. Who knows what might happen by tomorrow. I'm not the only person talking to Yingru."

Mariana, as was her custom, did not stay on the line to listen to Yora's thanks and hung up. Yora chose a dress, black and slightly newer than her other ones. Last year, it was too tight, but now it looked quite presentable. Black was not the best color for getting hired; you were supposed to give your prospective employer reasons to believe you were happy to have the opportunity, enjoyed life in general, etc., but Yora did not have a more appropriate dress.

Yingru would have to believe Mariana Schneider's recommendation. That's the kind of interview this was going to be—Yora's dress against Mariana's word.

Yora put on ankle boots, making sure she wrapped her feet—no longer bleeding and almost, one could say, normal looking—with fresh bandages. The boots, like the dress, were odd for the occasion, but anything else would make the bandages show, and who knew what questions that would prompt. But what if her feet, caught like fishes in the tight boots, started to ooze something through the bandages right in the middle of that yet-unseen office? Yora did not want to think about that. She dressed, put on the boots, and spent a long time making up her eyes.

* * *

The day was sunny but not warm; the river breathed cool moisture. The campus lawns were manicured. The biggest building pretended to be something Moorish, Oriental. Those who built the campus must have had peculiar tastes, because next to this oriental architecture sat brutalist structures, almost Le Corbusier.

Yora went into Barnett Hall, and it surprised her. The building looked immaculate from the outside, but inside the carpeting had threadbare patches, the tall windows were dirty, and it smelled of old age, as if an old man had his face lifted by an expert surgeon and the face was now smooth and glowing, but, beneath it, the rest of his body was still the same—an old liver, an old heart, a set of old tired blood vessels dotted with plaque. Yora, no longer nervous, found the right door and knocked.

LOVE LIFE 161

"Come in," a voice inside said, and she went in.

Yingru, exquisitely delicate and very pale, sat at a desk.

"You must be from Mariana?" she asked.

She had a definite but pleasant accent. Yingru got up, and Yora was able to take a better look at her. Yingru was dressed very elegantly and moved smoothly, like a dancer in a traditional Chinese theater performance. It was hard to tell how old she was. She could have been twenty-five or forty, but, of course, it was unlikely she would occupy the position she did at twenty-five.

"Julie will be here in just a moment, and she'll show you around." Yingru went to the file-cabinet and started looking for something.

A short energetic woman came into the office, the complete opposite of Yingru—she was dressed haphazardly, not at all like Yingru's magazine-cover style.

"Yes, great! Great to meet you. I'm Julie... I'll call HR."

"But... What about the interview?" Yora asked for some reason.

Julie and Yingru exchanged a look. Julie then burst out laughing, and Yingru's face reflected surprise mixed with a bit of scorn, as in, are we really hiring this idiot?

"Come with me," Julie said. "I'll show you where you will sit."

They went down the hallway, stopping at different rooms. Julie introduced Yora to other employees. The last room they visited was the mail room. Yora read the names she had just heard but didn't yet remember on mail slots like a strange poem—Evan Romanovich, Kelley Gillmore, Noah Balanza.

"You are not here," Julie said above her ear. "You'll be this, FINANCE. See? Right here. You are temporary, maybe Yingru will figure something out, if everything goes well, just try to make her like you and don't ask her too many questions, she knows everything, and for now your mail will be here, in this slot. I'll go call HR now, we have you from the beginning of March for the duration of the grant, until October 1st. What's today?" She glanced at the calendar. "We'll make it. They'll prepare your contract. Come back tomorrow. It's Friday, but we'll make it. That's it for now, you're free to go—it was a pleasure to meet you, and what's your name, by the way? Yora? That's an interesting name. Goodbye."

The entire introduction took no more than fifteen minutes.

Yora went outside, inhaled deeply, and smiled. The sun went in and out behind the clouds. Happy now, Yora marched down the immaculate sidewalk along the immaculate lawns. She was the same as everyone else—a woman with a modest job, and not the dying outcast she had been. Something made her walk past her parked car and turn onto the street that led to the bridge across the river. Here, in one of the stone buildings, was the student theater, famous across the entire city and, a few years ago, a giant coffeehouse with the pretentious name "Oxford" opened next door—two floors, a store with pseudo-colonial products where a curry-flavored chocolate bar could cost ten dollars and the shelves could not accommodate all the different kinds of tea. Yora, surprised at herself, automatically walked in; she had almost no money, stopping at a place like Oxford made no sense at all, but, for some reason, she got angry—at herself and the entire world—walked up to the counter, ordered a tea, and sat down at a table. She inhaled deeply, and then exhaled, once, twice, and for a third time.

How great it was to think that she was just like everyone else, just another woman in just another coffeehouse. And it was true! Why couldn't she think that? For the first time in a very long time Yora felt—no, not happy, that was too grand a word, and she might not ever be happy again—but content.

The sun, meanwhile, came out from behind a cloud, and, always bright in this part of the world, even in the cold season, shone through the window onto her face. Yora leaned into the light and smiled. The man who just then came up to Yora's table must have liked the expression on her face.

"You have a beautiful smile," he said, and Yora raised her eyes to him. "A beautiful smile and comfortable shoes," he went on, looking down. "Women these days wear all kinds of contraptions, but you are different, I could tell right away. Do you mind if I take a seat? There are no more seats left. This place is getting popular."

Yora just waved her hand at him. The man sat opposite her. He was older; he looked at least seventy, trim and with a spark in his eyes. He was dressed in a very expensive suit, one of those seemingly simple but extremely elegant garments that are not even sold in stores but custom-made from the best cloth.

"My name is Tripp," he introduced himself, extending his hand, warm and strong, and leaning across the table, so that Yora inhaled the cloud of his scent—sophisticated and unobtrusive, and, therefore, also expensive.

"Yora," Yora said.

"Do you work around here?"

"I don't know yet," Yora muttered, suddenly uncertain. She sort of did, but the paperwork hadn't gone through yet. "I think I'll be in an office here, at the college."

"Of course, you will be." Tripp smiled a wide smile. "How else? I'd like to see the idiot who wouldn't hire you."

Yora wondered if it were worth explaining to him the difference between employment at a private company, where one could run into a boss like himself, and working for a college where the pay was low, people like Yora were hired only for the duration of a grant, and even an unproven allegation of sexual harassment could cost one a long career.

"Thank you," was all she said. "They will let me know soon."

"I wonder if they haven't already." Tripp kept smiling. "The answer is probably in your inbox."

"I'll check when I get home," Yora promised.

"I used to work for this college, too," Tripp went on.

"Did you really?" Yora was surprised. He did not look like a professor—a professor would never parade across downtown in a suit like this and not because he couldn't afford it—some perfectly well could!—but because being rich was considered indecent in academic circles. And to display one's wealth would have been the apogee of indecency. Yora remembered the face Mariana Schneider made when she told them about a party hosted by the Sociology Department head last year; the man lived on the bay, in one of the most prestigious neighborhoods, right on Bayshore Boulevard, in a house with a white portico. Rumor had it he had inherited the house from a crazy aunt, but be that as it may, inviting your university colleagues over and forcing them to admire the bay, gently silvered by the full tide, from the house's gigantic deck was not decent. And neither was feeding them expensive Jamaican catering (shrimp with various sauces, blackened pork) instead of serving the usual celery sticks, crackers, and rotisserie chicken.

"I sat on the Board for four years," Tripp said, crossing his legs. He ran his hand over his still thick, although gray, hair and smiled again.

"So you are an entrepreneur?" Yora asked.

"Of course. And I'm not interested in retiring. My office is near here, across the street actually, see? It's a small office now, I mostly broker deals, and I've sold all the restaurants

LOVE LIFE 165

I used to own. Didn't want to waste any more time on that. I'm in planes now."

"Planes?"

"Well, I don't make them myself, of course." He laughed seeing the expression on her face. "I help sell them. Why not? Mister Sikes... You know, Mr. Sikes—the one who built the skyscraper named after him... There, look out the window, see? It says right on top... Yep, in giant letters, so you could see it from the highway. They're neon lit at night! How can you miss it? The whole town knows about Mr. Sikes... It was his uncle who built a Moorish-style hotel that's now a university building. What parties used to be thrown there! They wouldn't let you in if you weren't wearing a tuxedo. Music—only live. The three of us—myself, Mr. Sikes, and Doug Crumry—we were a team! All aces. Mr. Sikes is ill now, he's about ninety. I'm younger, so I'm still around. Mr. Sikes is one of my mentors. I've been very fortunate with mentors. I'm mentoring a lot of people now. You can learn a lot from me. I even wrote a book about it—it's about business, but more than that, you know, one needs a life strategy. But I keep talking about myself. Now you tell me something. What do you do?"

"Me? I'll probably be working in an office here at the college," Yora repeated her simple story.

"And do you like it?" Tripp asked almost with an accusing note in his voice.

Yora shrugged and said nothing.

"What do you do there? I mean, specifically? Pushing paper?"

"No one," Yora produced a weak smile, "pushes paper anymore, even at colleges. Everything's in Excel spreadsheets or in PowerPoint. Sometimes I prepare slides and presentations for the department."

"Oh, presentations!" He seemed happy to hear the word. "Let me tell you something. This one time, Doug Crumry asked me... Doug, my old pal, Entrepreneur of the Year... He asked me to talk about our new company, the one I own now, I have several partners. And I said okay, no problem, so I went and I'm telling them things, and the audience is fine, just people, but you know how it is, if you don't make people laugh, they'll fall asleep. Have they taught you that at college? No? I'll teach you. I'll be your mentor if you'd like. So, I tell them, in order to start a company, you have to be a superhero, and also a very sincere person. I'll show you what I mean, I say, and start unbuttoning my shirt. You should've seen their faces! They must have thought I was about to dance naked in front of them! Doug Crumry even closed his eyes, he was thinking, 'What have I done, I thought Tripp was my pal and won't let me down, and look at him now! I'll be the butt of every joke.' And I went—whoosh! And under the shirt I was wearing a Superman T-shirt. That, I said, is how you should fly and win people's hearts! They fell off their chairs laughing, everyone loved it, and Doug Crumry shook my hand for a very long time afterwards saying, 'Tripp, you are one of a kind!' You're smiling? That's the point. I told you I'm fun to be around."

He hadn't told her anything of the sort, not that she remembered, anyway. And she was not having fun, and if she did find something funny it wouldn't have been his story that immediately overshadowed anything Yora could tell him about her own life. Stories! What was it with people and stories? And why was she listening to him anyway, why hadn't she told him to get lost, Yora asked herself and found she was afraid of the answer.

"But I keep talking about myself. What about you? Tell me something about you. I can hear you have an accent, are you not from here? Where are you from?"

She told him.

"And what? Is your family here or back there?"

LOVE LIFE

"Over there."

"And you're here alone?"

"I am."

"Alone and without a good job." It looked like he'd just done some mental math.

Then he flashed his eyes at her. His eyes were still bright, very blue.

"You are a very beautiful woman."

"Thank you."

"Would you like to come to my office? It's right across the street, a two-minute walk. I'd be happy to give you a copy of my book. You might get something out of it, read something that helps you... I'd like to do something for you. I don't know what, but I came in here and I thought, that's a deserving girl. She has substance. I'd like to do something for her."

Tripp got to his feet and offered his hand.

"Come on. You won't regret it."

Yora could have told him she would go some other time, could have even given him her phone number or email address, knowing full well she would never respond and there would be no other time. There were plenty of other coffeehouses in this neighborhood, and she wasn't likely to have money to spend at coffeehouses, so she could be certain this was their first and last encounter, unless, of course, a mighty hand of fate interfered and brought them together again, but why? Doesn't the hand have plenty of other people to bring together? But Yora did not want this—she wanted to see this situation through. She did follow Sebastian that one time. An aching urge to walk the way of the cross again awoke in her, simply so she could see everything more clearly this time, with her vision defogged.

She got up, not touching Tripp's proffered hand, and said, "Alright."

From that point on she saw the two of them as if in a movie; a gray-haired man in an expensive suit and herself, in a black dress. Saw them leave the coffeehouse. Saw them wait for the light to change, saw them cross the street, saw them enter the glass doors of the office building and walk down an empty hallway—it looked like here, on the ground floor, there was nothing except a home-decorating store with sky-high prices and Tripp's office. She saw Tripp open the office door, saw them go inside, saw herself sit down on a leather couch and him pull up a chair and sit face-to-face with her so that their knees touched.

"So you were saying you are all alone?" Tripp asked.

"I have friends," she answered.

"What about a husband?"

"I don't have one."

"I know you don't," he said and took her hand.

Yora carefully withdrew it.

"I have a wife," Tripp said. "I love her very much, it's not like that. She is a very good woman. There's her photo there, on the wall." He pointed, but from her seat on the couch Yora couldn't see it. "She has her own business. I don't ask her what she does on those nights when her office is closed and she is not home... We take care of one another. She is younger than me. A beautiful woman, but we lead, how to put it, separate lives. But I'd never leave her. I know what it's like when you are left all alone, and she and I do need each other. Especially after everything that happened..."

"What happened?" Yora asked, but he did not answer.

"To put it simply, I need a friend," Tripp concluded. "Or a lady friend. Someone I could talk to, confide in, to take the burden off my shoulders. I would be a good friend to you."

"Thank you," Yora said. "I ..."

"Say, do you have a dream?" he interrupted, not giving her a chance to articulate the emotions that had surged

LOVE LIFE 169

inside her—a sudden empathy toward him and his wife she'd never seen, the common denominator of human existence.

"I'm not sure," Yora said, relenting.

"What do you want to do? Would you like to start your own business?" Tripp squinted.

"Not really."

"Do you write books?"

"No, I don't," Yora answered.

"What do you do then? How do you see the fullness of life?"

"I just feel it."

"Feel what?" Tripp asked, confused.

"Life."

He laughed. He leaned back in his chair and even stopped touching her knee with his.

"We all feel it. But no one pays you for that."

In that instant, Yora got angry with him—for the fact that he was so far away from her while he thought they were close.

"They don't?" she asked. "Would you like them to?"

"I sure wouldn't mind," he joked, still understanding nothing.

He sat closer and put a hand on her knee.

"I, by the way, feel lots of things. For example, right now. What about you? You must also feel it if you are not moving away? This is nice, isn't it? How much would such pleasure cost?"

Yora withdrew, then stood up, and he immediately changed his tune.

"Please, don't get upset, I didn't mean to offend you. I never want to offend anyone. I wouldn't hurt a fly, I swear. I like you, I mean it, very much. You are beautiful, and you have heart, and I would like us to be friends, you know, really close, real friends. I would be a good friend to you, loyal, I mean it. You live alone, don't you? I could come visit you. Sunday mornings are best, while my wife is at church."

Yora pictured Tripp coming to their emptied studio where there was no trace of Inga left, pictured him taking off his expensive suit right next to their pathetic mattress on the floor—the mattress that had seen her and Inga's bodies writhe in pain for so many nights; saw him transforming from a powerful entrepreneur into a naked old man, stripped of his clothes like during the Holocaust, saw him reach out his arms to her.

"I will always listen to you," Tripp went on. "You don't have to spare me, you can just tell me what's on your mind. Women need a friend, someone, a shoulder to cry on. I can see you would like to cry. So go ahead, here, lean on my shoulder, cry! We are lucky, you and I, lucky to have met each other. What a happy coincidence! It's a good thing—to cry sometimes. A woman who doesn't cry every so often is even worse than a woman who doesn't make love. Go ahead, cry! I can see you need it. I didn't mean to offend you, that's the farthest thing from my mind. I really want to help you. Not just to take something, but to give something in return. Just tell me what you want."

Tripp was now looking up at her, pleading. He really wanted her to cry.

"I'm running late," Yora said. "I have to go."

Tripp stood up and grabbed her in a tight embrace.

"Don't go, don't go," he whispered into her ear, and his hands traveled across her body, and this was also like in a movie, a movie about a woman who did not resist because she had lost all her strength. "Don't go, we'll be good together, everything will be great, I swear, just great, I'll get a hotel room, we'll go to Miami, I go to Miami all the time, do you like Miami? I can't leave you all alone in this huge

LOVE LIFE

country! It's hard without a mentor. And without money—I can see you don't have much. Don't reject me!" he begged. "I know all the important people in this city—come on, come on, kiss me! Kiss me! I'll let go, don't be afraid. If you want to marry someone, God bless, I'll sit in the first row in church, and be the first to wish you well. Oh, come on! Kiss me, kiss me, dear, kiss me, just take my lips in yours… take *him* into your hand, feel how hard *he* is, don't you want to fall on the couch with me and beg me to fuck you because you can't wait any longer?"

Yora tried to fight free, but it was hopeless—Tripp was much stronger than she was, taller, heavier, and he held her head as if in a vise grip.

"Don't go, don't go, let me at least kiss you… Like that… You'll like it, we'll both like it, just trust me, trust me, let me have your lips!"

She cried out, and instead of fighting to withdraw from him, did the opposite—pressed her entire weight into him so hard he had to step back and almost lost his balance. She pressed her face into his wide, fleshy chest, pressed hard and screamed somewhere into the depths of his body—desperately, like an animal caught in a trap. Then he finally heard her and let go.

"Say something, anything," he asked, but she said nothing, just tried to get around him and leave the office, but he blocked the exit and talked, talked—about the heart surgery he'd had three years ago, how this made him pay attention to his health, how his vice-president was the same age as he was but looked so much worse, and how, when he went to his school reunion, he was shocked to see how many of his classmates could no longer move without aid.

"Let me go!" Yora said firmly and loudly. "Tripp! Right now."

He stood up and looked down at her from his full height.

"Why then did you come here?" he said, hurt and disdainful at once. "Why did you agree to come with me? When a woman goes like that into a man's office it means she's prepared for anything. And a woman like that is not worth much."

"She's not worth much, you say?" Yora said. "That's it, isn't it! So you know that a woman who goes with you to your office is not worth much, don't you? But you still take her with you, right?"

* * *

At home, Yora, utterly exhausted, fell asleep in her clothes and slept for several hours straight. She dreamed of a woman in uniform who was in charge of cargo, and the cargo was—two other women, bound hand and foot. They were being loaded into a train carriage. All other passengers watched the procedure impassively and no one raised any objections. Yora did not object either, but not because she was scared, rather because, in her dream, she knew perfectly well: objections were futile. It was the same as with rain or a star shower—one did not dare object to something like that. After that, Yora found herself in a room where some people were sitting around a table and smoking, but she could not figure out who they were, couldn't even make out their faces, and the only person with a face there was Sebastian. He sat, incredibly beautiful, wrapped in a cloud of cigar smoke, and his gray eyes burned brightly. The fruit-pit bracelet hung on his wrist.

"Do you," Sebastian asked her, "do you really know what empathy is?"

"I really do," Yora answered mechanically, not pausing to consider the depth of the question—whether she really

LOVE LIFE 173

knew anything—and instead admiring Sebastian, who sat there as if made of smoke.

"How you disappointed me," he shook his sublime head.

"How, why?" she asked.

"You could have been with us, but now you can't."

"With whom?" Yora asked, surprised, and at the same instant, everything vanished—the room, the smoke, and Sebastian. Instead, she was outside, in a yard, watching birds—one in particular, large, looked like a person, because, it seemed, he actually was a person but was still considered a bird for some reason—he was trying to take flight, but his wings, meaning arms, did not obey him.

"Tell him, 'Move, move!'" a voice advised from behind Yora's back. "And he'll fly. But you have to keep saying that word, the entire time. He'll stay aloft only as long as you say it. He depends on you."

Yora nodded in agreement—and woke up. Instantly, she started crying—passionately, angrily. These men like Tripp and Sebastian did not leave her alone even in her dreams, and she kept obediently feeding them, like birds, from her open hand, but her hand was empty, and so they tore at her flesh. They were the only ones she knew how to talk to, only men like them. What about her sister? Or mother? She hadn't been picking up when her mother called, again. She saw her mother as if she were right there—sitting in the kitchen, peeling something at the table, or picking over the buckwheat for dinner. Her mother had her own life, didn't she? The life whose small particles Yora could not see but that made it up: movements, encounters, smells, and sounds. Her friends, perhaps, who came to tea, or her grandchildren, family, Yora's sister's family. They went to the river together. They had their own rhythm, a rhythm Yora could not perceive through the screen, could not glean from their voices, because their talks were only that—talk, but not actual life. There was the rhythm of their bodies, and Yora was no part of that at all. She only had Raven, the way she used to have Inga; she knew their rhythms, but no one else's.

She had not locked the door, and soon the sound of her crying brought Raven over. She sat next to Yora and hugged her shoulders.

"Why are you crying?"

"Because my mom has called me three times already and I can't talk to her. I just can't."

"That's alright, it's like that sometimes," Raven answered tentatively, clearly unsure how to comfort Yora. "Why can't you talk to her?"

"Because I'm afraid. She'll be able to tell that I'm not okay, and..."

"But it's good that she can tell."

"No, you don't understand, it isn't. They have their own life over there. She doesn't really know anything about me, and she'll think I'm making everything up. That's one thing. And second, if she does understand something about me, she'll worry. I'm so far away from her."

"Well, anyway, you should call her. It's not right."

"What am I going to tell her?"

"Ask what the weather is like."

"It's raining. Or raining and snowing."

"Do you not get nice weather over there?"

Yora thought of the streets where the wind chased clouds of dust, and the sun that would suddenly light up the sky, pale like the face of a sick child.

"We do. But what's the weather got to do with anything? I don't know what to tell them, I don't know where they go, what they eat, what occupies them, what they talk about at the dinner table, you know?"

"And you can't go see them?"

"What about the money?"

"You'll find the money later. Money has a way of turning up. You know that."

Yora thought she had left her mother and sister when she had in order not to become like them, not to live in a world like theirs. Well, now she wasn't.

"I don't see them, and they don't see me, so they don't know what's on my mind or how I live," Yora said, calmer now. "And it's a terrible thing."

"Oh, no," Raven disagreed. "It's actually a very good thing. It's good that everything that happened to you has happened now, and without them. Just think—you did the right thing that you left, that you are not with them. Think. It would've been hard for them to look at you. They would've just sat around you and cried their eyes out. And who knows what would've happened to them after that. It would have been intolerable if you were still a child. But you were lucky, you grew up and went away, and now you're getting better here little by little, not upsetting anybody. You should be happy that it all has happened to you now. You'll get through this now, and later will be better. Didn't Obike tell you so?"

These were strange ideas indeed, but they made a certain amount of sense.

"You think so? Do you really think so?"

"I think you are stupid to get so upset about it," Raven said. "That's not a good reason! Nothing there even to think about. Just call them. Look, just press this button, it's not hard at all. Come on, call. I can sit with you if you want."

"Easy for you to say! You're different," Yora went on. She was starting to like that she was being comforted, and wanted more of it, although it would probably be smart to quit while she was ahead. "At least your mom is somewhere here, in this country. You have someone—"

"No," Raven interrupted. "I don't."

"What do you mean, you don't? You told me about her."

"She died, three years ago. She had cancer."

"Wait... She would have been very young!"

"She was. But she still died. We had a hard life, she and I, never had any money, but then things got better, and she even sent me to college. I had a boyfriend there, Emmanuel, he... Well, he graduated, and then he decided he had no use for this education since it came from white people, don't ask, it's a long story... He helps me out sometimes—he and his people, like Obike. And then I... Well, anyway. And this cancer happened. It was so abrupt, without any in-between—she wasn't even in the hospital, just in total pain, went to hospice, because it was the end. There was no beginning, but there was the end. She lay there in her room and cried—couldn't death wait? She wanted one thing—for death to wait. Things were just starting to get better finally, her child was in college, why couldn't death just wait? Maybe it would have been better if she could die happy and content, maybe it would've been easier for her. Or maybe not. Maybe it makes no difference. When Mom finally died, her face was so serene. The skin sort of freezes then into these little waves and ridges, and they can't be smoothed out. You've seen dead people, haven't you? So you know. And that's that. That's the story."

"What about you?" Yora asked, shocked. "How are you... now?"

"Me? I've been living the way you see me living since then. I start nothing, and I finish nothing."

"Why?"

"What do you mean, why? Do you really not get it?"

"I... I'm not sure."

"So that I can remember that my mom died. No, 'remember' is not the right word. The dead need... to be lived, right? I don't know how to put it another way. Everyone wants me to forget about it. Forget it, move on, start living.

LOVE LIFE 177

Take off your mourning clothes. And I don't want to take off my mourning, because when I do—no one else will put it on, you see? It's not like there are mourning shifts out there, one person takes it off, another one puts it on, and it goes on uninterrupted, as would be fair. And everyone will forget about my mom, and I will forget about her. Maybe I'll pull out a picture of hers once in a blue moon, some snapshot no one wants, and sigh, oh, yes, I did have a mom, but it's okay, I'm over the loss and am marching bravely on. Because that's what everyone expects me to do, so they can shake their heads and say, oh yes, you are doing everything right, and your mom would've been proud of you. Except what's there for her to be proud of? The fact that I've forgotten her?"

Yora said nothing, stunned into silence.

"Actually," Raven spoke again, in a different voice. "Actually, I'm going to give you one great piece of advice."

Yora had gotten used to Raven's sudden mood swings, when she could go from deep, as it appeared, sincerity straight to mockery, hidden but implicit. She could then mock with impunity, and it was impossible to tell how and what exactly she was mocking.

"Alright, let's hear it," Yora said, agreeing to the game.

"Actually, you should go see people... People who will help you."

"Are you talking about a therapist? I don't have money for one. And the free ones, you know, are not worth the time," Yora answered, speaking actually about *something else*—but what this was, the two of them, by mutual agreement, decided not to articulate.

"You crazy!" Raven scoffed. "What moron goes to shrinks, free or not?"

"I thought everyone here went."

"Morons do. And you are right, there are plenty of morons around. On behalf of the still-sane inhabitants of this loony bin, I would like to apologize to you—it's become impossible to live here."

Raven, as was her custom, spread out on the bed. She lay on her back and said, "Have I ever told you how I went to see a witch?"

"Ew." Yora made a face. And then, laughing a little, just like Raven did a moment ago, she said, "You have told me, no need to repeat."

"Nah," Raven smiled at her gently. "I told you about the Black Mass. Right?"

"Yeah," Yora agreed.

"That's different. That was my mom's story, but I wanted to tell you one of my own."

"You'll be lying again," Yora sighed and threw a pillow at Raven.

"Who? Me? I'd never! I only tell the truth... Do you not believe me?"

"I don't!"

"That's alright, you will when you hear it."

"Let me guess. You went to see a witch, and the witch told you to—"

"Hey, that's not fair! Wait. We'll get to that. So, when my mom died... Right, now you feel sorry for me, but you shouldn't. Listen and learn. When things get really bad, you'll know where to go. I'll tell you an important thing now. How to become really powerful! There are people out there—they can give you power."

"Do you mean Obike? But he said they don't—"

"Obike told you the truth, he doesn't do things like that. You'd have to call on Papa Legba himself!"

"Does this papa go to the same church?"

Raven nearly choked laughing.

"Oh, this is precious! Do go on, please! Oh, I can't even... Papa Legba goes to church! Oh!"

LOVE LIFE 179

"Why are you laughing? How am I supposed to know about this papa of yours?" Yora laughed along, already guessing the truth.

"Of course you aren't," Raven went on, once she stopped laughing. "Because you spent your entire life on some nonsense and only listened to your very serious friend who eloped with Ronald McDonald. And what does she know? She doesn't know how to live here. So, Papa Legba in your own, European terms is, quite simply, the devil."

Raven, either serious or joking, was watching Yora's reaction quite closely.

"The devil?" Yora repeated, affecting innocence. "And they call him Papa around here?"

"What difference does it make? The devil is the devil. And it's not here they call him that, but in the Caribbean. Or in New Orleans. He is one of the Loa."

"What are those?"

"You can go read about them in your very serious books. So, this one time, I went to them—"

"To whom?"

"To whom, to whom! To the people who talk to him. There's a lady here in the Black neighborhood."

"No, there isn't. You are making everything up!" Yora teased.

"Yes, there is. Emmanuel knows all those people, that's his job."

"Is he, like, a gangster?"

"No."

"A pastor?"

"No again."

"What does he do?"

"He *grows vegan bread*," Raven said with emphasis and pursed her lips.

"Wha-at?"

"Wha-at?" Raven mocked back. "He is restoring the strength of the earth! Someone has to do that, not everyone gets to live in Babylon and care about nothing except their bank account."

"What do you mean?"

"You don't get it? He is one of those who build."

"A new world?" Yora asked, instantly reminded of something.

"New? I don't know... More like the old one," Raven said, doubtfully. "People have forgotten how to live, the way they used to. But you might be right. Maybe it's a new world. Or maybe it's the same thing."

"Maybe."

"That's why he knows everyone... You'll meet him, he's supposed to stop by. I don't even know if I should let you, because he'll probably like you... But we'll deal with that later," she summed up gravely. And went on with her story.

"So, I got ready, did everything they told me I should, they also got ready, I borrowed some money, and so on—"

"What did they tell you to do? How did you get ready?"

"Aha, now you want to know! I can see you do."

"I don't! It's just you'd never shut up. So, everyone got ready, and?"

"Getting ready is a very individual thing. Everyone has to do something different. So my experience will not be relevant for you."

"Good Lord, why would I want your experience?"

"Don't utter the Lord's name in vain, especially in the company of..."

"No, *you* don't! I'm not the one keeping company to..."

"So, I got all ready, got on the bus, went where they told me to, and it was already dark. I found the right house, knocked, and they let me in. They sat me down in a dark room and told me to wait. This lady would come, and she

LOVE LIFE

would summon Papa Legba. And I could ask him for whatever I wanted."

"And did you see him? What did he look like?"

"Wait!"

"I can't wait! That's quite a story. You're about to meet the devil himself face-to-face and I'm supposed to wait! What happened next?"

"Well, I sat there for a while, took a good look around, listened to these people, and realized I had nothing to ask him for. So I got up and left."

"And that's it?"

"That's it."

"You mean, you didn't see him?"

"Nope. I didn't stay long enough. I just thought it was kind of funny—me sitting on a stool in the middle of a dark room, hoping for who knows what. And there he'd be... And I'd be like, oh, you're Papa Legba! And what would he say to me? I'd have a good laugh if I were him. It's funny."

For some reason, Yora also found it funny. She pictured Raven on that little stool, all serious and intent, skinny and small in the middle of someone else's room, and she couldn't help it—she burst out laughing.

It could have been anyone in Raven's place, even her, Yora. People did all kinds of things when they were desperate. Raven snorted, too. They looked at each other—and laughed together.

"That's one way to get out of a bind!"

"Worked for me!"

"Anything's not right—you go ahead and call Papa Legba, let him adopt you!"

"Papa Legba!"

"Papa Legba, ha-ha-ha!"

"Oh, I can't even, I'm gonna burst, Papa Legba, ha-ha-ha, Papa Legba, ha-ha-ha!"

They shouted his name like a new, powerful spell and laughed so loudly that the walls seemed to shake.

"Are you finally going to tell me what happened?" Raven asked later when they were going to bed together on Yora's bed. "With that man?"

"Oh, that," Yora said, feeling suddenly that Sebastian did not matter to her anymore. She had no interest in him; he was no one, a dead man on the other side of life. "I'd go to his home, and we'd... You know..."

"For how long?"

"Several weeks. A month. Maybe two. I'm not sure."

"And then?"

"And then he told me about Bonnie."

"Another woman?"

"He had several."

"Several other women? Are you for real?" Raven whistled.

"Sure, why not. He had the time for it."

"How often would you see each other?"

"Twice a week... Sometimes three times."

"And you said he used to be an actor?"

"Uh-huh."

"How old was he?"

"I'm not sure. About fifty?"

"He's fifty, he is seeing you two or three times a week, you spend the night there, and he'd still like to convince you that he has some Bonnie? Or three?"

Raven thought about it for a moment, squinted, and then said, "Okay, he can afford Viagra. And he has plenty of free time. But something's not right here, I don't believe him."

"Why?" Yora asked. Something in her soul quickened, like a small flame in the dark. As if Romeo had found Juliet and noticed that she was waking up, and now, in the middle of the frigid tomb, he prepared to take Juliet into his arms, because death had been canceled. Until the next play.

LOVE LIFE

"What did you say to him? When he—"

"When he told me about Bonnie? Nothing. What was there to say?"

"Lots," Raven said.

"What would you have said?" Yora asked.

"Me? I probably would have bargained with him."

"How do you mean, bargained? I don't know how to do that."

"That's a problem." Raven said gravely. "You told him that was terrible, turned around, and left. Am I right?"

"Basically, yes."

"See! That was a mistake."

"What was I supposed to do?"

"Toy with him! You should have toyed with him. That's what he was counting on. That you would play along, purse your lips, and insist you were better. He thought you—you, and all his other Bonnies—would fall over each other trying to please him, so that he would choose—in his heart—just one, and that would be you, you alone. That way, he wouldn't have to do any work, because, let's be honest, for a man, winning over a woman is hard work. And, in his mind, he was being honest. Because he hadn't promised you anything... And I bet, before you, women just went along with it."

"He did mention something about that..."

"That's it! Is he good-looking? Well, there you are. He thinks this is how things should be. And he would have gotten used to you—men do get used to women, what did you think? And he wouldn't have gone anywhere. You were supposed to kiss him on the shoulder, laugh a little—as in, what a load of nonsense—and keep drinking your coffee. Because such things are so far below you that you couldn't care less. Because he is your territory, and you have no wish to recognize this homeless Bonnie as an equal. She is no one. She doesn't exist. Bonnie—and all his other Bonnies—they are girls, he buys them pretty dresses, and they go happily on, bragging to their friends, look what my sugar daddy got me! He knows they don't give a hoot about him. And you—no, you are different, and he knew it from the very start. You mattered to him. You should have laughed. He would have seen your strength then. And you, instead, let him see that you were hurt."

"I couldn't have gone on like that," Yora said. "I'm a poor actress. It would have hurt anyway. How was I supposed to keep up the act, for such a long time, so close to him? Watch that Bonnie and not care? Watch them together? Or would you have me chat with the two of them, in the living room, with the floor lamp on? Look at the pond with them? Like, look, what a pretty sunset? Have breakfast with them, and say, 'Oh, yes, I can't come this Saturday, because you'll have Bonnie here,' and he would say, 'Ah, yes, Bonnie will be here, but I like you very much, too, don't think I don't. And could you pour me some more coffee?' Or I'd have to go to bed with him? How?"

Yora said all that, feeling like the hope, which Raven's words had so suddenly kindled inside her, ought to be extinguished by what she was saying, her bitter and somehow comical words, but this hope, for some reason, did not die. On the contrary, it now burned brighter.

Yora slipped into sleep easily that night. In her dreams, she flew and saw a strange earth below. From the depths of this earth, black rays reached out toward her, but they were not scary—they were protecting, defending her. And, in her sleep, Yora wept with gratitude.

How stupid had she been this entire time—she had thought she was so terribly alone! An air current kept carrying her. Yora closed her eyes and let it do what it wished. Then she opened her eyes and wanted to look for the sky, but realized it was impossible, because the sky was all around

LOVE LIFE

her. A sky black and burning, dark and hot—she swam in its plasma, moving not up but *into it*, deeper into previously unknown dimensions of it, through waves, to its very center where, Yora now knew, grew that one magic flower she needed, the flower of the world's wound, a part of which everyone carries inside them, not knowing how to keep it inside and how to heal it.

Yora's own wound did not need to hide anymore; this unbearable wound that she had so long watered with her tears in silence, entirely alone with it, now led her unerringly, carried her as if on a pair of mighty wings, forward, ahead, to where she could become one with the wound of the world, collide with it and, by doing so, bring about healing, a restoration, and not just hers, Yora's, but for everyone, all the people in the world, known and unknown, and at whose existence she could only guess. Not yet today, but soon.

New worlds formed from the heavenly rock before her eyes and fell apart again into sheaves of stellar bodies, and then flashed with the spirit of life in order to fall deep into the cosmos and rise again from it as pillars of fire.

* * *

The following day, Yora still did not call her mother despite the fact that she had promised Raven she would, and she fully intended to do so; she just ended up having an unexpectedly busy day.

In the morning, Yora got behind the wheel and drove to the college. Julie and Yingru were waiting for her, and then on-boarding took longer than Yora had expected—first, she had to fill out countless forms for HR, all on a computer, then another endless series of them for her specific department, then there were two safety and security trainings, also to be done on a computer and each taking almost an hour, and finally she had to go to be issued her keys and keypad codes from a tiny facility that was hidden on a different street, near the post office. And, at every step, she had to wait for someone important. Julie told Yora it wasn't like this all the time, but in Yora's case, they were in a hurry because they had to hire her officially immediately.

"Stay, we're having a party. It's Barbara's birthday, there will be pizza. Barbara has no idea," said Julie when it was already after five and Yora was about to leave. "It's a surprise party. Yingru is keeping Barbara busy while we set the table." And Julie patted Yora on the shoulder. It was too late for Yora to call Mom—nearly midnight back in Europe.

Everyone bustled in and out. People set the table; Julie called to order pizza. Yora stood alone off to the side of the commotion; she did not know anyone and hesitated to offer to help. Someone brought in colorful balloons and let them go; they flew up and bunched at the ceiling. Presents in bright packages were laid out on the tables. Yora realized she did not even know who Barbara was, which one of them—she didn't even remember seeing that name on the labels in the mail room. It was strange, though, that everyone decided to stay for a party after work—usually people left as soon as they could at the end of the day, because the commute home took at least half an hour, and almost everyone had a family waiting for them. Well, perhaps, Barbara did not have a family and was in no hurry to get home. Perhaps Julie and Yingru also did not have to rush home, and they stayed late at the office all the time. Yora herself didn't have any family, unless one counted Raven.

"We're almost ready," Julie said, running past her. "The pizza is on the way, and the cake is over there."

LOVE LIFE

Everyone who worked there came into the room, a dozen people or so; someone turned off the lights. In the dark room, Yora could hear people's breathing and muffled giggles.

"I have pulled those files already, let me show you," they heard Yingru's even voice from the hallway, and then her steps, and then the door opened, the lights flashed back on, and everyone shouted together, "Surprise!"

Barbara, a very thin woman of about fifty-five, startled happily, but her happiness was affected, rehearsed—even Yora could see that. Had her colleagues not thrown this party, Barbara would have been very unhappy, but being truly happy was no longer something she could do. Her face looked desiccated, her eyelids were heavy, and her smile quite weary.

"Her husband died a year ago," Julie whispered into Yora's ear. And added, even though Yora asked no questions, not wishing to pry, "He drank a lot."

"Ah," Yora said. "I see."

Julie then rushed into the middle of the room.

"But what about the cake! The cake!" she cried.

Someone lit the candles.

"Blow them out, Barbara, make a wish!"

Everyone sang. Barbara tightened her lips, then filled her chest with air and blew out the candles; everyone clapped.

"Thank you, thank you," Barbara said. She pressed her hand to her heart, made other theatrical gestures and smiled at everyone around, twisting her lips.

The pizza went quickly; someone got started on the cake. Yora was hungry, so she took a slice of pizza, even though she generally disliked such food. To her great surprise, the party involved wine—despite the fact that it was a dry campus.

"Is it actually," Yora asked a man standing next to her, "real wine?"

The man smiled and answered, with emphasis:"Of course! It's Yingru, after all."

From this answer, Yora concluded that she might, indeed, have gotten lucky, and Mariana had been right. Yingru had a certain power in this world.

"I'm Albert," the man went on. "What's your name?"

"Yora."

"Are you new?"

"Yes."

"You are lucky. This is a great place to work."

"Albert, how many have you had already?" someone asked.

"I'm Kelly."

"I'm Noah."

"Why don't you finish your wine?" Albert said to Yora, smiling. "I told you it's the real deal—don't you believe me?"

Yora thought about telling him she was taking medication but didn't. Why shouldn't she, after all, have a drink.

The wine spread through her body in a surprising wave and seemed to give her new energy. It wasn't that bad. There were people, laughter, wine, this pizza, even this cake with its acid-blue frosting and tiny candles, the cake she had no intention of eating but which was proof they were celebrating.

Why couldn't people celebrate once in a while? It had been such a long time since she had anything to celebrate; she only had tears, but how long could one go on like that? How beautiful it was—people coming together, having a good time eating and drinking. It was so great that Julie had invited her. Yora looked out the window where the dusk was almost dark. The river was very close, and a few streets over, the dark bay began, and it smelled sharply of seaweed. But the darkness did not scare Yora, as it usually did.

LOVE LIFE

"What," Yora felt like saying to the darkness, "have you got there at the bottom of the well? I've cut your thread, haven't I? So, what now?"

But the darkening sky was silent. Yora, as if hypnotized, moved closer to the window—and suddenly saw the moon. She looked closer—an uneven, chipped disc, it was yellow and humongous, as it often is in the tropics. It hung, like a phantom, very low above the ground, and looked straight at Yora with its single blind eye.

It was dark by the time she left the building. Yora's car was parked nearby, near Oxford, which was closed for the night. Yora got into her car and started the engine, and it suddenly responded with a deep, throaty sound. It did start, but something was wrong, she could feel it without a doubt, but she did not know what exactly. The car moved slowly; the streets around the college were empty. Kennedy Street, however, where the bridge across the river began, was packed. Yora sat in a traffic jam for a while, and when the cars finally moved, luck wasn't on her side—the light ahead switched from green to yellow to red, and she didn't make it through the intersection. The engine growled suspiciously, then gave a sort of quack, and instantly stalled. Yora started the car again. The car started, but when the light changed, it would not move. Yora pressed on the accelerator as hard as she could; the car stood still. She was in the left-turn lane. If she were turning right, she could've gone on red, but, in this direction, you had to wait forever for the light, and the green arrow only turned on for a few seconds. The cars behind her began to honk. Yora tensed up—as if her tension meant something, as if she could galvanize her dead—obviously, dead!—car, kicked at the pedal, and made the turn on yellow. She exhaled with relief, and right then her car stalled again, as if it were indeed Yora's will and not its sophisticated mechanisms that had kept it moving for this entire trip and, perhaps, for months before. The Honda rolled a few more yards, purely on momentum—just enough to stop in a very inconvenient spot, next to a hotel. Instantly, a policeman approached.

"My car won't go," Yora explained.

The policeman nodded, called for a security guard and a few other men with him, and together (except the policeman) they leaned in and pushed the car a few yards forward, where the policeman let her stay.

"But don't leave your car," he said. "Or we'll give you a ticket. There's no parking here."

Having said that, he vanished as if he'd never been there. Yora reached for her phone; in better times, she used to have AAA. A glance at her phone made her shake her head—she had about seven percent of battery left. She had no charger that she could use in the car. Yora had a low-budget Android smartphone; an iPhone would have gotten her through till morning even on three percent, but this phone was going to die in half an hour if she made a single call. And she would still have to wait for the tow truck. That service was reliable, but slow.

Yora felt a terror shoot through her. Not because she was lost in a phoneless desert; she could get the security guard's attention, or borrow a phone from one of the young men at the hotel, worst case—get out of the car and talk to a policeman, of whom there were always plenty downtown; none of this would have been difficult, no; none of it was what scared her.

The dark sky she could not see out of her car had to be looking down on her with scorn. "What are you doing, fighting death, fighting with the concrete well, with the Gray Rose? Death will win anyway. Did you really think you could run away? Close your accounts? One little tug on this thread—and you're gone," the toothless thing deep inside

LOVE LIFE

191

her mocked. "Where will you run to escape from death? It is everywhere, it surrounds you like the ocean surrounds this Peninsula, there's no point in running."

Yora shook involuntarily. She clenched her teeth, trying to control herself, to get control of her terror. She dialed AAA. She had to wait for an intolerably long time, anxious about her battery dying.

"Your membership number?" a female operator finally asked.

Yora read it out to her.

"Where are you?"

The woman took a long, an eternally long time looking up something in her system—while the battery percentage melted and melted away.

"For God's sake, could you hurry up?" Yora asked. "My phone is about to die."

"No problem," the woman said. "Just stay on the line for another minute, so I don't have to call you back, I'm looking for a tow truck for you."

In a minute or two—really, quite fast, she added, "Forty minutes. The driver will call you, but even if he can't reach you, he has your car information, so don't worry, he'll find you."

Yora was now parked on the side of the street, in a fairly safe place, and, however funny it was, right next to a round skyscraper labeled "Sikes Enterprises." The skyscraper was belted with lights—the fourth, seventh, and fifteenth floor were lit up, each a different color. From the car, Yora could not see anything above that. Somewhere up there, at the top, at the very pinnacle of it, in the best penthouse apartment in the world lived the invisible powers that be, Tripp and his mentor, the mighty Mr. Sikes, Doug Crumry, Entrepreneur of the Year, as well as Raven's father who, perhaps, had finally gotten all the might he so desperately wanted. It would not even occur to them to look down, and even if it did, they wouldn't really see anything from the windows of their tower. And if they did—what would they have seen? Yora in her dead car? It was a shame, she thought, that her feet were, for the first time in a long time, unbandaged, or she could have played doctor-and-hospital like Tripp at his school reunion. That would've made Tripp happy! He'd be thrilled to have his own, much older feet, in much better order.

Cars sped past Yora's stalled Honda, their bodies gleaming and their headlights flashing; people sat inside their cars. To the right of "Sikes Enterprises," on Ashley Street, were the fountains, the ones where Carlos used to meet up with Inga, and past the fountains rolled the murky, stone-clad river.

It got cold. So cold that Yora's teeth clattered. She tried to press her frozen body hard into the body of the car that had always been so warm. She really did not appreciate her unfortunate little car! She should've taken better care of it. Yora used to think the car was just another object, a thing, but now, wiser, she knew that even cars were not mere objects. "How could it be just a thing if it brought me food, carried me around, warmed me up?" Yora thought. This car was a cosmic cow, a kind and warm body. "Please don't leave me!" She begged. "Don't leave me." When a cow dies, you can at least take her hide—wasn't that what people had done since times immemorial? They asked for the cow's forgiveness and used its pelt to keep warm, warm.

Suddenly, madness, on tiptoe, snuck up on Yora. She would always be visible to death now, to this sniper so drawn to the wounds on her feet, never mind they were now healed and all but invisible. But death knew they were there, and it knew about the virus in Yora's body, that traitor, that Judas. How easy it was to go mad in an enclosed space. Because the truth was that no one was going to help her; the tow truck,

LOVE LIFE

other people—that was an illusion. She had to at least start counting to a hundred, had to do something, anything, anything not to lose her mind, finally and completely, in this dusk, among these lights that flew at her like bullets that could not kill her.

Yora felt her feet go numb. She recalled Neya Fernandes's instructions about circulation, sighed, and began to move. There was something unnatural about this, moving inside a stalled car. One, two, one-two-three, she counted in a whisper, rotating her feet clockwise and then in the opposite direction and moving her feet as if to stand on tiptoe. Several years ago, she used to have friends, Maryna and her husband Volodya; Volodya was the one who taught Yora to drive. Maryna, like Inga, was getting her master's degree, and Volodya did not study anywhere; he cooked Maryna's meals and made a little money buying old cars, repairing them, detailing them, and then selling them for more than he had paid. At home, he was a Ukrainian literature scholar and could easily quote Nechui-Levytskyi when appropriate; he'd call a nice car "the poppy of the patch," like in the works of Ukrainian authors from the 19th century, but had loved everything mechanical since he was a child, passionately and devotedly, and it loved him back. Americans worshiped him like a great wizard.

"Come on," Volodya told Yora who was living at the time, like Volodya and Maryna, next to the college—not the one downtown, but the other, larger one, where she used to work for Mariana or in other similar offices and took the college shuttle to work. "Come on, let me teach you to drive, you'll have your own car one day." Yora resisted—she was scared. She could not see herself ever owning a car; she made very little money. But then a friend of Volodya's decided to let his Honda, old as the world itself, go for next to nothing, and Volodya convinced Yora to buy it.

"Don't worry… I can always tune it up for you," Volodya promised and, in fact, after his ministrations, the car that only a madman would buy ran just fine. "Just take it to the shop regularly and make sure to change the oil," Volodya advised. Yora's first practice runs were terrible. Not only did the cars around her move in solid columns and she had to figure out how to maneuver between them at high speed, but Volodya, next to her, drilled her without mercy. With rough kindness, he instructed: "Put your heel down and roll your foot, don't take your foot off the floor when you change pedals, on your heel, I said, on your heel…"

One time Yora had to interrupt.

"Are you a mechanic or a ballet teacher?"

But Volodya did not take offense. He was incapable of being offended. Gradually, Yora got used to his drills, and to the streets, and the highways, and got behind the wheel cheerfully, happy to be a particle in the rivers of cars with their flashes of headlights. She was thrilled by her own sudden power, when she sat ensconced in her seat, like a warrior in a chariot, and sped ahead.

Maryna and Volodya later moved to a different city; they wrote at first—they had gone to an *Okean Elzy* concert, taken a trip to the mountains—but then stopped, or maybe she was the one who stopped, who could remember? And now there she was, doing her ballet moves, alone in her Honda, heel-toe, heel-toe, one-two, one-two-three, syncing up with the changing traffic light.

She did not feel any warmer, but her feet felt less numb. Wait, how was she going to get to work now that her Honda had breathed its last, and Volodya was no longer around? Admittedly, she wasn't going to start for another week, when the term of the grant began, but where was she going to get a car if she had no money? She had no money for anything else, either, but other things could wait, even food—she still

LOVE LIFE 195

had her tuna—but a car... She couldn't walk, could she? It didn't seem far on the highway—ten miles, but that was by car. Biking was out of the question; the roads weren't made for it. She could potentially take the bus, but buses in this city, as in nearly every city in the south or out west, were highly unreliable and used either by people in dire need or those who had had their drivers' licenses revoked for drunk driving. A bus, she knew from experience, could take two or three hours to get to the same destination a car would reach in twenty minutes; the routes were never straight.

Yora's phone rang. The screen showed one percent of battery power left. Yora answered.

"Good evening! This is your tow truck driver," a man's voice said, tired and bare, without the defense of the usual automatic courtesy, or corporate pretense, or even aggression at the end of a long day. "I'm coming, forty minutes, tops. The operator told me your phone is low and will probably turn off. I'm calling to tell you not to worry, I have everything I need, and I'll find you even if your phone dies."

"Thank you," Yora said.

Gratitude made her throat tight. That woman operator, somewhere in a different state, a woman who had never and would never meet her, cared about her and gave her information to this driver. And the driver, who was probably about to finish his shift, cared about her so much he called her to tell her when he was coming. And his voice was full of real tenderness. Because real tenderness—it's not only the time when adoring lovers touch each other's skin; tenderness was being tired at the end of the day and yet loving everyone out there, everyone without exception.

Finally, the tow truck lights shone through Yora's back window. Yora did not notice him approach. She opened the door carefully and stepped out onto the nighttime asphalt. The tow truck driver had also gotten out of his vehicle and was now studying Yora's Honda, evidently trying to figure out how best to approach it. He looked at Yora once, sideways, and instantly looked away; Yora's sixth sense told her he liked her. The driver shifted his weight from one foot to another, then tilted his head back as if to absorb the downtown light, and then, apparently, decided he was acting like a savage, and it would be a good idea to stop. He came up to Yora.

"Good evening again," he said, extending his hand. "My name is Jimmy."

"Yora."

"Let me come at it from the front. Just wait here. Or, you could hop into my truck, if you'd like, it's warmer in there."

"It's okay, I'll stand here."

Jimmy's eyes were clear and green, his body—a touch overweight because of his sedentary job, and his voice the same as it had been on the phone—defenseless.

He worked to attach chains to the Honda and then pressed various levers to lift it onto the truck. Yora stood nearby, not approaching him, and not talking to him, because he was busy. Finally, he was done, and went to get in. Yora followed. It was warm inside the truck's cab.

"That's it," Jimmy said, giving Yora another look with his green eyes.

"Thank you," she answered.

"Do you know where you want to go? First five miles is free."

"I don't have a regular mechanic," she muttered.

Jimmy sighed, started the engine, and began driving.

"It's alright, I know a guy, I send everyone to him. His name is Willis Figuera. You can tell him I sent you in the morning."

Yora did not protest. This mechanic or any other—all there was left to do was to divvy up what the scrap metal

LOVE LIFE

company would pay for her Honda. There was, in all likelihood, no point in fixing it. The tow truck moved heavily through the downtown streets, then crawled onto a narrow road that led to the highway, and that's where they got stuck. The street was packed; everyone downtown was going home.

"Traffic jam," Jimmy said.

"Sure is," Yora said. She would have liked to add something, but she could not think of anything to say. None of the tow truck drivers she'd met before were very talkative, and she sat there quietly, not daring to strike up a conversation. On the other hand, Jimmy had been so nice to her that not saying anything did not feel right either; she didn't want him to think her rude. Feeling very shy, she pulled out her phone, a dead little bird, as if the warmth of her hands could bring it back to life. Jimmy, seeing it, without a word handed her the black cord of the charger plugged into a generator.

"Will it fit my model?" Yora asked.

"If it's an Android, it will," Jimmy said softly.

Yora carefully connected her phone to the power source. Usually, a little red light would come on in one corner, proof that the bird was still alive, only battered, but this time, either the charger did not fit the model, or Yora was just having that kind of a day—the phone remained black and silent.

No matter. Death must have been toying with her again, sending her a kind operator, a kind tow truck driver—but these were only ripples on the surface of life, grimaces of Death, that old actor, affected to dull Yora's vigilance. It was still there, at the bottom of the well, pulling invisible threads. Invisible, but powerful; stronger, in any case, than the black cord of the charger which could not wake up Yora's phone.

"Doesn't work?" Jimmy asked.

"No," Yora said, swallowing tears, so he wouldn't notice anything.

"Give it a minute," he advised. "This happens if the phone has been dead for a while."

They were still stuck in traffic, inching toward the highway.

"Do you work here?" Jimmy nodded to imply the whole of downtown, its glamorous essence.

"Yeah, at the college over there," she replied.

"Is it a good job?"

"It's okay."

"What happened to your car?"

"I'm not sure," Yora shrugged. "I have no idea."

"They are good cars, those old Hondas. They don't make them like that anymore."

"That's very true," Yora said.

She was ready to start screaming for the whole world to hear, because everything was lost, the Honda did not matter anymore, even if it could be fixed, because Death could not be overcome and everyone it had set its sights on even once was doomed, so all there was left to do was to give in and die quickly and with dignity—if that were even possible! And all at once the road before them suddenly cleared. Jimmy stepped on the gas, the truck lurched forward, and they merged onto the highway. At the same moment, the little red eye came on in the corner of the phone. The tiny light pulsed.

"Oh, Lord," Yora said, barely audible, and brushed off a tear before Jimmy could see it. And if he did see it, he said nothing. Yora kept crying—with relief, because tension had gone all at once from her body, and every muscle that had been so intolerably taut seemed now to rejoice and relax.

She had escaped Death one more time, and even the moon, the shapeless rag that hung above the earth on its cosmic tether, this spy who had just found her with its Cyclops' eye and betrayed her to the Gray Rose, even it could do nothing to her.

LOVE LIFE

The tow truck carried Yora into a safe zone, somewhere Death could not reach her, neither her nor her poor exhausted Honda, and even the bird of her black phone was alive. Jimmy rescued them all. They got stuck in traffic again, but it no longer mattered.

Jimmy, otherwise so calm, jumped out of the truck anxiously time and again to wipe his windshield with special wipes.

"I can't stand those spots," he explained to Yora, and she just nodded. The spots did not go away because the highway was windy and dusty. In fact, the road was quite dirty.

"I hate spots," Jimmy muttered. "I want a windshield I can see through."

Yora agreed and caught more tears with the tips of her fingers and her knuckles, while tears rolled and rolled, obscuring the world for her.

Finally, she felt calmer. The traffic was finally moving, and they drove faster. City landscapes floated outside the windows. Here and there, she could see scattered low buildings without windows, far from each other. Giant billboards glowed in the dark.

"You're my last one tonight," Jimmy said, looking at Yora sideways.

"That's good to hear, you must be tired—it's a hard job."

"It is," he smiled. "But I enjoy it. I've told myself, 'You know, Jimmy, what would you do if you could be doing anything else?' But I don't want anything else. I get tired at the end of the day, of course, but it's a good tired. I drive around like this all day, I get to see all kinds of things. Only these spots bother me, and I know what you must think about me, but I can't help it."

"It's nothing," Yora said. "I understand. They would drive me nuts, too."

"Really?"

"Of course."

She had to say something else to him, had to make an effort to keep the conversation going.

"Are you from around here?" She suddenly remembered a psychologist's advice from a workshop a long time ago. When you don't know how to start a conversation, ask the other person where they are from, and that will always work. It worked this time, too.

"Me? Yes, I am. Born and raised, went to school here, too. We had a good school, I can't complain. We used to go to the beach all the time. We had the time, you know, and fishing, too."

Yora never even thought about her school. Was it good or bad—who knew? Perhaps, if she, like Jimmy, were living where she had been born, her school memories, like all other memories of her childhood, would have meant something entirely different to her. Here, everything was strange, and memories did not thrive.

"Did you go to a good school?" Jimmy asked, as if overhearing her thoughts.

"I guess it depends," she said slowly. "Seemed alright at the time." But her voice, like an X-ray snapshot, showed shadows.

Jimmy laughed, understanding—in this country, school mattered very much indeed, because that's where you learned to get along with other people.

"I know what you mean... High school," he said. "It's not a walk in the park. But you graduated."

"Of course," Yora answered.

He must have thought that Yora had been bullied by the more popular girls, but there was no such thing as popular girls back in that country at that time. Popular girls were lucky if they had something to eat, because the only thing on the shelves in grocery stores was vinegar. And then the girls

LOVE LIFE 201

got a bit older and wanted to leave the country. But Jimmy didn't know that, and that was just fine.

"Do you like it here?"

"Very much."

"And where are you from?"

She told him.

"You have such an uncommon name..."

"Thank you."

"Do you live far from work?"

"Far enough," Yora said. "And now my Honda's dead."

"Willis will fix it, he's an expert, don't worry. Don't worry so much. You are not alone, trust him, he'll do everything right."

"What about you? Do you live far away?"

"In the woods," he smiled. "Okay, not in the woods exactly, but right next to the nature preserve." He named it. The preserve was in the east side of the city, far from the sea, the beaches, and the expensive neighborhoods and closer to the center of the Peninsula, the farms, and poor homesteads. There were no highways there, except the 301, a narrow and sometimes potholed road, much abused by large trucks and lined with unmown grass. Behind the wall of grass, small houses began, with small tractors and old car parts in their yards.

"It's very quiet there. Even deer come into my back yard. I wouldn't live anywhere else, only there, you can make a fire at night or just sit and look at the stars."

They exited the highway and did not talk any more until they reached the right street. The space in front of Willis Figuera's garage was empty and dark, and only a pharmacy entrance was lit up on the other side of the street. Jimmy stopped the truck, got out, and started moving the various levers to lower the Honda to the ground. Yora stood beside him, watching the action with a hangdog look.

Jimmy saw Yora's expression and decided to cheer her up.

"They are sure to fix it. At the very least, they will tell you what's wrong."

"But it won't be free, so I'm standing here wondering if I should ask you to take it straight to the junkyard."

"No, no. I know this place, they can take a look at it for free. I told you. Ask for Willis, tell him Jimmy sent you."

"How much do I owe you?" Yora still had to pay for the tow, although it came with a significant discount. Jimmy would have to account for his services with the company that sent him.

"Thirty," he said, hesitating. "You know, I wouldn't charge you anything, but the company..."

Yora sighed.

"Or you know what? Let me give you an invoice, and you can send us a check, or something."

"Thank you," Yora said, blushing. She had no choice, though; she had no cash at all.

"I can give you a ride home," Jimmy offered. "If you'd like."

"No, don't worry... I..." She felt instantly lost and thought she would call Raven to come get her. "I have someone I could... Who could..."

"It's the end of my shift anyway."

"But you don't live in my part of town, it's way out of the way for you..."

He hesitated, and then said: "Would you like some water? I have a fridge here."

Jimmy reached for another lever and opened a little door on the side of the truck. He pulled out a bottle of water, handed it to Yora and stood looking at her. Sometimes, he smiled, and she noticed he was missing a few teeth on the left side of his mouth. She could not see that while he was driving.

LOVE LIFE

"Well," she said. "Have a great evening, and thank you very much again!"

"You're welcome," he said and climbed into the cab.

Yora walked a few yards away from his truck and pulled out her partially charged phone to call Raven, then suddenly changed her mind.

It was dark, with only the pharmacy lighting the street and the flickering of a weak neon sign "Willis Figuera's Auto Body Shop." The "e" was missing, there was a gaping hole in its place. Yora's Honda stood in the parking lot. But beside this, her poor cosmic cow, her shed carapace, Yora still had her freedom, the night, and this city—and all of this was a great treasure she could not afford to squander. Never, never before had she been in possession of such treasures. She breathed easily. The past would be left here, and she had nothing to worry about.

Yora laughed to herself. She sent Raven a text, put her phone away, walked up decisively to the truck, and waved at Jimmy. He reached across from his seat to open the door for her.

"Yes?"

"Yes, please, do give me a ride."

"Get in."

Jimmy started the engine, and they drove. They started talking again, and this was already a different conversation, although neither its tone nor the words had changed.

"How long has it been since you moved here?" he asked.

"A while," she said. "About ten years."

"I wanted to ask—you said you worked at that college. You teach, right?"

"No, not at all. I'm not a professor."

"It's a nice place to work anyway. What are you going to do when you get home? Make dinner for your family?" He gave her another sideways look.

"Oh, no, I live alone. What about you?"

"I've got my daughter. I have a daughter and a son from different mothers, my ex-wives. My daughter lives with me, and my son... I haven't seen him in four years. You know what the laws are like. The mother can be a complete psychopath and the court will still give her custody. She took him all the way to Ohio."

Jimmy spoke with correct grammar, and only his merciless accent betrayed him as a Southerner and a man from a working-class background.

"So, you are divorced?" Yora asked, rather stupidly—it was clear he was. But they were already talking about something different indeed.

"Uh-huh," he blurted out, quickly, like a man touching boiling water. Then he added, seeing that nothing terrible had happened, "Twice. I'm single. Just me and my daughter. It's the two of us that like sitting by a fire. What about you?"

"Me... I've been divorced twice, too," she said, thinking of Sebastian and Inga.

"Uh-huh," he said, slowly. "I understand. Actually, if I'm being honest, I don't. How could anyone divorce such a beautiful woman?"

By now, they had passed Fifty-Sixth Street and were driving down Fletcher Avenue, from where they needed to take a right onto Yora's street.

"Jimmy," she said. "Listen, I..."

Her tone made him start and turn somewhere completely wrong, into a parking lot of a research center or the VA, where he braked and stopped. Then, not turning off the engine, he turned his entire body to her and...

"Jimmy, I..."

She could see he very much wanted to kiss her but did not dare because she had not given him a clear signal, had not done anything that would convince lawyers later, if

LOVE LIFE   205

things were to end badly. He swallowed, hard. His Adam's apple moved.

"Listen..." he said and stopped.

Yora wanted to help him out somehow, to say something that would reassure him, show him she was his ally, but was feeling too many things at once to find the right words.

"...Let's go to my place," he said, finally.

"What about your daughter?"

"She's with her mother until next week. I'll take you wherever you want in the morning. I don't start until after noon tomorrow."

"Alright," she agreed. He stepped on the pedal, turned the truck around, and drove; there were only a few small intersections between them and Yora's street. If she wanted, she probably could have walked the remaining distance, but she hadn't yet challenged herself with so much walking after being sick.

They did not have to drive for very long. From Fletcher Avenue, Jimmy turned onto Morris Bridge, empty at that hour, and from there right onto the 301 which took him past the preserve, the tall grass, and the tractors. There were several rail crossings—small trains ran here, supplying farmers with construction materials and fertilizer.

"I live here," he said quietly once they'd parked and gotten out of the truck.

His was a typical rental house. It was darker here than downtown with all its lights, or even on Fletcher Avenue. Dogs barked—a forgotten sound; in the city, dogs were kept inside apartments, but this was the country. Jimmy opened the door and let Yora in ahead of him. This was against the rules of etiquette; the rules said he should have gone in first to make her feel safe. But Jimmy did not know etiquette.

She entered. She went into the darkness, but she was not scared, and moved ahead, not knowing where, not caring whether he turned on the lights. He did not, and followed her as if she were the mistress of the house and he were the guest. Yora stopped, waited, and drew him toward her. She reached for his eyes and kissed his eyes, thinking that perhaps she shouldn't; back home, they believed kissing someone on the eyes meant you would soon part with them. "Only dead people are kissed on the eyes," her grandmother used to say. But who knew if she was ever going to see this Jimmy again. She had been afraid to kiss Sebastian's eyes. In the dark, she would see their gleam and be afraid to kiss them. Now she knew, she shouldn't have feared, could have gone ahead and kissed them. She should kiss whoever she wanted wherever she wanted.

This was now true tenderness, her hands, her lips full of it. She had not felt this much even toward Sebastian, and touched this man's face in the dark, and opened herself to him because she did not want to be a mystery anymore. Let him see her and know her as others perhaps will see and know her later—or no one will ever again. Somehow, she had to manage all these silenced, invisible treasures—the treasure of her body, the treasure of desire, the treasure of love; they were capital that would disappear unless it was used, its banknotes turned to dust, its coins defaced. And the man next to her, in the dark, responded with his own tenderness—just as full and fearless, and perhaps, he, too, was looking for someone he had lost in Yora's face, but, if so, it didn't upset either one of them, quite the opposite—love lived everywhere, in every cell of the world, and it did not matter to whom they were about to give it. Sooner or later, love would circle back and embrace those who first fell into its gravitational field; love had always been there. And would always remain.

Afterwards, after everything, Yora, smiling in the dark, thought about Sebastian—she realized he did not love her at all and smiled at the idea. What would it have been like—if

LOVE LIFE

he had? She never felt like she had enough of him; it always seemed to her like something important hadn't happened between them but one day it certainly would and waiting for this "something" had fulfilled her, warmed her, and given her hope. Perhaps, this willingness to wait—this was love? But he did not love her back.

Yora wasn't used to thinking about Sebastian in those terms. It was laughable, really—he loved me, he loved me not... Or perhaps she should have been thinking exactly in these terms, in these simple words. Perhaps she had been afraid to. Now she understood something and was no longer afraid, so did that mean that understanding became, in itself, like love?

There was another idea in there, something very important, and not just about Sebastian, but, at that moment, the man beside her moved and said, "Lemme turn on the light for a second. Would you like a towel, to shower?"

And Yora felt ashamed. They had let each other out of their arms, the time of fleeting love was over. But why was Yora thinking about another man if she were in bed next to Jimmy?

Light cut through the darkness. The room was poor, like the neighborhood, but the towel clean albeit worn. Yora took it and went into the bathroom. The bathtub was typical, white, a little chipped, like in all rented houses, hidden behind a shower curtain with fishes on it, bought probably not even at IKEA but at the nearest Target. Yora couldn't help it and thought of Sebastian again—his bathroom tiled in black and white, and not with common tile, but the expensive, small subway rectangles. The pipes at his house were old and the water took a long time to warm up; Sebastian would turn on the faucet and wait for several minutes, testing the water with his hand; only when he was sure it was warm enough would he let Yora into the shower.

"Go ahead," he would say. "Don't spend too much time in there—you never know when the boiler is going to turn itself off. I'm only a renter here, so I can't make them fix it."

Yora would step into the shower, and the warm water would wrap around her body. The tile was also warm, and feeling it with her bare feet made her warm.

Afterwards, Yora would step out of the shower into a black—and also warm—towel, because Sebastian was partial to black towels, and wrapped up like that would return to Sebastian in the bedroom.

And now she returned to the bedroom and lay down next to Jimmy.

He also went to take a shower, then came back to bed, and held her against him. For a few minutes, they lay peacefully in their shared warmth. Suddenly, there were someone's steps in the hallway. A door opened and closed, then another one.

"Who is that?" Yora asked. "You said your kid was..."

Someone was scratching at their door. Jimmy muttered something in the dark, then got up and headed to the entrance. His lack of alacrity told Yora there was nothing serious to worry about.

"Get out of here! Do you hear me?" Jimmy said to someone through the door.

"Who is it?" Yora asked.

"An idiot," Jimmy said irritably. "Go away! Didn't you hear me?"

But the idiot apparently did not. Jimmy came back to the bedroom, picked up his clothes and pulled them on, intending to go out. Yora, just in case, put her dress on as well. Jimmy opened the door, went outside and spoke angrily to someone she could not see.

"Oh," she heard a voice. "You've got a lady here. I want to meet her, too."

"Go to hell."

LOVE LIFE 209

"Don't be so stubborn."

Following this, the door opened, and a man of about thirty followed Jimmy into the room. The man was naked above the waist and had short hair, almost a military buzz-cut; his body was also military-like, his shoulders covered in tattoos. Baggy pants hung off his hips, held up by a belt, and above the belt, there was a strip of plaid maroon underwear, very ghetto-style. He was, however, white. The man proceeded to lie down on the bed at Yora's feet.

"Who is this?" Yora asked Jimmy.

Jimmy came back to bed, lay down, like Yora, on top of the bedspread, sighed and closed his eyes.

"Listen, Jimmy," she said again. "This is not funny. Why'd you let him in here? Who is this? Jimmy? Are you listening to me? Jimmy?" She raised her voice because Jimmy seemed to be falling asleep. "Are we going to fall asleep altogether? Or pretend this dude is not here?"

"This is Justin," Jimmy finally said, opening his eyes.

"How are you doing?" said the man, either to her or to Jimmy. He was very friendly.

"How about you just get lost," Jimmy suggested, without conviction.

"Right, on my way already," Justin said, but kept lying on the bed. He lay there as if the three of them were old friends or siblings.

"What is he doing here? You said you lived alone," Yora said.

"He's always lying," Justin said and yawned. "You shouldn't believe everything he tells you."

Yora gave Jimmy a quizzical look.

"Jesus Christ! Don't listen to this idiot, he's the one lying," Jimmy said.

"Well, one of you is. I'm just trying to figure out which one."

"Hey, she's cool," Justin said. "Looks like she really gave it to you. About time someone did."

"I'll explain everything," Jimmy said, hugging her—he didn't want her to be afraid of Justin, but she wasn't anyway. Something about him was the complete opposite of scary. "Justin is here temporarily, he's a friend of mine from the old days, and he's had some trouble. He's got nowhere to go at the moment. And today," Jimmy said, glaring at Justin and raising his head from the pillow for emphasis, "today, he was supposed to be staying somewhere else. Weren't you going to Sean's for the barbecue?"

"I was, but they weren't drinking."

"How'd you get home?"

"You know," Justin said. "They dropped me off."

"He doesn't have a license," Jimmy explained to Yora. "He can't drive."

"Did he lose it? Or was it revoked?"

"No, it's not like that. Someone stole his identity."

"What does that mean?"

"You know. I could have had a different name before," the new man said. "But now I'm Justin. Or, no, wait, I've always been Justin, but now I've got no ID, so how do I know who I am, right?"

"So," Jimmy went on. "This dumbass now sits here all day long looking at porn on the internet."

"Not just porn," Justin corrected, pretending to be offended. "The kind of porn you have to pay for. I know a few other people who could benefit from watching some, or you'll be bored to death with him." He winked at Yora.

"You see, he's just had bad luck. He got phished."

"Bad luck? That's the understatement of the year," Justin said.

"Fished how?" Yora asked.

LOVE LIFE 211

"Phished, you know, by the people who grab your credit card and then everything else. And then it turns out that Justin Mendoza is not me, but some other guy from Southern California who's been making wine for years. And I'm— no one knows who."

"He's really a winemaker?"

"Well, I haven't been at his place... yet..."

"Why would he need your identity?"

"Who knows! Maybe his is no good."

"And you can't file a report with the police?"

"I could, but then again, I don't exist. I'd give them my social security number and they'd see his wine-making mug in the system. And they'd be like, 'Wait, did you steal this man's identity?' And I'd be like, 'Shit, no, he stole mine.' And they'd be like, 'Aha, and who are you?' And who am I then?"

"You're a dumbass," Jimmy said, and they all laughed.

"That was fun," Justin said after they were done. He ran his hand over his buzzed skull. "I got really cold today, it was as cold as hell. Aren't you cold?"

"Did you maybe forget to turn the heat on?" Jimmy asked. Jimmy was falling asleep again. He'd doze off and then wake up. He'd spent the day in the tow truck—he had a reason to be tired.

"Nah," Justin said. He rolled onto his side and rested his head on his arm, like an odalisque, although, of course, that's the last thing he resembled at the moment. "What's your name?"

"Yora."

"Cool."

"How long have you been living here?" Yora asked.

"Five days... If you could call it life, with this penguin," Justin said, referring, obviously, to Jimmy.

Jimmy kicked him. Justin laughed and fell onto the floor.

"What are you doing? You start kicking me, I'll drink all your beer, Sleeping Beauty," he threatened.

"Then you'll have to go get more. And I'll make you walk there," Jimmy said, good-naturedly, and kicked Justin again.

This time, Justin fell onto Yora's feet.

"You're pretty," he said.

"Thank you," she felt shy.

"Shit," Justin went on. "It's always the same. Jimmy brings someone home, and what about me?"

"You should bring someone home, too," Yora suggested.

"Girls don't like me."

"Why not? You're good-looking."

"He's got the looks, but not the brains," Jimmy chimed in. "Girls generally like people who aren't so dumb."

"There, that's the truth from Jimmy, for once in his life," Justin snorted. "I'm kind of dumb."

"Dumb?" Yora objected. "Why would you talk about yourself like that?"

"Would you go home with me?"

"Me? But I'm with Jimmy!" This was a surreal claim indeed, as if in a movie without a script—she was not really with Jimmy, she was supposed to be asleep in her own bed in her own studio, and what the hell was she doing here, in this house, on these dirty sheets, with two strange men, trying to convince the guy she'd just met that she had some sort of connection to the other one? How exactly? With a black charger cord?

"What's Jimmy got to do with anything?" Justin said, as if reading her thoughts. "Plus, I could be anyone right now. I could be Jimmy if you'd like. Come on!"

"Oh, drop it!"

"Have you not heard about the thirty halves?"

"What thirty halves? Thirty halves of what?"

"What do you mean, what? You, of course? Have you not read about the halves? That was Plato, right?"

LOVE LIFE 213

"You're a Plato fan now?"

"Not a fan," Justin shrugged. "Just something we covered in school. He's alright, basically. Then I read more on the internet."

"And what did you read on the internet?"

"I read that Plato was wrong. That each of us has not just one missing half, but thirty of them, at least. And you— no, don't say anything—you haven't had all thirty of them. You've got to go find some. I'm right, don't think I'm not because I'm dumb. And even if you'd had all thirty, then what's the chance, mathematically speaking, that one of them was not actually your half but just someone random?"

"I don't know," Yora said. "I'm not a mathematician."

She suddenly felt an urge to run her hand over Justin's head, to feel what his hair was like.

"I don't know either," Justin agreed. "But to hell with it. Love life—it's complicated, you never know anything. Shit, are you sure you don't want to do it with me?"

"I'm with Jimmy," Yora repeated, uncertainly. Jimmy was sound asleep. Justin got up, went to the wall, and turned off the lights.

***

That night, Yora dreamed she and Inga were together, and Inga never left because there was never any Donald, and they were renting a boat to go to an island, one of the many islands scattered along the shore. At first, Inga and Yora saw this island from a bird's-eye view—the houses, the paths, the palm trees; Yora even wondered if it were Sanibel again, but it wasn't. Then they were down on the very warm and very white sand, as if sifted through a sieve, right by the sea that lazily rolled waves to their feet and, in the dream, they realized this was the blessed Indonesia, their lost home. They walked along the beach and admired the waves until the police came up and demanded to see their IDs.

"What do you mean, IDs," she and Inga said, "we live right over there." They waved toward the Peninsula spread in the middle of the ocean like a petrified reptile.

"Go back there," the policemen said, sweating in their uniforms. "You can't be here."

"Okay," Inga and Yora said and went to their boat, but somehow couldn't get to it. Instead, they were now in the middle of the island, lost; this was absurd because the island was not at all large in size, and they should have, one way or the other, crossed it by now and come out to another beach, but the paths wound and wound away from them among palm trees and flowers...

It was already getting dark when Yora and Inga came to a small cottage, and an older woman came out to greet them, an Indonesian woman. She invited them in. She spoke her own language, but they could understand her easily and were very happy to be in her presence, happy as children to be invited in. They came into the cottage and sat at the table, and the Indonesian woman fussed over them because they got badly sunburned during their day of wandering the island, lost. The woman put some ointment on their faces and bare shoulders, speaking kindly in her tongue, and her words miraculously cohered in their minds into something they understood. Yora and Inga held on to this woman like children and said, "Mama! Mama!" while she kissed their hair and answered their "Mama! Mama!" and hugged them. They breathed in her smell and basked in her embrace, and time ceased to exist for them—it shrank to fit on the tines of a fork, or stretched to the size of a galaxy, or simply got tired and lay down to sleep, nestled next to the Peninsula they could no longer see. But even what was left of it was enough for wounds to begin to scar over, for burns to heal, and for souls to gain new strength. Their exile was over; they had come home. After a reunion like this, one could live a long time, a thousand years. And somewhere above the sea, a giant angel stood to his full, tremendous height: he raised his open wings and wrapped them around the water, and the land, and the black sky, to give them all a peaceful night. No trouble was going to touch anyone in the world because not even the tiniest bit of evil could sneak through the shield of his wings. A bright heavenly star flashed brightly on the angel's forehead, but he knew that no one could see it—as no one could see him, either, because no one had ever been this far, beyond the edge of the world. He was the edge of the world. Yora and Inga did not see him either. The old Indonesian woman lit a lamp because the house had gone dark. Night sounds reigned over the island, the rustle of sand and wind in the crowns of the trees, the footsteps of animals and the sighing of the spirits of the dead.

There was a knock at the door, and it was, of course, the diligent police that had finally found them.

"Pack up," they said. "We've found your boat."

"Where was it?" Yora asked. "We looked for it all day and couldn't find it."

"It's here, in a harbor, right next to this house," the policemen said. "We don't know how you managed to miss it." The old Indonesian woman got up from the table and said a few words angrily to the policemen, and they started explaining something to her in the same language, and this time Yora and Inga did not understand what they were saying. They had understood the policemen and the old Indonesian woman just fine, but only when they spoke directly to Yora and Inga. Finally, the Indonesian woman kicked the unwanted guests out of her house, and they loitered outside, waiting for the young women to come out, so they could escort them to the boat and make sure they left. A wind blew above the sea and rattled the windowpanes. The Indonesian woman laughed and said, "They can wait." Yora and Inga could understand her again. The lamp above the table glowed with a yellow light, and she put a round flatbread into its light, a circle inside a circle.

"Have some," she invited, and they reached for the bread and tore pieces of it and ate. The bread was warm; it could be said to have been delicious, but the word seemed too simple and common for the experience; the bread was not just delicious—it was alive, but not like a living thing that had been killed and devoured, that they themselves killed and devoured like cannibals, but like a tremulous substance that possessed life. They stuffed their mouths full of this bread and stopped worrying about the police and the dark sea they were about to cross in their borrowed boat; their impending separation from the old Indonesian woman no longer upset them, and many, many other causes of anxiety, large and small, of which there had been myriad, now vanished like popped soap bubbles. None of these things mattered. They had been lucky, they had always been lucky because only the best possible things happened to them and would keep happening to them. On the entire island, only the window of the cottage glowed with light like a star on earth, and the bread glowed on the table, and they sat around it.

Yora woke up in the morning, in this strange house, easily and happily, with light on her eyelids, like she used to wake up at Sebastian's.

Sebastian again!—Sebastian would not leave her. He manifested in this new house as if in a photograph, but Yora no longer felt guilty simply because she thought about him—instead, she accepted his presence. So what if someone else

LOVE LIFE 217

lived here? Now, between another man's sheets, in another man's warmth, he was neither a ghost nor a cause for nostalgia. Yora did not quite know how to name what Sebastian was—she only knew that he was not beside her, and, most likely, would never be, and she could live with that knowledge. He was both a part of Yora and a void, but a void could be a part of a person just like other parts.

Yora thought of Sebastian's face—for the first time, without pain—and smiled. There was Yora, still half-blind in the morning, and there was her smile, transparent and incomprehensible to anyone else, and somewhere else there was Sebastian, but his existence no longer had to be entwined with Yora's.

His existence did not keep her suspended on the thread of Death. His existence was discrete and separate.

The thought made Yora jump to her feet. It was still very early. Jimmy slept in his bed, and Justin was asleep on the floor, wrapped comically in a blanket that covered his head.

"Justin," she said, reaching out toward him. "Justin, come on, wake up."

He freed an arm and hugged her, half-asleep.

"Is that you, baby?" he said in a voice of a TV character Yora did not recognize.

"Justin, can I borrow your car for a few hours? I'll just run where I need to and come right back. You don't have a license anyway, you won't be going anywhere today."

"Uh-huh, right. You'll run away from us," he flirted and played with her hair.

"No, I won't run, what are you talking about? Let me have your car, baby, come on, sweetie, just let me." She cuddled him like she'd never cuddled anyone before, played with him, kissed his tattooed shoulders and his neck, rubbed the tip of her nose against his cheek and smothered giggles so as not to wake up Jimmy.

"Oh, baby," Justin groaned under her caresses, defeated. "Baby, God's already punished me plenty, so go ahead, steal my car."

"No, sweetie, don't say that, I'll just run out and be right back."

"And what will I get for this?"

"Let's talk about it when I come back—I promise I will make it worth your while."

"Baby... baby, ah! No, don't kiss me there... Ah, what are you doing to me! I can't risk like that... With, shit, my stock... I promised my millionaire aunt that I wouldn't play the market... It's... ah... indecent for a rich heir like me."

"Oh, but risk it, baby... It's worth it... It's really worth it."

"You say it's worth it?" Justin asked later, once he caught his breath and lifted himself on one elbow. He kissed her on the top of her head and groaned again. "Oh, I would like to know how I'm supposed to say 'no' to you... Alright, but come back soon, I'll fix you a bad-ass smoothie in the blender. Penguin got a pretty decent blender two days ago. The keys are in the living room, the Dodge."

"Of course, baby! Thank you!" Yora put her black dress back on and ran to get the keys.

In the car, she felt an urge to laugh out loud—not like before, in the bedroom, but really loudly, so that the skies would hear, the sun itself would hear out in the high heavens above the Peninsula. Laughter tore her apart. Everything was funny—this morning, and the night before, and the blender, and her abrupt and total, transportless poverty—she hoped there was enough gas in the car!—and her new job at—as Jimmy put it—such a nice place, and the 301 she had so rarely taken before, and even Sebastian himself.

For months, she had been so afraid to go to his place! Why? Now, being afraid made no sense. He had advised her to become like him and, up to a point, considering her

LOVE LIFE

recent experiences, she had done exactly that. Now, in the worst case, they'd just chat like two equals. But that was not the reason she wanted so much to see him.

Or was Raven right—and Yora really had mattered to Sebastian? Why, then, did he never tell her she had? Why hadn't she said anything to him? Perhaps it wasn't too late yet, only now they could say things without generating hope, or expectations? They would be both not together and yet together, because they would talk. Could anything really prevent them from just talking?

Yora recalled their last phone conversation, him telling her coldly he had no feelings for anyone, and her heart skipped a beat again, but she chased the memory away. Not like that. Not like that. The world could be changed, everything could be changed. They would talk and grieve together what could have been and had not come to be. Why not?

She could no longer be with him—he had gone somewhere far away, in the shadow—but she could still talk to the shadow. Not make love, no, just talk. He could just talk to her, too, couldn't he? This was somehow a very important moment in Yora's life. "I'll have to tell Raven later," she thought. Raven understood her. Raven was the one who told her that the dead had to be "lived". But the living had to be "lived," too.

So, they would talk and these would be honest, real words. It happens so rarely. Usually, words and reality exist separately from each other. But, sometimes, a word can come in touch with reality, fit it like a groove made specifically for it, and then the word and reality become one. This is how the word becomes body. The order of things changes; you become invisible to yourself and visible to others.

Yora herself, her blood, her existence will guarantee the reality of her words. He will have to recognize that. There was no fear in her anymore, and perhaps this, not having fear inside you, was one of the ways of doing good. Perhaps one could have their sins forgiven for this, too. She did not want anything from him, only to have him share in her joy, the simple joy of living. When this joy filled her so much, how could her words fail to help it fill Sebastian, too? They would rejoice together, rejoice at being alive and forget about time, and all their troubles and difficulties, and would think only of the sun, lazy and grateful, like children, and the shadows of the trees, and the fact that they had met each other—this would be their happiness, and nothing could be greater; nothing was ever greater, wasn't it? And who could dare take this happiness away from them, so powerful? Who would dare tell them it was not real once they had determined to experience it so fully and deeply?

Gratitude to the universe filled Yora. To Raven, to Mariana Schneider, to Obike, to Jimmy, to Justin, to Volodya who had taught her to drive, to everyone with whom fate had brought her together, and to everyone she was yet to meet. She hadn't understood anything until now, but everything that happened to her made sense! Only Sebastian was left, like the last chord in this symphony, and then a new life would begin, beyond, on the other side. She knew everything, everything, she had never known so much in her entire life. Soon, right now, they will break the spell cast upon both of them, and then everything will be alright. So very soon.

She drove down the 301, getting ready to turn west, onto the road that would take her to the sea and to Sebastian, and looked at everything around her with great emotion. The sun was shining and, in its light, everything was new because spring had come, spring came even to the tropics and even here it performed miracles; everything green got greener, everything magnificent—even more magnificent. The nature preserve on both sides of the road was lush. There were almost no cars at this early hour. Yora pulled over

LOVE LIFE 221

for a minute and rolled down her window. Birds sang, and the world filled with sound. A seagull shrieked somewhere nearby—she was getting closer to the sea.

Yora drove on. She was already in Sebastian's neighborhood when the sun suddenly went behind a cloud. The streets here, near the bay, were threaded with fog, and the air was cooler than farther east, among the moist palm trees of the preserve that held onto the ground securely with their resilient roots. Yora parked the car on Sebastian's street, which was small and, therefore, very cozy, and got out. The cobblestone was covered with fallen leaves, as if it were still autumn. The half-dead leaves lay over the entire street; it was odd that no one had picked them up—usually the neighbors took turns or did it all together. The leaves rustled under Yora's feet. Trees in the tropics lived by their own rules, different from those of the north. Yora in her black dress slowly walked toward Sebastian's home.

The trees stood as if made of glass, and dead leaves that had not fallen hung off their branches. The wind came and made the leaves sway like dried Christmas decorations that someone had forgotten to take down. The sun still did not show, only its light filtered through the milky cloud.

Yora could hear no birds. Actually, she could hear nothing except the beating of her own heart, as if in a vacuum. Spring seemed to have forgotten to come here, into this muteness, leaving this street untouched, conserved as an eternal space of timelessness.

Someone had put up a sign on Sebastian's unmown lawn. Yora came closer. A gust of wind made the sign swing hard on its wire hinges; the hinges creaked. The wind died down as abruptly as it had come. Yora read the sign—the house was for rent. A real estate agent's number was provided. Yora looked down. The grass under her feet lay yellowed, gossamer-thin, cold.

So, Sebastian was not here anymore.

Yora walked across the lawn toward the house and looked around the corner. The pond lay dark there, the very lake they so loved to look at from the veranda, a very common thing, a hole in the ground filled with motionless water. A dead piece of glass. Yora saw a man come out of the neighbor's house; he was either humpbacked or severely hunched over, and older. The man was looking at her. Neighborhoods like these had old-fashioned customs—people tended to look out for their neighbors and did not care for strangers very much. The man might very well yell at Yora for walking on the lawn. No, Yora dismissed the thought. He wouldn't yell at her, that was a fiction of her own mind. People didn't yell at people for something like that in this country; plus, the man was looking at her rather sympathetically.

"Are you looking to rent the house?" he asked, coming closer, and yet hesitating, which gave his voice an insincere note.

"No," she said.

"That's what I thought. Then you must be looking for the man who used to live here."

"Did he move?"

The neighbor looked around as if afraid someone was going to overhear him—but the street was entirely empty.

"I'm not sure if I should tell you..."

"Please do," Yora said, knowing already the news would be bad.

"You remember," the man started, pulling his head deeper between his shoulders, "what a rainy winter we had. It was so cold—very unlike the tropics! I've been living here forty years and I've never seen anything like it, except maybe in ninety-three. That was a very cold winter, too, and we went to visit my wife's brother in Miami. Of course, it was

LOVE LIFE

223

hot there, but Miami is a different world, even flowers smell different over there. And the man you are looking for, he came to live here, and we thought he was nice," the neighbor went on without any transition. "A good-looking man, he had a face for the movies, I'd tell you."

"You said, *had?*" Yora asked quietly.

The neighbor looked around again, and spoke in a lower voice, too.

"That's what I'm saying—he died. I'm just telling you what happened. All that rain in the winter, remember? It rained and rained, like the biblical flood! Me and my wife, we thought, that's it, that's the end of our Peninsula, people were right when they said it'd be the first to flood when global warming really kicked in! It was the last to rise from the sea and it would be the first to sink back into it, and I'm just praying we have a chance to die before then. And the man, the one you are looking for, he stood out there every night and looked at the water. I mean the lake. It was overflowing then. The water came up the grass almost to the door. He'd stand there and look, and just stand there, in the rain, not moving. I've seen everything in my life, but I won't lie to you, I've never seen a man stand like that in a tropical downpour. And, one time, it was already so cold, and it was coming down really hard, so I came out, and took an umbrella—but you know how it is, an umbrella is not much use—and wanted to give it to him. Let him, I thought, at least stand under an umbrella. 'Don't stand here,' I said to him. 'It's too cold outside. Or at least take my umbrella, you can give it back later, when the season is over, we have others.' And he just stood with his arms across his chest, all stiff like that, and looked right in front of him. And then he looked at me. His eyes burned—I'd never seen eyes like that on a man—as if he had fallen into the hand of a living God. I remember I told him, please, take my umbrella, and he just looked at me and said, 'No, thank you, I won't, I don't want to.' And that was all I got out of him."

"I went back home and looked out the window," the neighbor continued, "and he was still standing there, looking at the lake, just stood in the rain and did not move. He'd done it for a few nights already, every night. And, on Sunday, I did not see him, and my wife went and knocked on his door, but he didn't answer, and we did not want to bother him, and he did not come again, and a few days later he died—cars came, he must have managed to call an ambulance, or someone else called it for him, we don't even know. They carried him out of the house with his face covered."

"Then his friends came—our neighbors who rented out the house to him—and took his furniture. We asked them what happened, but they only said he got sick. Megan cried a lot, and Steve didn't say much. That night, I stopped by Steve and Megan's again, and asked about the funeral, and they said the man had an adult son in New York, and the son would take care of it, and then the next day we wanted to ask when the service would be because we felt sorry for him, even though we didn't know him very well, who knows if he was a good man, although, maybe, everyone is good before they die—but we felt very sorry for him because he was a tortured soul. But there was no one in the house anymore, Steven and Megan had gone like someone was after them, didn't even say goodbye, it's very unlike them, I worry now if Megan's had some trouble, she cried so much, so much... Who knows who that man was to them, I don't know how they knew him... I wrote to Steve later—and Steve wrote back right away to say they'd already buried the man, it was all done very fast, his son took care of it. Had him cremated. And the ashes, I don't know if he'd taken them back to New York or scattered them above the sea because Steve said that the man wasn't interred here. It's a good thing, I said to my

LOVE LIFE

wife, his son came, although it's not right he did the funeral in secret, didn't even tell his neighbors, that's not right. But it was good he came, because it's not right to have the body on ice forever, like it happens. When old Mrs. Gillmore died, we had to wait for her granddaughter to come from Arizona, and she said, I can't, I've got exams the next two weeks, so for two weeks we waited, we did."

Yora said nothing.

"Did you... Did you say you used to know him?" the neighbor asked.

Yora wanted to lie, but no, she could not.

"I did," she said, and then asked herself the same question—did she really know Sebastian?

"That's what I thought. I'm sorry if I..." the neighbor muttered.

His face seemed to say—I understand there's something here, and I can see you need to be alone, but I can't say it out loud because it would be impolite and I don't want to intrude on your private matter, but I understand you very well, I just don't know how to tell you.

He seemed like a decent man who was ashamed to peek in on someone else's death. For an instant, Yora thought he might cry.

"Goodbye," the neighbor said, waved, and walked off, hunched over.

Yora watched him go; in the deafening muteness of the street he crossed his lawn, went into the house, and locked the heavy wooden door with a glass insert.

The grass lay before Yora faded after the winter, crumpled. "It's because it rained so hard," Yora thought. The downpours suddenly separated one eternal summer from another. Only the low bushes of palmetto were still green, only they were untouched by the unexpected tropical winter. They looked up, just like Sebastian used to do when he turned his sublime angelic face free of any expression heavenward.

But did anyone see his face before he was cremated, and if so, who was it? Did his son want to take one last look at his father, with whom he was not, perhaps, particularly close? Or were there only the nurses and assistants at the hospital where the body was taken? Or only the undertakers? Did the person who sucked the innards from Sebastian's body with a special syringe look at his face? Or the one who made up his eyes and covered the yellow spots below them and on his cheeks with foundation? Or did Sebastian not even have that—was he just pulled out of the freezer, packed into a white shirt and a black suit, and rolled out—without roses, or mourners—into the crematorium where the eternal flame burned?

Someone said love could be found on the other side of sex. But, in fact, love was on the other side of the unknown, and no one could say anything else about it.

> Job has no words left anymore, no complaints,
> everything's left him, even language itself,
> only his skin keeps burning, covered in scabs,
> longs for heaven, abandons the bone and flesh
>
> to soar like a wild bird under the clouds,
> to beg for a shepherd to be sent for the flocks,
> to cry the bird's cry through the bird's small throat,
> through the heaven's blackberry thorns.

The Key to *Love Life*

for professional players of the glass bead game[1]

This part is an optional read for those so inclined. Tarot was used as one of the matrices of the novel, but I refrained from telling the reader which person, theme, or motif corresponds to which card. In a way, to step beyond the limits of Tarot is to step beyond the confines of the novel (and the possibilities of the Book altogether).[2]

The Major Arcana

0. The Fool

The Fool traditionally symbolizes a new beginning; they are the one in pursuit of new experiences, a lover of beauty. They are a beginner, or a symbol of the beginning; a child who is leaving the parental Eden; a human being on a path of spiritual growth. In a narrower sense, they are someone who follows the path of Tarot. In the reversed position, the Fool means recklessness. They are depicted as stepping off a cliff into the abyss: certainly a courageous step, but one

---

[1] *Das Glasperlenspiel* (The Glass Bead Game, 1943), Hermann Hesse's last novel.

[2] Blumenberg, Hans. *The Readability of the World*. Trans. Robert Savage and David Roberts. Ithaca, Cornell University Press, 2022.

that profoundly lacks foresight. In the novel, more than one character can be associated with this card.

1. The Magician
In the Tarot system, the Magician is the one who orders the flowers to bloom; the divine in a human; Hermes Trismegistus; the Messiah; *Mundus Novus*, meaning the new world and new life that must come. In the novel, the Magician does not appear directly. He is intentionally placed outside the frame, in someone's narrative, because, while he may be the *Mundus Novus*, he is still a man, and his version of the world considered "new" is a man's version, and this is a woman's story.[3]

2. The High Priestess
She is the keeper of secrets and secret knowledge, possibly, the knowledge of female power; she is a woman who serves the subterranean gods, "a perfect woman," or, in another interpretation, a woman that does not need a man to be complete. She can "see" others with her spiritual gaze. The spiritual gaze is associated with empathy but not identical to it; its essence is permanent, rather than occasional, compassion which might not appear to be what it is. Her attitude toward the world is non-utilitarian, "motherly"; it is, essentially, unconditional love. In the novel, she may be someone bestowed with the gift of foretelling, prophesy, energy reading, and visions that help her interpret the past or see the future.

3. The Empress
Traditionally, the Empress represents Isis, as well as the mother of the Dying and Resurrecting God who is associated with the Hanged Man. In the reversed position, she

---

[3] Sjoo, Monica, and Barbara Mor. *The Great Cosmic Mother: Rediscovering the Religion of the Earth*. San Francisco: Harper Collins, 2013.

LOVE LIFE   229

indicates the object of desire, the love of flesh. Here one
might recall Gaston Bachelard's analysis of the earth as
a substance that, on the one hand, gives birth to all living
beings and, on the other, absorbs, swallows her creations
into itself, which means it is both a generative and a de-
structive force.[4] In the novel, the Empress is reversed—
she is not "the Mother of the World" but "the Grave of the
World." She is the prescribed ideal of Body that is propagat-
ed by magazines and screens, the Body of a model as well
as a Model-body, while in reality she is anything but a body,
since she is stripped of any individuality and incapable of
experiencing pain.

4. The Emperor

The Emperor symbolizes stability, but Emperor reversed
means stagnation, cruelty, absence of flexibility, patriar-
chy; the Emperor is traditionally connected to card thirteen,
Death. The reversed position shows his inflexibility and the
inevitability of his demise. Usually, his "kingdom" is impenetrable: even the change of seasons cannot touch it, everything here is frozen in an absence of time. Sex for him is but
a manifestation of power. His words are a conglomeration
of lies, because Logos (the symbolic Word that created the
world) is his personal enemy.

5. The High Priest

He is a bridge between Heaven and Earth; unlike the Hanged
Man, whose body is a physical bridge, the Priest represents
spiritual connection. The Priest also symbolizes religion. His
number is five, as in the five senses, and that is precisely why
all five senses would be evoked in the scene featuring him.

---

[4] Bachelard, Gaston. *Earth and Reveries of Will: an Essay on the Imagination
of Matter.* Dallas: Dallas Institute of Humanities and Culture, 2002.

6. The Lovers

In Tarot, this card is, on the one hand, very positive since it symbolizes love (or bodily desire) but, at the same time, very dramatic because it implies a choice, a fork in the road, the expulsion from Eden and the entry into adult life. The choice is not necessarily between this person or object of desire and a different one, but, to put it crudely, between good and evil, or at least between that which constitutes good and evil *for the duration of the novel*.

7. The Chariot

The Chariot signifies victory in battle. In the novel, it is in the reversed position—that is, a Pyrrhic victory. The Chariot belongs to a warrior like Achilles—powerful but solitary and acting on a whim. It may be that the Chariot keeps rolling but the rider is dead (recall Hector's body tied behind a chariot). The rider will have the epic poem written about him, but he will not survive the battle unless he finds a way to overcome his pride and call for help. This card symbolizes the need for feedback, a warning, an invitation to call for help and put pride aside. In a certain sense, the person driving the Chariot is "a hero of our times," a psychopath (a person who lacks empathy). No interaction with a psychopath can ever be cathartic. A psychopath gives nothing—they only take, thus disturbing the cosmic balance. In this lies a rebellion against the order of things: a psychopath robs the other of the catharsis inherent in relations. To destroy the chains of universal interconnectedness, to block the channels of interaction is, then, the definition and the task of psychopathy which remains practically undiagnosed in interpersonal relations and still believed to be the "normal" egotism of "the Western world." In the novel, the Chariot is part of several characters' stories, but in all cases it is in the reversed position.

LOVE LIFE 231

8. Justice
Justice refers to morality, duty; sometimes it can signify empathy, the end of hostilities. In the novel, it is a theme rather than a person.

9. The Hermit
The Hermit points to introspection, a withdrawal from the world, contemplation. The Hermit is someone who has recognized the sting of the ego inside himself or herself and has chosen to study this internal foe and to fight him alone, thus protecting others who could be harmed if the weapon were allowed to break through his or her chest and aim at the outside world. The Hermit is a heroic figure; but theirs is the everyday heroism of a regular person. In the novel, the Hermit is present in more than one character's story.

10. The Wheel of Fortune
The Wheel of Fortune symbolizes the journey through life; partially, luck; the path of the Fool; new experiences. The movement of the text remains circular, and an angel with a fiery sword stands guard at the edge of the text and will not let anyone out of its boundary (or circle).

11. Strength
This card indicates friendship, with all its complexities, and support. The card depicts a woman with a lion—a dangerous animal who may be a friend or may (symbolically) maul her, like early Christians were in a Roman circus, with an emphasis put on the spectacle (we could say perhaps that "the abandoned woman" is a performance of our age, not unlike the people on the arena eaten by wild animals). Another aspect of Strength is being a mirror to a friend (or foe): each person acts like the mirror of the Other.

12. The Hanged Man
This card signifies patience, living up to one's true destiny, self-destruction, Odin's meditation (upside down), a change of perspective, and deliberate choice of the harder spiritual path. In the novel, the card pertains to at least two characters.

13. Death
Death is the end of a cycle, a transition, a re-birth. It can signify, in its reversed position, a source of narcissism. It is the Great Void that negates not only the possibility of life after death, but the sense and direction of life itself. In the novel, it is connected to the card of the Emperor.

14. Temperance
Despite its positive connotations, this is a card of the underworld; it signifies the death of the ego (in Buddhist terms) and, sometimes, the unconscious. It also signifies contentment. This is the guardian angel, the maternal; a certain ending and rest after hostilities; possibly death.

15. The Devil
This card signifies self-indulgence, the attachment to material or sensual pleasures, the lack of spontaneity, money and power in the hands of the wrong person. In the novel, the Devil appears in several guises: look for pride, inflexibility, and lack of knowledge or awareness.

16. The Tower
The Tower is a symbol of destruction of illusions, liberation from deceit at the cost of great pain. The collapse here is a positive development because this was a house of lies, the Tower of Babylon. In the novel, it is a certain building.

17. The Star
This card means hope, the end of the storm caused by the Devil and the Tower, good fortune, and the guardian angel. It also signifies integration, the movement towards synthesis; at least the movement towards a holistic picture of the heavenly bodies (which, according to Dante, are moved by love). In the novel, it is both a person (a harbinger of good news) and a theme.

18. The Moon
The Moon occupies the realm of sleep, nightmares, fears, difficult times, and the subconscious as a threat. It also foretells the final liberation through destruction. Enlightenment in this context does not mean "becoming better" or "leading a more pleasant life"; rather, enlightenment involves a passage through tremendous pain, a new birth, the phase of Lazarus. In the novel, the Moon makes a cameo appearance as itself.

19. The Sun
Apollo, light, energy, or the sheer joy of salvation. We might say, the Sun also makes a cameo experience, but the card is also present more broadly, as a theme.

20. The Last Judgment
This card signifies life after death, the Last Judgment that comes without warning, and a sudden change. In the novel, this is a motif rather than a person.

21. The World
The World means the end of the cycle (before a new one begins again, with the Fool) and Sophia (Wisdom) as an aspect of Christ and the purpose of a spiritual quest. This is the Fool's complete journey—the journey of whoever follows the path of Tarot. In the hermeneutic sense, the World is this entire novel.

The Minor Arcana

Aces
Supervisors, moneybags—think of four of those mentioned in the novel.

Kings
Worldly powers of a more empathetic nature, not deities—episodic characters who have any kind of worldly power, or look and sound regal. These can be people or even animals.

Queens
The maternal—important women or maternal kin.

Knights
Protectors—these may come in any gender, not just as men.

Pages
Messengers, sometimes unreliable—those who bring forth any kind of news, good or bad.

From tens to twos
Minor and episodic characters, usually unnamed.

Recent Titles in the Series
Harvard Library of Ukrainian Literature

Forest Song: A Fairy Play in Three Acts
Lesia Ukrainka (Larysa Kosach)

Translated by Virlana Tkacz and Wanda Phipps
Introduced by George G. Grabowicz

This play represents the crowning achievement of Lesia Ukrainka's (Larysa Kosach's) mature period and is a uniquely powerful poetic text. Here, the author presents a symbolist meditation on the interaction of mankind and nature set in a world of primal forces and pure feelings as seen through childhood memories and the re-creation of local Volhynian folklore.

2024	appr. 240 pp.	
ISBN 9780674291874 (cloth)		$29.95
9780674291881 (paperback)		$19.95
9780674291898 (epub)		
9780674291904 (PDF)		

Harvard Library of Ukrainian Literature, vol. 13

Read the book online

Cecil the Lion Had to Die: A Novel
Olena Stiazhkina

Translated by Dominique Hoffman

This novel follows the fate of four families as the world around them undergoes radical transformations when the Soviet Union unexpectedly implodes, independent Ukraine emerges, and neoimperial Russia begins its war by occupying Ukraine's Crimea and parts of the Donbas. A tour de force of stylistic registers and intertwining stories, ironic voices and sincere discoveries, this novel is a must-read for those who seek to deeper understand Ukrainians from the Donbas, and how history and local identity have shaped the current war with Russia.

2024	248 pp.	
ISBN 9780674291645 (cloth)		$39.95
9780674291669 (paperback)		$19.95
9780674291676 (epub)		
9780674291683 (PDF)		

Harvard Library of Ukrainian Literature, vol. 11

Read the book online

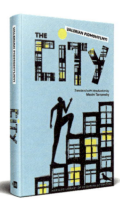

The City: A Novel
Valerian Pidmohylnyi

Translated with an introduction by Maxim Tarnawsky

This novel was a landmark event in the history of Ukrainian literature. Written by a master craftsman in full control of the texture, rhythm, and tone of the text, the novel tells the story of Stepan, a young man from the provinces who moves to the capital of Ukraine, Kyiv, and achieves success as a writer through a succession of romantic encounters with women.

2024	496 pp.	
ISBN 9780674291119 (cloth)		$39.95
9780674291126 (paperback)		$19.95
9780674291133 (epub)		
9780674291140 (PDF)		

Harvard Library of Ukrainian Literature, vol. 10

Read the book online

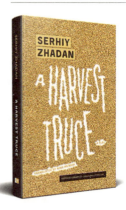

A Harvest Truce: A Play
Serhiy Zhadan

Translated by Nina Murray

Brothers Anton and Tolik reunite at their family home to bury their recently deceased mother. An otherwise natural ritual unfolds under extraordinary circumstances: their house is on the front line of a war ignited by Russian-backed separatists in eastern Ukraine. Isolated without power or running water, the brothers' best hope for success and survival lies in the declared cease fire—the harvest truce.

Spring 2024	196 pp.	
ISBN 9780674291997 (hardcover)		$29.95
9780674292017 (paperback)		$19.95
9780674292024 (epub)		
9780674292031 (PDF)		

Harvard Library of Ukrainian Literature, vol. 9

Read the book online

Cassandra: A Dramatic Poem,

Lesia Ukrainka (Larysa Kosach)

Translated by Nina Murray, introduction by Marko Pavlyshyn

The classic myth of Cassandra turns into much more in Lesia Ukrainka's rendering: Cassandra's prophecies are uttered in highly poetic language—fitting to the genre of the dramatic poem that Ukrainka crafts for this work—and are not believed for that very reason, rather than because of Apollo's curse. Cassandra's being a poet and a woman are therefore the two focal points of the drama.

2024	263 pp, bilingual ed. (Ukrainian, English)
ISBN 9780674291775 (hardcover)	$29.95
9780674291782 (paperback)	$19.95
9780674291799 (epub)	
9780674291805 (PDF)	

Harvard Library of Ukrainian Literature, vol. 8

Read the book online

Ukraine, War, Love: A Donetsk Diary

Olena Stiazhkina

Translated by Anne O. Fisher

In this war-time diary, Olena Stiazhkina depicts day-to-day developments in and around her beloved hometown during Russia's 2014 invasion and occupation of the Ukrainian city of Donetsk.

Summer 2023	
ISBN 9780674291690 (hardcover)	$39.95
9780674291706 (paperback)	$19.95
9780674291713 (epub)	
9780674291768 (PDF)	

Harvard Library of Ukrainian Literature, vol. 7

Read the book online

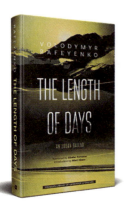

The Length of Days: An Urban Ballad

Volodymyr Rafeyenko

Translated by Sibelan Forrester
Afterword and interview with the author by Marci Shore

This novel is set mostly in the composite Donbas city of Z—an uncanny foretelling of what this letter has come to symbolize since February 24, 2022, when Russia launched a full-scale invasion of Ukraine. Several embedded narratives attributed to an alcoholic chemist-turned-massage therapist give insight into the funny, ironic, or tragic lives of people who remained in the occupied Donbas after Russia's initial aggression in 2014.

2023	349 pp.	
ISBN 780674291201 (cloth)		$39.95
9780674291218 (paper)		$19.95
9780674291225 (epub)		
9780674291232 (PDF)		

Harvard Library of Ukrainian Literature, vol. 6

Read the book online

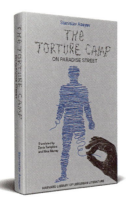

The Torture Camp on Paradise Street

Stanislav Aseyev

Translated by Zenia Tompkins and Nina Murray

Ukrainian journalist and writer Stanislav Aseyev details his experience as a prisoner from 2015 to 2017 in a modern-day concentration camp overseen by the Federal Security Bureau of the Russian Federation (FSB) in the Russian-controlled city of Donetsk. This memoir recounts an endless ordeal of psychological and physical abuse, including torture and rape, inflicted upon the author and his fellow inmates over the course of nearly three years of illegal incarceration spent largely in the prison called Izoliatsiia (Isolation).

2023	300 pp., 1 map, 18 ill.	
ISBN 9780674291072 (cloth)		$39.95
9780674291089 (paper)		$19.95
9780674291102 (epub)		
9780674291096 (PDF)		

Harvard Library of Ukrainian Literature, vol. 5

Read the book online